Gabriel's Hope

RHYN ETERNAL, BOOK ONE

Lizzy Ford

http://www.guerrillawordfare.com/

Cover art by Regina, Mae I Design
http://www.maeidesign.com/

ISBN-13: 978-1-62378-067-8
ISBN-10: 1623780675

Acknowledgments

This one is for Jenn Pringle,

My sweet friend, whose judicious use of the shock collar controller keeps Lizzyland on track.

Chapter One

Deidre rubbed her hands on her legs. The papery hospital gown was rough beneath her palms, the dark room too cold. She sat on the table in the exam room facing a line of backlit x-rays and cat scans on the wall. Gazing at the obvious mass in her brain, she knew the results were bad, but were they *worse?*

Impatiently waiting for her longtime surgeon, she pushed herself off the table and crossed to the desk, where a small folder sat. If its contents were like the reports she'd seen in the past, it would be full medical nonsense. She was able to decipher some of it after all the tests she'd been through. She flipped it open. The summary of results might as well have been in a foreign language with the medical terminology, abbreviations and sprinkling of what seemed like random numbers.

"Come *on,*" she muttered at the file. Skimming it, her gaze settled on the last line of the first page.

When patient presents, inform of advanced deterioration of tumor stability. Recommended local hospices attached to report.

Hospice? They wanted to shove her away for the last few months of her life? Deidre closed the file, chewing her lip. Dr. Wynn knew better. Every week, he asked how many things she checked off her bucket list. She wasn't the kind who sat around waiting to die, not when she wanted so badly to enjoy every day until she was no longer able to.

Which would be soon. She blinked away tears. She didn't want to die. At twenty-six years old, she must've done something pretty bad in a past life to deserve this. Karma was a bitch, but it wasn't indiscriminate, was it?

Dr. Wynn knocked and opened the door. He was tall and slender with cocoa skin, dazzling blue eyes and prematurely white hair that made him appear twice his age. His features were heavy and roughly hewn. Though not traditionally handsome, he moved and spoke with a diplomat's grace. He kissed her cheeks and waited for her to heft herself back onto the table. Instead of seating himself on the traditional doctor's stool, Dr. Wynn sat beside her on the table, hands folded across one knee.

His smile didn't reach his eyes. It never had. She'd thought him cold and distant at first, until she learned his background. He was one of those medical prodigies that mentally existed on a level too removed for most people to follow. He'd stuck by her for over three years, though. It had to mean something.

"It's not good, is it?" she asked.

"No," he replied in the smooth, velvety voice that talked her down from hysterics several times many times.

She swallowed hard and gazed at the charts on the wall. She already knew, but it seemed worse when a doctor said it.

"There really is nothing I can do this time," he said. "We've been through every option."

"How long?" she whispered.

"Three months at most."

Deidre nodded, not sure how to respond. He'd told her the chances were slim long ago, but she wasn't ready for him to admit defeat quite yet. She'd been anticipating this moment for awhile. Sitting through it, she didn't think it was ever possible to be prepared for the news.

"I am very sorry, Deidre. You are a sweet girl," he said.

"No worries," she said, forcing a smile. "We all have to go at some point. At least I know how and when, right? You've …done so …" She couldn't finish it through the sudden tears.

Dr. Wynn hesitated then hugged her. Deidre closed her eyes and rested against him, trying to imagine what the last days of her life would be like. She'd let herself grieve for a day – maybe two – and then fill her world with as much sunshine as possible. She'd been on the verge of death for years. She could handle this turn of events.

"Logan won't take this well," he said, referring to her boyfriend of almost two years. "I will always meet you both for dinner again to explain, if it helps you."

Deidre drew a shuddering breath then groaned.

"If there is a Logan still?"

"More or less," she said. "He seems to be waiting for the inevitable while I try to check off my bucket list. He doesn't get that I'm not going to waste my time mourning when I can *live*."

"It's a difficult time for both of you."

"Yeah." She moved away from him, wiping her face. "I think he feels guilty for wanting to leave his dying girlfriend. Most days, I just want to tell him to get it over with and move on." She rolled her eyes.

"You've lived on your terms the past few years. No one will fault you for taking that one step further and cleaning house," Dr. Wynn said with a faint smile.

"Are you saying he's the dead weight and not me?"

"Your humor is morbid, darling," he said, though he chuckled. "I was thinking more along the lines that he can have no objection when I ask you to dinner, if he's out of the picture."

A laugh bubbled up. "You're insane, Doc. You've always been a little sweet on me, haven't you?"

"I've yet to meet someone as brave in the face of death as you are. I admire your joie de vivre and am always fascinated by your perspective on life."

She wiped her face, affected by his words. That a cultured medical genius found her inspiring was beyond flattering. His gentle flirting reminded her of how charismatic he could be, when not telling her she was getting ready to die.

"I also regret you choosing Logan over me," he said, rising.

"You're a good man, Doc," she said with a watery smile.

"Wynn," he corrected her. "You've been more than a patient for months now." He held her gaze for a moment too long before looking away.

Their history was too personal for her to feel uncomfortable standing near-naked to a man who'd had a crush on her for awhile. He'd cut her open and seen her from the inside out. There was nothing she kept from him. If anything, she felt lucky to have a doctor who saw her as more than a case.

"Okay, then, Wynn," she said. "I'm headed to the coast this weekend. Logan's taking off work early today, so we can have a long weekend at the beach. I've always wanted to stay in a beach house. If your girlfriend was going to dump you, wouldn't you rather it happen at a beach house?"

He raised an eyebrow.

"I'm joking."

"Are you?"

"I haven't decided yet," she admitted. "If I do, I'll call you for that dinner date when I get back."

"I'll await your call."

Always polite, always a gentleman. He'd never liked Logan, but he'd never say it directly. Something about his proper responses made her smile.

"There may be signs soon of deterioration, Deidre," he said with gravity.

"I know, Doc," she replied then recited. "Hallucinations, incurable pain, loss of muscular control, cognitive dysfunction. It'll be a slow, painful death."

For the first time in their history, a flicker of emotion crossed the features of her surgeon. He rubbed his jaw.

"Yes," he said at last. "It will be. For which I feel entirely responsible."

"Omigod, Doc," she said. "Don't get all emotional on me now. One of us has to keep the other calm, and it won't be me."

"Deidre, for what little this is worth, I apologize for not being good enough or smart enough or quick enough to prevent the inevitable."

"Ah, Wynn," she said, touched by his subtle emotion. "You have nothing to apologize for. You've been the one constant in my life since this mess started. I wouldn't trade you for anyone."

"Perhaps I'm the dead weight in this relationship."

"You can be so charming when you want to be." She smiled and reached out to squeeze his arm. Most of the times, conversation with Dr. Wynn was like talking to a robot. Today, he was human. "Remember: no apologies, no regrets. Got it?"

He chuckled, this smile the largest she'd seen yet.

"Wynn, I will call you for dinner when I get back," she said. "Promise."

"I hope you do," he said. The façade returned, and he moved towards the door. "Have a nice weekend, Deidre."

"You, too, Wynn."

He left her alone. If nothing else, Wynn was going to make a terrific friend during the last leg of her life, which comforted her a little. She stared at the charts again. It was hard to imagine she had a tumor in her brain the half the size of her fist. She was happy to be functional, though that wasn't likely going to last long.

She wasn't going to let things get worse. She lived on her terms; she'd die on her terms. Her hands trembled as she got dressed. The decision made to face death soon, the only thing she hadn't quite worked out was how she planned to do it. Did she tell Wynn what she planned? Ask him for help? Or just disappear one day? Somehow, it seemed wrong not to warn him.

Deep in thought, she left the hospital. The spring air was heavy and humid already in Atlanta; it felt like summer. She walked from the hospital campus to a crowded sidewalk that ran beside a main street. The scents of food from street vendors and car exhaust filled the air outside the quiet hospital grounds. It was lunchtime, and the sidewalk was packed with people in business attire headed to the small bistros, cafes and other eateries lining the business district of downtown Atlanta.

Pausing at her normal bus stop, Deidre debated walking instead of taking the bus. Soon, she wasn't going to have the option of walking. She needed to put more effort into taking advantage of life while she could. She moved away from the bus stop and joined the crowds on the sidewalk.

She waited until she reached a quieter side street before dialing her boyfriend. Logan picked up on the third ring.

"Hey." He sounded distracted.

"Hello to you, too!" she said cheerfully.

"I'm running behind. Anything new?"

"Not really." She frowned at his tone. "Got word the inevitable is coming in three months or so."

Logan was silent. She heard him typing in the background. He didn't respond.

"You still there?" she prompted.

"Sorry. New client brought in a dump truck full of receipts and needs his return done by close of business today. I'm trying to wrap up everything as fast as I can," Logan said.

"You didn't hear what I said."

"No, Dee," Logan sighed. "I've got a lot going on. Did Dr. Wynn have good news?"

She hesitated, agitated. "The usual."

"Maybe you need a new surgeon. He hasn't done anything for you in awhile," Logan suggested.

I'd dump you before Dr. Wynn, she replied silently.

"If we got married, you'd have health insurance. You could find a good doctor," Logan added.

"We've discussed this. We're not getting married when I'm on my deathbed, and Dr. Wynn is the best there is!" she snapped. Deidre stopped in the middle of the busy sidewalk, too angry at the idea of losing her friend and doctor to care when someone jostled by her.

"The best there is doesn't take on charity cases, Dee."

"You know, Logan, maybe he likes me enough to want to help me. There are a lot of good people in the world."

"He likes you too much, in my opinion. I told you I got a bad vibe from him when we had dinner a few weeks ago."

"Whatever. You've got work to do and I need to pack," she said. "You care which shirts I pack for you?"

"Leave out the one you got me for my birthday. I'll wear it tonight."

"Okay. Good luck with the tax stuff. I'll have everything ready for when you get back," she said.

"See you tonight." He hung up before she could say farewell.

Deidre glared at the phone, comparing Logan's unconcerned response with Dr. Wynn's kindness. She joined a few others at a corner waiting to cross the street. She pulled up Dr. Wynn's office number on her cell, tempted to invite him to the beach this weekend instead of Logan.

Someone near her gasped, and Deidre glanced up, expecting to see a fender bender or similar issue in the street. A woman nearby was staring at her. Deidre saw the strange flash of a red, glowing tattoo on the lady's exposed neck. It faded when she looked directly at it.

"Are you here for me?" the woman asked in a hushed tone.

Deidre turned to see if there was someone behind her the stranger spoke to. There wasn't.

"Um, no," she replied. "I'm just ... waiting for the green light."

"You must be here for someone. As long as it's not me." The woman was smartly dressed in a suit. She didn't seem like the lunatic kind. She beamed a smile and faced the street again.

Deidre shook her head. She'd been asked that question more than once while out and didn't understand it, unless it was some sort of odd Southern greeting. As soon as the signal to walk flashed, she put some distance between her and the crazy woman.

It took five blocks before her agitation at Logan faded, and she started paying attention to the world around her. Her angry march turned into a stroll. Deidre stopped to admire bouquets being sold on a street corner. Most of them were wilting in the Atlanta heat.

Like me. She grinned at the thought.

Taking pity on the sad flowers, she bought a bunch before continuing on her journey home. She commiserated with the brown-tinged blossoms left behind by other customers who didn't want to be so close to death. The petals were like silk, their scent strong and sweet.

"You're still beautiful to me," she told them. "Logan won't agree. What a jerk. Maybe you all can go with me to the beach and we'll leave him at home."

Entertained by her pep talk with the flowers, Deidre reached her towering apartment building a short time later and paused to collect the mail. Her gaze fell to the envelope from *South Peachtree Mortuary Services.* She'd bought her casket months ago and was on a payment plan. Holding the bill made her hands sweat and her heart beat faster. She wanted to burn or shred the sign of her impending demise. How many twenty-six-year-olds planned their own funerals?

"Don't worry, flowers," she murmured as she entered the elevator. "We've got a better plan, right?"

The other occupant of the elevator glanced at her. She smiled and shoved the bill into her purse. She could pay it this month or put the three hundred dollars towards a one-way ticket to wherever she wanted to be when she died.

She liked the latter plan much better.

The apartment was quiet when she entered a few minutes later. She tossed her keys on the counter and set down the flowers. She dug out the envelope from the funeral home and tore it in half. The sight of it lying in two pieces was gratifying. Unable to outmaneuver death, she could at least take out her grief and anger on a poor little piece of mail.

Bottle of wine in one hand, Deidre retreated to her bedroom to pack. She caught her reflection in the mirror and admired her hair. Naturally white-blonde, she'd dyed it pink on a whim last weekend. Logan hated it, but she loved it.

She drank straight from the bottle as she moved around the room, gathering and piling clothing into a small suitcase. She left out the shirt bearing Logan's initials as he requested then glared at it.

"Sorry, Logan," she told the shirt. "We're through after this weekend. I got too many things on my bucket list."

Deidre wiped away more tears and went to her messy desk, where a red-covered notebook sat on a pile of paper. She opened it and reviewed the to-do list of things she wanted to experience before she died. Some of them were crossed out. Most were not. She added yet another item to the growing queue.

Dump Logan. Her attention lingered on it for a moment before she wrote one more.

Ask Wynn to dinner.

Satisfied, she closed the notebook. The end of her life started this weekend. She was going to enjoy it, no matter what.

Dr. Wynn stood in the middle of his office. His heart was pounding harder than ever. Deidre's tears burned through his shirt to his skin, and he couldn't dismiss the expression on her face from his thoughts. She'd made a decision in front of him, one that warned him this might be his last chance to reveal his secret. He'd wanted to tell her not to go to the beach with Logan, to spend the weekend with him instead of some stupid human that had no idea how to appreciate a woman like her. He walked away, because it was the *right* thing to do.

Wynn didn't do what was *right* in this life or the last, unless it benefited him directly. He wanted her. It didn't matter if she felt the same or if she had someone else.

One minute, Dr. Wynn was headed back towards Deidre's exam room. The next, his foot sank into sand. Fluorescent lighting overhead morphed to an expansive blue sky and brilliant sunlight that made him squint. The air-conditioned hospital corridor gave way to the balmy heat of the Caribbean island on which he stood. He glanced down at the expensive loafers that now contained tiny grains of sand he'd never be able to flush out of the seams.

"Where might you be going?" a warm voice asked from behind him.

Wynn was still for a long moment. It was not every day he was summoned by a deity. Reincarnation left his power stunted and him far less brash in how he used what remained.

"You do not normally demean yourself by talking to someone as lowly as I am," he replied, turning.

Barefooted and relaxed, Fate flashed a wide smile. His brown hair was tousled from the ocean breeze, and he was dressed in jeans and a loose shirt fastened across the golden skin of his chest by one button.

"A doctor this time around?"

"It's an honorable trade," Wynn replied.

"An honorable trade for a man with no honor," Fate said.

"Better than preying on the free will of humans."

"Speaking of preying on those weaker than you, I have an interest in your … patient."

"You and many others." Wynn removed his shoes and sat nearby, uneasy but unwilling to show it. Deities did not summon formerly dead-dead Immortals to them without a compelling reason.

"Vengeance is a strong motivator, even for me," Fate began. "I am curious, *doctor,* did you know she would come to you or did you stumble upon her?"

"You know the answer," Wynn said. "Let's not play games with one another today. I cannot possibly have anything you want."

"I monitor and balance potential outcomes and free will. There's room for curiosity about the motivations of others," Fate said.

Wynn met the deity's gaze, which flickered between all the colors in the universe. He'd met Fate once. It was impossible to forget Fate or Death or any other deity once one crossed their paths or to deny that such creatures not only existed, but played a game no one else understood or had a chance of winning. Wynn didn't like being out of control, at the mercy of one he couldn't predict or manipulate.

"For example, before you ran into her in the mortal world, there was a ninety seven percent chance you would've killed her the first time you met. Now, there's less than a one percent chance," Fate continued. "You've gone so far as to eliminate some of the enemies who likewise stumbled across her."

"I do not need to explain my actions to you." Wynn looked away. "What do you want from me?"

"You are close to crossing the line where you mess with the Future. You have been for awhile."

"You have a preferred outcome," Wynn said, suddenly comprehending why he'd been involuntarily summoned. "You don't want me to influence it."

"Some laws from the time-before-time cannot be broken," Fate replied.

"Those rules are very few."

"You will have to trust me when I say this is one of them."

"Will you tell me one thing?" Wynn asked. "What is your motivation to interfere now?"

"I have no motivation." Fate smiled. "Ask what you mean to ask, Wynn. I may answer it."

Wynn's jaw clenched. No, he didn't miss this aspect of his past life. Dealing with deities was a nightmare. He hated the idea of being vulnerable, and concern for another was vulnerability.

"Are you going to save her?" He forced the words out.

"From what?" Fate asked with faux innocence.

"I made a mistake. I cannot fix it."

"It's not so bad to admit you were wrong, is it?"

"How do you think it feels to live with the regret that stems from having done something beyond reparation to someone as beautiful as she is in this life?" Wynn asked in barely controlled anger.

"No idea. I'll never have that problem," Fate said with a shrug.

"If you are finished with me, I have work to do." Wynn rose, fed up.

"Her destiny lies with Death."

Wynn debated the meaning behind the words. There was more than one interpretation, and he admitted at last he wasn't certain what Fate was telling him.

"She brought me back for a reason," Wynn said. "I'd like to think there's greater meaning to both of us being reincarnated."

"It's not lost on me that you repay her for that favor by killing her," Fate said. "Slowly, while you hold her hand and lower her into eternal rest. Beautiful, Wynn. I've been watching the events unfold with no small amount of entertainment."

"It was a kinder revenge than she deserved," he replied. "I know you agree with me."

"Very much so, especially when you consider she stole your heart not once but twice."

"She has a way about her."

"She will never be yours."

Wynn's breath caught at the stark pronouncement from the enigmatic deity. His body was tense, his memories flowing unabated. He hadn't expected anything different when he met the reincarnated Deidre a few years ago and started down this path. When his mind changed from vengeance to compassion, he wasn't certain. Perhaps the day he realized what he'd done was irreparable, and he was going to lose her twice.

Fate knew what Wynn intended to do, had he left his office to find Deidre before she left the hospital. The deity dragged Wynn here to warn him against altering his plan for revenge. Wynn lost this round.

"I understand," he managed. "I will not interfere in that regard. Anything else?"

"No."

Wynn nodded once. He took a step and was back in the hallway. Fate dropped him in front of the door to Deidre's exam room, a twisting of the knife in his heart. With a deep breath, Wynn turned away and retreated to his office.

No apologies. No regrets.

Chapter Two

Death was almost seven feet tall, built more solid than a tree trunk with hair and eyes darker than a moonless night. The weapons lining his body and tucked into pockets of his trench coat were items of comfort rather than necessity; his hands alone had ended the lives of more humans and Immortals than there were stars in the sky he stared into. Dawn lined the horizon in faint yellow. He watched his expelled breath float away from him, his calm features hiding the anger in his blood.

"Cancel all contracts. We've got to figure out this shit," he told the female death-dealer beside him.

"Gabriel, *why* does this keep happening?" the red-headed assassin asked, frustration in her voice.

His gaze went from the sky to her to the body at her feet. A competent, methodical assassin, she didn't make the mistake of trying to collect from someone not on the list. And yet, this wasn't the human she came for. Just like every other soul collector Gabriel sent out the past week, Harmony had gone on a mission and returned empty-handed. It was better than the alternative: returning with the wrong soul, which almost happened twice today.

Immortal Code, Rule 5329: Death shall not knowingly claim a soul not on the list, he recited silently.

In the matter of seven days, Gabriel had come close to breaking more Immortal Codes governing Death's actions in the mortal world than his predecessor did over hundreds of thousands of millennia. His predecessor, referred to as *past-Death* by his collectors, made exactly two mistakes, the second of which landed Gabriel his new gig ruling the underworld. Four months after becoming Death, Gabriel was trying to salvage what he could of the underworld as it crashed and burned. He followed all the rules in the Code, but he couldn't help thinking he was doing something ...wrong.

"I went to the soul I heard," the assassin said. "I swear it. I came right here, where the radar brought me. It's not here. This guy isn't even on the list." She wiped her face and paced. "I failed you. I messed up."

"You didn't fail me, Harmony," Gabriel said. "You broke no part of the Immortal Code, and you followed our procedures. The radar led you astray. It's outside of your control." *Like every other part of my life.* This part he kept silent for fear of spooking someone he was supposed to be leading.

"But if this guy wasn't supposed to die tonight, where is the soul I came for?"

They were in the middle of the desert in New Mexico. It was cold, sandy – and completely void of any other signs of life for miles. Death-dealers operated off a sense of soul radar that pulled them like magnets to the lives that were on Death's list to be ended. Except, a week ago, all the radars of his army of grim reapers had gone haywire. Sometimes, the souls they sought were a few feet from the ones they claimed. Sometimes, the humans or Immortals targeted for extermination or soul extraction were on the other side of the world.

"I don't know this guy from Adam," he said.

"Adam who?" she asked, confused.

Gabe glanced at her. "It was an attempt at levity."

"This is no time for a joke!"

"He'll show up downstairs eventually," he said, referring to his underworldly domain. "Everyone does."

Harmony's frown was fierce. Not many people appreciated a sense of humor crafted over millennia as a sanctioned killer for Death. Most Immortals had no mirth in the first place. As the sole living resident of the underworld with human origins, Gabriel was often reminded of how different he remained. Right now, he was too frazzled to know what else to do aside from make a joke to ease some of the tension.

"If you feel the need to expel me for almost breaking the Code, I will go where you bid," Harmony said in a quieter voice. "Or cast myself into the Lake of Souls."

"The Lake's at capacity," he replied.

"Very well. When the Lake has subsided, I will throw myself in." The determination in Harmony's voice left him no doubt she'd do it.

Gabriel chuckled. "No, you won't. Relax. Thank you for calling me."

"I must. It's my duty."

"I'm more concerned with why this guy has no soul. The demons beat us here again," Gabriel shifted. "The last thing I need is an Army of Souls in the hands of those bastards. I can't figure out how they're tracking the dead."

"Darkyn is very powerful." Harmony's voice held a hushed note of reverence that irked Gabriel.

"He's a demon lord but not a deity," he pointed out.

"Oh, sorry Gabriel. I keep forgetting you are now."

"Thanks," he said drily.

"I didn't mean … you're really trying … um, and doing your best." She met his gaze at last, a red flush creeping across her face. With forest colored eyes and an athletic body, she towered over most men. The top of her head reached his chin.

"Appreciate the encouragement."

"Sorry, Gabe," she mumbled. "Where do I sleep tonight?"

He assessed her. While he wanted nothing more than to kill past-Death over and over for fucking him over, he was forced to admit the death-dealers that survived the recent demon attacks were loyal, honorable and ruthless. All traits he admired. His predecessor chose the best, like the cautious and steady Immortal awaiting his decision. There was no spontaneity – or surprises – to her. He never had to wonder how many men were rotating through her bed or when she was planning to stab him in the back or decipher the riddles she gave him as answers to important questions. His last lover – the only other he'd ever taken – had been the opposite of Harmony.

He never wanted to deal with the unexpected in his personal life again. At least, he thought he didn't when he invited Harmony to his bed. Most nights, she wasn't enough to settle his restless blood. He had sex and went back to work, unable to sleep knowing all the issues he couldn't fix. Though he never felt that way sleeping with past-Death, he valued trusting the woman in his bed over potential rejection.

"Where you've slept every night for the past two months," he answered.

She appeared relieved.

"I'll be late," he said. "Don't wait up. Grab this guy and take him downstairs in case his soul pops up later."

"Will do." Harmony bent and lifted the dead man in a fireman's carry. She called forth a portal, and what looked like a cave opened in the air before them.

Gabriel followed her into it. Portals to various places in the mortal and underworlds glowed in the in-between shadow realm. Mortal portals were like sunshine, the underworld the color of a storm cloud, and the portal to Hell blacker than Gabe's eyes. Harmony disappeared through the gray portal while Gabe took one of the yellow portals.

He emerged at the Caribbean Sanctuary, one of four places that connected the mortal and immortal worlds. Governed by Death, the Sanctuaries were located on islands protected by magic and tended by convents of Immortal nuns, who helped any who came to them.

The room of the Sanctuary where he materialized consisted of nothing more than a lectern holding a massive book possessed by a long-dead Oracle. In its pages, the events of the Past were recorded, the Present written and the Future a blur of potential outcomes.

Not that he could see the Future. He'd hoped to be granted the same level of power as his predecessor. Instead, he'd found his vision unchanged. Gabe strode to the lectern and watched the words of the Present being written across the pages. They leapt from the pages to create visions before him that then swirled and turned back into words. He could see the Past and Present. Never the Future.

The balmy morning breeze drifting in from the small window was fragrant with the scents of the ocean and bread from the Sanctuary's kitchens.

"Any news today?" he asked the Oracle.

More visions formed. These were of demons gathering the souls of dead mortals while death-dealers missed the lives meant to be ended. The Oracle was re-writing the present, based on who was killed and who had lived that wasn't supposed to.

"Yeah, I know," he said. "Anything more useful?"

The images returned to the pages. The Oracle was quiet, scribbling words. As he watched, the words reached the page on the right, the one reserved for the Future. Interested, he read the message addressed to him.

Did you not receive my first summons? You cannot avoid me forever.

The scribbling stopped with an image that left him irritated. What kind of deity added a smiley face to its messages?

Gabriel crossed his arms. Fate was getting more persistent. Gabriel was too busy to answer. At least, he told himself he was. He didn't look forward to meeting the deity past-Death considered viler than the Dark One.

A knock kept him from cursing the book and Fate out loud. The door opened to reveal Daniela, the headmistress, a severe-looking woman wearing the brown robes of the convent.

"You are in time for tea," she said. "Unless you want to blow up my Sanctuary again?"

Immortal Code, Rule 35: Sanctuaries and the shadow world between places are part of Death's domain to protect.

"Tea sounds good." Gabriel sighed. No one ever spoke to his predecessor that way. They'd been either enamored by her beauty or terrified of her, rightly so.

The stern woman whirled away from the door, leaving it open for him to follow. With a last look at the Oracle, Gabe trailed. His gaze took in the new wall they'd installed after the last one was destroyed by his best friend, Rhyn. The ultimate peacekeepers, the nuns running the Sanctuary would likely never let him forget the day the half-demon took out their wall.

The cafeteria where she led him looked medieval at best, a stone hall with lines of crude picnic tables and dark hearths. The only difference was the electricity powering lights in the heavy iron and wood chandeliers overhead and the intercom system installed into the walls beside each entrance. Located right off the kitchens, the cafeteria was awash with the smells of bread, fruit pies and the jerk-spiced meat the Caribbean was renowned for.

She poured them each a cup of steaming tea. Gabriel didn't touch his.

They sat and stared at each other. A man of few words, Gabriel hadn't gotten used to the political side of his job yet. Someone his size with his specific skills didn't ask for favors or need to be polite. Past-Death had only played nice with those she needed something from. Thus far, he didn't know what it was he was supposed to need from the nun in front of him, and he was too cautious to set this bridge on fire.

"You don't even like tea," Daniela accused him finally.

"No."

"Then why do you come here?"

"I'm maintaining Death's routine."

Daniela's eyes narrowed. "Friendship isn't a routine."

"She had no friends," he replied. "And the ones she did, she fucked over twice as bad as her enemies, like dumping her job on me with no instruction manual."

"The Code is an instruction manual."

"There's nothing in the Code about what I'm dealing with," he said.

"What *are* you dealing with?" Daniela folded her hands in her lap, her irritation at him replaced by interest.

Gabriel hesitated. "Our radars are broken. We're missing souls and fighting off demons to get to the dead."

"And the Lake of Souls?"

"Still bubbling."

"Two very separate issues," she said, pensive. "Maybe the problem is you. A former-human running Death's domain? What's the world coming to?"

"Not helpful," he said. "The Immortal Code, rule seventy four states that my status as a former-human has no relevance, once I was made Immortal."

"It was an attempt at humor, but I can see you have none," she replied flatly. "If Andre the Ancient was still around, he'd be able to help you with the demons. He was the most gifted tracker in the history of Immortals."

"Also not helpful, since he's dead-dead."

"You're Death. Bring him back."

Was she joking or not? She had to know raising the dead-dead broke *thousands* of rules! What little patience he had was waning fast. Gabriel stared at her stonily.

Daniela shook her head. "Past-Death would've figured it out. But if *you* can't do your job, then go back to the way it was originally, before past-Deaths hired on all that help. You fetch souls instead of the death-dealers. When in doubt, go back to the basics."

Surprised at the casual wisdom of her words, Gabriel was quiet.

"Use your compass instead of the radar. Maybe it'll reset things." Daniela sipped her tea.

"What compass?"

"The soul compass. It was what she used long before your time. I'm sure she left it there for you."

Gabriel didn't say what he wanted, that if his predecessor knew he needed something, she'd probably torched it before she left. He'd roamed the palace that was his home many times before returning to live out of the tiny cabin he preferred in the Everdark forest. He never thought twice about searching the rooms for something he didn't know existed.

"That's probably why she told me about it," Daniela smiled. "To tell you. I wondered at the time. Maybe I'm your instruction manual."

He looked at her hard. It wasn't out of the realm of the possible that the information he needed was hidden in some sort of sadistic treasure hunt created by the sociopathic goddess who held the title of Death before him.

"You miss her, don't you?" Daniela asked.

"Not the way you think," he answered, standing. "I'll see you next time."

"You're welcome," Daniela said.

Intent on hunting down his first real lead since things started going wrong, Gabe called open a portal to return to his underworld and the shopping mall-sized palace in the center of the living forest. The palace acted as a barracks for his assassins, who were trudging in after he ordered their contracts all cancelled. They moved out of his way as he strode through the wide hallways to the stairwell leading to the top floor, Death's floor.

He stopped in front of the closed door to the massive set of chambers that were supposed to be his. He'd entered twice since assuming his duties. There were too many memories inside, and he hadn't been able to return. Which past-Death probably knew, meaning any secrets she hid were within.

"I'm done with you," he muttered. He opened the door to the rooms he knew as well as his cabin. After all, he spent much time here, making love to her on the round bed down the hallway to his left.

It was the last place he wanted to visit, so it became the first place he went. Gabe paused as he entered the bedroom. It was bright, the windows open to the soft underworld breeze and curtains fluttering. The room was utterly feminine, from the pale colors to the silk and lace accents and carved furniture. It smelled sweet and spicy, a scent that always reminded him of pecan pie.

He frowned, noticing for the first time that the bed was unmade. It wasn't like past-Death to leave something a mess. Not that it mattered. She probably knew it was her last day and decided not to make the bed.

He stopped in front of a door near the far corner. It bore another note from Fate, written in elegant script on parchment and pinned to the door with a knife. Gabe pried the knife free and tossed it on the bed, reading the message.

Come on in and meet me.

Fate wasn't going to leave him alone, but this door ...

Gabriel stepped back. He'd been everywhere in the underworld and mortal worlds, but never through this door. His predecessor once told him that if he entered, he'd become like her in every way. He'd loved and hated her his whole life, a beautiful woman with neither mercy nor honor, who viewed mortals and Immortals alike as toys.

No, Gabriel would *never* go through that door. The fact Fate wanted him to made him more determined, for past-Death was always in some sort of ugly struggle against Fate.

Shaking his head, he walked once around the room, trying to determine where she'd hide something he needed. Somewhere he'd never look otherwise. Gabriel went to her jewelry box. Considering she lived for hundreds of millennia and her status as a deity, she didn't own anything fancy. Her jewelry box was tiny and wooden. It looked ancient, and he opened it carefully. It contained three items: a tarnished ring, a soul and a delicate silver necklace with a compass on the end. He lifted the compass first. Instead of pointing to the four directions, its edges were lined with ancient symbols he took to be writing from the time-before-time. He couldn't read them.

Guessing the compass only worked in the mortal world, Gabe emplaced it around his neck before picking up the green emerald – the form a soul took after death – and peering at it. Whoever owned the soul, he or she was important to find their way to Death's jewelry box. He replaced it and picked up the ring. It was old, silver, and covered with Celtic knots. He'd given it to her hundreds of years ago. She'd rejected him but kept the ring.

The memories were closing in on him again. He'd loved her once, and he would've bet his soul she loved him. When he did turn over his soul to her, she dumped him.

Immortal Code, Rule 2,000,010: Death shall not return a soul It has claimed.

He put the ring back and closed the jewelry box, wishing he could shut off his memories as easily.

He left for the mortal world and emerged in an alley in some large city. The list – a scrolling queue of names that lined his left forearm – was always changing. The next name up for claiming appeared. He plucked the compass from his chest and waited to see what it did.

Nothing.

Gabe dropped it and touched his forearm, willing the soul radar to guide him to the right place. A portal opened in front of him and he crossed through it, emerging in what looked like the Pacific Northwest. If the radar was working, the soul would be within a few feet of him.

There was nothing at all within a few feet of him, aside from knee-high wild flowers waving happily in the spring breeze.

"Dammit!" he roared. He flung one of his knives at the tree line, not caring if he hit anything or not.

The compass grew hot against his chest. He looked down and saw the arrow pointed towards one of the symbols. The name on his arm lit up again. He went through the routine: touch, portal, emerge somewhere new. This time, he was on a dirt road near a tiny village.

There was a body at his feet. He'd never been so thrilled to see a dead man as he was that moment. It was not just any dead man, but the *right* one. The name on his forearm disappeared as he knelt.

"Come out, you little bastard," he said. It wasn't the normal greeting Death gave souls, but he was too frustrated to care.

Green smoke swirled from the man's ears and mouth, forming a fog around Gabe's hand before crystallizing into a small emerald.

"One down," he said with a glance at his forearm. He didn't bother to try to count how many were waiting for him. He sensed the silent appearance of his friend and drew a breath. "I hope your week was better than mine."

"Probably not."

Gabe shifted in time to see the portal close behind the half-demon, Rhyn, whose muscular form, crackling aura and cunning, liquid silver eyes sent most people running the opposite direction.

"Did you send a message?" Gabe asked, frowning.

"Five. A day," Rhyn replied. "Maybe six. I hate waiting."

"I'll add the message system to the list of shit I have to fix."

"I'm stacking up bodies for you. No rush. Whenever you've got time."

"I'll send someone up to collect," Gabe replied. "You at the castle again?"

"Demon free for a month." Rhyn's chuckle was like a low growl, his sharp eyes traveling over Gabriel in what Gabe knew was brotherly concern. "You look like shit."

"Haven't slept in weeks," Gabe grunted and rose, tucking the soul in his pocket. "What's up?"

"I have a name for you," Rhyn continued. "Logan Myers."

Gabe glanced at his forearm. "On the list. You need him dead-dead?"

"Yeah, I guess," Rhyn muttered.

Gabriel stared at him. "If I didn't know better, I'd say you're trying to keep a secret."

"We spotted some strange demon activity last week. Shape-shifter demons, Gabe. They're stalking a couple of mortals."

"Hate those things," Gabe said.

"One of them might be targeting Logan Myers," Rhyn said. "We're watching, but it's not easy balancing the Council, demons and a pregnant mate."

Gabe smiled at the look on Rhyn's face. "I need to visit more often."

"Dude, you have no fucking idea. I'd take a herd of demons over this shit. One day, she's begging me to fuck her every five minutes. The next, it's my fault she's gained twenty pounds. I told her to lay off the ice cream. Been on the couch for a week. I don't know where you're going, Gabe, but take me with you."

Gabe laughed. Despite Rhyn's frustration, there was affection on his face as he talked about his mate.

"I admit, I'd rather deal with the shit I'm dealing with than a woman," Gabe said.

"Still with Harmony?"

"Yeah."

"Hmmm." Rhyn was studying him again.

"Don't look at me like that. She's a good girl. Stable and ..."

"Boring?"

"I was going to say drama-free," Gabe replied.

"Whatever."

"Like you know shit about relationships."

"I know that you'll know when it's right," Rhyn shot back. "I've been fucked since then, but I got my Katie. You need your Katie. You're driving yourself into the grave."

"Good one," Gabe said, appreciative of his friend's humor.

Finding a mate wasn't a priority, not when he was trying to fix his world. He'd watched Rhyn and Katie's relationship unfold from its rocky beginning, when Katie inadvertently rescued Rhyn from his sentence in Hell. Gabriel gave up his soul to help Rhyn and would do it again, especially seeing how strong their bond had become. Their world was far from perfect, but they were handling it together, as a team.

Immortal Code, Rule 3: The bond between an Immortal and its mate is sacred, unbreakable.

While he envied them, Gabriel really didn't want to go through all that shit with his own mate. Life was simpler without emotional attachments. Aside from drama, it was going to take half an eternity to straighten out the underworld without the distraction of a woman in his life.

"When do you need Logan taken care of?" he asked.

"When you have the time. We're trying to figure out what Darkyn is doing planting a shape-shifter demon on the mortal realm," Rhyn said, referring to the demon lord who wanted both their heads on pikes.

"I'll send someone up tonight."

"Uh, yeah, this guy has a connection to you. You need to go."

Rhyn was trying to be casual about it, but the half-demon had never asked Gabe for anything and was incapable of subtlety. This was important. Gabe had never heard of Logan Myers and didn't know what connection he might have, considering he had no living relatives or friends, aside from Rhyn and Katie.

"I don't know this guy from Adam," Gabe said then waited.

Rhyn grinned then laughed.

"It's funny, right?" Gabe said.

"Yeah."

Satisfied someone got his humor when none of the death-dealers did, Gabe grew thoughtful. They were all serious, absorbed with following the Immortal Code and performing their duties. They lived for nothing more. He'd been like that once. He changed so gradually, he didn't notice how much different he'd become, until he realized how much he was enjoying talking to his friend.

Rhyn was right. The death-dealers were boring to talk to.

"You're not gonna tell me why?" he asked with the same casual tone Rhyn used.

"Sometimes the head of the Council That Was Seven has to be discreet." Rhyn said through clenched teeth with a look of distaste.

"I can't get used to the political side of the job, either," Gabe said. "And you're welcome for rescuing you, and Katie and your unborn hatchling from the demons and –"

"He's connected to your ex-girlfriend." Rhyn threw up his hands in surrender. "You didn't hear it from me. I'm out."

Gabe watched him disappear through a portal, not understanding. He only had one ex-girlfriend, past-Death, and she was presumed dead. She had to be, or he wouldn't have been able to assume her role as Death. On the smallest of chances she was alive, she would've had to find a loophole to surrender her duty without losing her soul. While he could see her figuring it out, he couldn't see her choosing the mortal world. Her biggest issue with him had always been what she perceived as his *weakness:* his humanity and compassion for others.

Unless she came to the mortal world to torment more humans. *That* he saw happening.

He shook his head. Though he didn't know what connection past-Death had to some human, he trusted Rhyn above everyone. If nothing else, he'd check out this Logan guy this evening and see whatever it was Rhyn wanted him to see. In the meantime, he'd learn to use the compass better and decipher the symbols.

Twelve hours and forty three souls later, Gabriel gave up on the icons. No matter where the compass pointed, it led him to the correct body. The symbols were useless to him. He knelt over the latest body with a glance at his forearm.

Logan Myers had been dead for a couple of days at least. His body was hidden in the brush near a beach. Rhyn was right about the demons; Gabe smelled demon blood and saw the gashes across Logan's throat. He hadn't been attacked by anything remotely human or animal. A demon tore off his neck and face and drained him of blood. It'd be hard to spot the shape-shifter demon posing as Logan with his face shredded.

"At least they didn't eat you," Gabe consoled the dead man quietly. "Hard to get a soul that way. Come on out."

The green fog appeared at his words. He watched the green gem form in his palm and rose. He put it with the others in his pocket. The sound of the ocean was calming under the full moon, the steady ebb and flow of waves drawing him to sit on the beach.

Why was he disappointed not to find …more? Some reminder of past-Death, a sign she cared for him, a hint at the connection between this Logan and the woman Gabriel knew.

"The soul radar takes me to you, if nowhere else."

Gabe glanced up at Harmony's voice. He patted the sand beside him.

"Business or pleasure?" he asked.

"Business," his second-in-command and current lover said, seating herself.

"What broke this time?"

"The portal. I was delivering your orders and tried to get home but couldn't."

"How many are trapped up here?" he asked, irritated.

"Maybe twenty."

"I'll get it fixed," he said. He had no clue how and hoped the portal still worked for him. After all, the underworld was his. It couldn't deny its master.

Harmony was looking at him. "Don't you want to try it?"

"In a minute. I'm taking a break."

"Oh."

He doubted his night – or his next few thousand years – was going to get any better than this. He glanced at Harmony, whose green gaze was on the ocean. She was gorgeous in the moonlight, and desire stirred his blood.

"Since we might not make it back tonight, you wanna, you know, do something here?" he asked.

"There are four hundred and thirty three people within five kilometers waiting for Death," she said. "Though how accurate –"

"I wasn't talking about work," he said.

"You mean…" She was skeptical. "On the beach? Is that where humans do it?"

"Never mind," he said. For some reason, he felt more disappointed. He stood and offered her his hand. "We'll try the portal." He pulled her up and called a portal. The gray door to the underworld was present for him.

"I tried several times," Harmony said. "A few of us did."

"I believe you. Go home. I'll find the others."

She hesitated. "Gabriel, I can stay with you, on the beach. If you want."

"Don't worry about it," he replied. "We'll have time after I rescue the rest of the assassins."

"I'll wait up." She smiled and walked through the portal to the underworld.

Gabe faced the ocean. His gaze went back to the dead man Rhyn wanted him to find. Puzzled, restless, he returned and crouched beside Logan Myers. If Rhyn's Immortals were watching Logan, they'd have known he was dead when Rhyn found Gabe this morning. What was he supposed to be looking for?

With another look around, Gabe left. He had twenty assassins to rescue and countless souls waiting to be claimed. He'd come back later.

Duty first, as usual.

Chapter Three

By Saturday morning, Deidre was certain she never wanted to leave the ocean. She plopped an omelet onto Logan's plate then turned around to make her own.

"I don't know what's gotten into you, but I like it," she said, grinning.

"Nothing has gotten into me," he replied in a deadpan voice. He ate without waiting for her, his eyes either glued to her or the door.

"I guess the sea breeze is good for the libido," she continued. "You're a demon in the sack this weekend. Reminds me of when we just met."

"You think I'm a demon?"

She glanced at him. Was he offended or surprised? Deidre rolled her eyes without answering and went back to cooking her breakfast. She breathed in the ocean air. The bungalow cost as much as to rent for the weekend as a month of her apartment, but she'd never been happier.

"I never realized how much I missed nature. I've lived in Atlanta since I started college. Do you ever miss the countryside?" she asked.

"No."

"I really like it here."

She should definitely stay longer. She thought about it as she sprinkled cheese into the skillet. It wasn't like she was saving her money for anything. She'd be dead soon anyway.

No apologies, no regrets, she repeated the mantra she adopted when Wynn first diagnosed her as terminal.

"You want to stay here for the whole week?" she asked.

"Do you?"

"Yeah, I think so. Isn't it the most beautiful place you've ever seen?"

"The lack of security is unsettling. There are no locks on the doors or windows, and only one route of egress in the case of an emergency."

Okay, the sex was phenomenal last night, but their conversations had gone further downhill. Logan was an accountant, not a security guard, yet he barricaded the doors with furniture before bed in case there were criminals wandering the beach. He flat out refused to go out after dark last night.

"Whatever. It's a full moon tonight," she said hopefully.

"Yes." His voice was thoughtful.

She dumped her omelet onto her plate and faced him, leaning against the counter to eat. He'd inhaled his breakfast. His green eyes were distant. At under six feet tall, Logan was still almost half a foot taller than she was.

"Bonfire?" she prodded. "Or, you know, just a quickie in the moonlight."

"No, I think I'm going to town tonight."

"Good idea. We can go out."

"No, just me."

"Care to explain why you want to go out on a Saturday night without your girlfriend?" she asked, raising her eyebrow.

"I'm ah … not sure." He didn't look at her. "I'll be back Monday."

And then it hit her. Monday was their two year anniversary. He was going to propose. Deidre almost dropped her breakfast. She told him a million times there was no way she was going to marry him then turn around and die. They argued about marriage for weeks before he finally went silent on the matter. She'd thought he dropped it; maybe he hadn't. Maybe he figured she'd change her mind if she saw a ring.

He was in for a surprise if he tried. Angry at him again, she realized she'd been trying to work up the courage to break up with him for weeks. She had a private bucket list she didn't show him, one with things on it she wasn't sure she should want. Like, hooking up with a stranger at a bar like they did in movies and a few sex positions she'd been subtly trying to talk him into.

Unsuccessfully.

She was a few weeks out from never having these opportunities again.

"Okay," she said. "Have fun."

He looked relieved. She *felt* relieved. As much as she cared for him, he was driving her crazy the past few months. He didn't seem to get it. Her bucket list was getting longer while her time was getting shorter. He wanted to mourn and tread water until the inevitable. She wanted to do everything she'd ever wanted.

"You want to walk to the farmer's market this morning?" she asked.

He hesitated then said, "No."

"Okay," she said cheerfully. "I'll see you later."

She couldn't really be irritated with him. He was, after all, taking time off work during the busiest time of the year for an accountant to be with her. It counted for something but did nothing to soothe her anger.

Dressed in a sundress and sandals, Deidre left the bungalow on the beach and walked down the long driveway to the small road. She marveled at the world, the gentle sunshine, beautiful sky, the fragrant ocean breeze that ruffled her pink-striped blond hair, the soft crunch of gravel beneath her shoes. This was the most perfect place in the world.

The farmers market was teeming with the locals and makeshift booths lining a cordoned off section of the beach town nearby. She meandered through it, absorbing the life around her. Fresh produce, homemade foods, handmade crafts and soaps. She touched, smelled and tasted everything she could, determined to remember every pleasurable part of every day she had left. The homemade ice cream stand drew her attention, and she crossed to it.

"Can I help ..." he stopped.

Deidre glanced up with a smile. The guy behind the counter was staring at her, his mouth lax and his eyes wide. For the second time in as many days, she thought she saw red tattoos flash. They faded as she looked directly at them. Were these the first of the hallucinations Dr. Wynn warned her about?

"Are you here for me?" he whispered.

"Um, no," she turned to make sure he wasn't talking to someone else. "Just for ice cream."

"You're sure?"

"That's kinda why I came to an ice cream stand," she said with a laugh.

"What flavor?"

"Surprise me."

"No. I don't want to upset you."

Deidre looked over the flavors. She pointed out two finally. His hands shook as he scooped them into a bowl. She took it and handed him a five dollar bill.

"On me."

"Oh, thanks."

"Just, ah, remember that. Make it quick when I'm up."

Flustered, Deidre nodded and walked away with her ice cream. The woman she saw in downtown Atlanta had reacted to her the same way. Unwilling to let the weirdness ruin her day, Deidre dismissed the strange exchange, distracted by the smells coming from a display of homemade candles. She went down the line, smelling everything, until one candle in particular caught her attention.

"Smells good enough to eat!" she said to the lady sitting behind the table.

"Pecan pie."

She bought it then moved on. She passed three face painting clowns before she gave in and decided to have her own done. By the time she reached the beach house, her face was Smurf blue and she was laboring under the weight of the treasures she'd found. She walked in and paused in the doorway, listening.

"Logan?"

No answer. He hadn't texted her to say he was going out before heading to Atlanta this evening.

"This is getting old, Logan," she said with a sigh. Deidre piled everything on the kitchen counters and pulled out the candle. She lit it and set it on the back porch. Sitting down with a book, she propped her feet up on the table and relaxed, calmed by the sounds of the ocean and the warm sun. Eventually, she dozed off.

The candle's wick popped loudly enough to wake her awhile later. It was past dusk, and bonfires were springing up down the beach. Deidre grunted at how stiff her legs were. She twisted to see into the beach house. The lights were off. Logan wasn't home. A glance at her phone made her roll her eyes.

She was beginning to think he wasn't going to propose. He'd walked out on her. The hot sex, strange distance he put between them, sudden disappearance.

Yeah, he wasn't coming back.

She wasn't sure she cared. Deidre flipped on the lights in the bungalow and made herself stir fry with the fresh veggies she'd bought that day. The neighbors were having a party around a huge bonfire. The muffled beats of music thumped through her open windows. She watched them with a smile as she cooked.

She ate her dinner on the back porch then wandered out onto the beach barefooted. The ocean was cold, and wet sand squished between her toes. She walked down the beach opposite the party, gaze alternating between the ocean at her feet and the full moon climbing into the sky. Wind tossed her hair, and she tied it up in a bun. The sweet scent of rotting seaweed made her nose wrinkle. She glanced towards the brush and shrubs of an unkempt lot, where a crumbling foundation of an old beach house remained.

The beach ahead of her was open and dark. She grinned, pretending it was all hers. Deidre sat and dropped onto her back, staring up at the sky. She lay there for a few minutes, content.

"It's not safe out here for you to be alone." The voice was low and quiet. She didn't hear him approach, but he sounded close.

She rolled onto her stomach to see who spoke. The man standing in the weedy area of the lot was tall and thick, dressed in a trench coat, black clothing and heavy boots. His features were partially illuminated by the moonlight: a chiseled jaw and cheekbones, dark eyes and neatly trimmed, dark hair. The other half of his face was stuck in the shadows, giving him a surreal appearance, as if he had one foot in a different world. The breeze ruffling the curls that escaped from her bun went around him, not touching his coat.

"I'm good," she said.

"Famous last words."

She laughed, knowing he couldn't possibly understand why she found it funny.

"Water sprite or human?" He sounded genuinely puzzled.

"What? Why ...Ooohhh." she touched her face, recalling the stop at the clown's booth. Her face was stiff and blue while her hair was hot pink. "It's face paint."

"Interesting."

She ducked her head to hide her smile. The way he said it, he didn't find it interesting at all.

"Sorry to disappoint you." She rolled onto her back again. "Sit with me?"

"No."

"Alright."

There was a pause. "You're going to ignore my warning, aren't you?"

"Yeah." The stars were brilliant this evening. Absorbed by the sight, she began to think he left as quietly as he arrived. The stranger's dark form came into her peripheral. He sat a couple of feet from her.

He was bigger than he looked from a distance, the size of a linebacker. His elbows were propped on his knees, the trench falling back to show a lean body, flat stomach and muscular thighs outlined by the soft material of his pants. She thought she saw the glint of weapons lining his trench. While she didn't fear dying anymore, she was in no hurry to die, either. She'd passed through that stage after a few months and decided to make – and fulfill – her bucket list.

"Have you ever met a water sprite?" she asked.

"Once."

Yeah, the serial killer lunatic was probably going to kill her tonight. Did she have any regrets? She thought for a long moment. Just one: not dumping Logan before coming to the beach this weekend. Her eyes went to the chiseled features of the man sitting near her. He was handsome, with olive skin and eyes that looked as dark as the ocean. He was also too grave to appreciate the gorgeous night.

"What're you thinking about?" she asked.

"The day job."

"Oh, no," she told him. "The moon is full, the sky full of stars." She breathed in deeply. "I love the smell of the ocean. You can't sit here on such a beautiful night and think about the day job."

"I suppose."

"I'm going to guess you kill people for a living," she said, eyes on what was definitely a line of small throwing knives and was that a sword lining the thigh on the far side? "Not judging. Just saying, take a break and look around."

He looked at her hard. She returned her gaze to the sky at the awkward silence that fell.

"Are you drunk?" he asked at last.

"No. Just happy to be alive."

"That makes one of us." The dry note in his voice made her think he had his own inside joke. "You're not drunk. You're not a water sprite, and you're not afraid to be alone on a beach with a man you think murders people."

"You know pretty much everything there is to know about me," she said, laughing. "My turn. You're an off-duty serial killer with an affinity for weapons with blades who believes in imaginary creatures and takes the time to talk to crazy women lying on the beach."

"Everything but off-duty."

"That does not bode well for me."

"You're not on my list tonight."

"Glad to hear. Not fearing for my life is a total turn on," she retorted.

He laughed. The sound was rough, as if he didn't laugh often.

"There you go," she said. "Life's too short to waste a night like this."

He met her gaze. Deidre was surprised to feel her body grow warm from the inside out. She'd never been turned on by a look, though if anyone could do it, the intense man beside her could. Her face grew hot under his scrutiny, and she was grateful for the face paint covering her blush.

"You're right," he said at last, a trace of a smile pulling up the corners of his full lips. "What're you thinking about?"

"Oh, you don't want to know," she said with a sigh.

"I asked, didn't I?" It came out as a growl.

"You don't talk to women much, do you?"

"Answer, woman."

She smiled. "Death. I'm thinking about death."

He went still, the humor fading from his features.

"Kinda puts a damper on any conversation," she said. "I've got a few things left on my bucket list. I was thinking about working a couple of them in this week."

"Why?"

"Obvious, isn't it? I'm dying."

"Then why are you so happy?"

"Because I'm not dead yet," she said.

His gaze went to the ocean. Deidre felt bummed. He was disturbed. She'd pushed down his walls then driven them back up.

"You're brave," he said.

"I realized that to appreciate what I had left, I had to let go of everything," she said with a shrug. "No apologies, no regrets."

"What's on your bucket list?"

She was quiet for a moment, thinking. "I want to go skydiving. And successfully make a soufflé. Visit the Grand Canyon, travel to Scotland, hot air balloon ride. You know those Christmas lights that are shaped like red chili peppers?"

He snorted. "Yeah."

"I want those in my kitchen. I've always liked those," she murmured, pensive.

"What else?"

"Some of them are really stupid."

"People who say that mean the opposite."

"You really want to know?" she asked.

"Yeah."

"Okay then. Skinny dipping. Making love in the moonlight on the beach. Sex in a hot tub or shower. You know I've never been on top? I bookmarked a few pages in the Kamasutra for things I'd like to try, but I'm too afraid to show anyone." She stopped. "I should *not* have mentioned that. I made this really awkward."

"It's just getting interesting," he replied. "I like this bucket list better. Bet I could show you a few things you won't find in the Kamasutra."

"Well, what're we waiting for?" she replied without thinking. "Let's go!"

"I'm game," he said, laughing quietly. "Though I'm wondering why you're alone on a beach in the moonlight without someone to make love to you with a bucket list like that."

"Oh, god. I've humiliated myself," she mumbled.

Suddenly self-conscious, she touched her face. It felt hot. She couldn't remember the last time she'd been so honest or embarrassed, and in front of a complete stranger! No wonder he asked her if she was drunk. Something about him made her feel comfortable, or she wouldn't be sitting alone with a man dressed like the angel of death on the beach after dark, revealing secrets she didn't tell her boyfriend of two years.

"I'm so sorry. I think I'm gonna go." Deidre stood to leave. He caught her wrist, and a strange energy moved up her arm. She paused, the unfamiliar sensation a combination of adrenaline that made her blood quicken and electricity that made her skin tingle. It fascinated her.

"Stay. Please," he said, letting her go. "This is the first good night I've had in forever."

She shivered, as much from the warm current working its way through her body as the cold ocean breeze. The sense he wasn't wholly of this world returned. It should've scared her. Instead, it made him different enough to be like her: a shadow on the fringe of society. Without knowing anything about him, she had the uncanny impression they were a lot alike in how alone they were.

He was the first real person she'd ever met.

She sat near him. The man stretched out his legs in front of him. He pulled her closer to him, until their sides were pressed together, then released her as the weird energy fluttered through her. Her sense of self-consciousness grew as the physical contact made her appreciative of the size and heat of his body. His strength was the kind she could almost imagine herself melting into. Unlike Logan, this man wouldn't hesitate or complain about holding her on the days when the pain was too much. His strength was constant but steady. He took in the world with thought.

Why did she feel like she knew him?

"How are you going to do it?" he asked.

Startled, Deidre's gaze went from the muscular legs to his face. He was looking at her, as if he already knew.

"I'm guessing in a week. Maybe two," he said.

She said nothing.

"Something simple and quick. You're brave, but you're terrified as well. You don't want to give yourself a second chance to think it over."

He held her gaze as he spoke. His dark eyes were fathomless in the moonlight. He saw through her, pushed down the barriers of her soul and stepped back to examine it. The sensation left her feeling exposed.

"Your face may be blue and your hair pink, but I don't see you doing anything messy, like taking a shotgun to the head." He considered her. "You'll go somewhere on your bucket list. Grand Canyon. You're a jumper."

Who the hell was this guy?

"Bingo," he said, reading the expression on her face. He looked out to sea again.

Deidre felt the release of whatever strange magic he had. Part of her wanted to lean against him, knowing he wouldn't turn her away. She resisted, already too aware of him physically.

"What gave it away?" she asked in a hushed tone.

"Nothing anyone else can see."

His response made her think she wasn't far off in thinking he'd at least read her mind.

"If it helps, death is indiscriminate," he added. "Everyone dies. It's nothing personal."

"Spoken like someone on the other end of the equation," she said, offended by his casual dismissal. "So you figured out my plan." She moved to face him, distracted by the fact he shifted his body to keep from breaking their physical contact. Though she'd rather not be trapped by the eyes that made her blood quicken, she forced herself to look at him.

He studied her, waiting.

"Death is the most universal experience possible, true, but it's also the most personal. There's nothing else on the planet that forces you to really see and accept who you are as the day the doctor says you're dying. You have to make a choice that day: to continue living or to start mourning," she started angrily.

The stranger was silent, gaze riveted to her.

"Death lets you see the stars and the moon instead of how dark the night is. It teaches compassion, because sitting on the bus, I know the person beside me is someday going to have to search his soul the same way I did, so I don't mind that he's spilling his coffee on my shoes. My *new* shoes." She grimaced at the memory. "Knowing what's coming, I've never felt more alive than I do now."

When she stopped, the sound of waves filled the quiet.

"I made this awkward again, didn't I?" she said, embarrassed once more by the passion she put into her speech.

"Not for me," he replied. His eyes were warm, his features losing their gravity as he gave a genuine smile. "I don't know why our paths crossed tonight, but I'm glad they did."

"Really? I'm not freaking you out?"

"I admire your spirit and your passion. You make me feel human again."

"Good, I think," she replied.

They gazed at one another, the tension growing thicker.

"Is kissing a stranger on the beach under the full moon on your bucket list?" he whispered.

Definitely. Warmth bloomed within her while her heart beat with more excitement than a moth outside a lighted window. Surprised at her body's eagerness, Deidre said nothing.

"I'll take that as a yes."

She nodded. She found herself leaning into him in anticipation. Her time was too short to turn away a tall, dark, handsome, intriguing, dangerous stranger she met on the beach in the moonlight who smelled good. She closed her eyes.

The stranger's kiss was light, his full lips warm and soft. The strange energy hummed through her again, and she became aware of new sensations she'd never noticed with anyone else. He smelled like dark chocolate, spices and man, a combination that ensnared her senses and made her want to taste him. The heat of his body sank through her clothes, and the idea of his hot skin pressed to hers made her lower belly burn.

He withdrew long before she was ready for him to. She opened her eyes. Their faces were inches away, his fingers tracing a line of warm electricity down her jaw.

"Okay?" he asked, voice husky.

"Yeah."

"I got time. You got a one night stand on your bucket list?"

Her breath caught in her chest.

"You can be on top," he added. "Once. There's a few other things I have I mind."

Deidre laughed, uncertain what else to do. This was too crazy, even for her, and yet she *wanted* to unwrap the mysterious man before her and experience his heat, his strength. She wanted to feel his large hands on her body and to find out what it was about him that made her feel like he was the only real person she'd ever met.

"You'll face down death but not spend the night with me?" he teased.

She kissed him. His response was hungrier, deeper. He opened to her, and she was thrilled to find he tasted as good as he smelled. He wrapped an arm around her and pulled her into his body. Deidre yielded, alarmed but yearning. The desire lighting her body was hot and aching, as if her body innately knew how well he'd satisfy her.

She was lost in a haze of heat and dark spices, of his hot kisses and solid strength, until his touch left her. Dazed, she was surprised to find they were standing in the bedroom of the bungalow. She didn't remember walking there. Moonlight streamed through one window while the rest of the house was dark. Before she could ponder how they'd gotten there, she felt his heat again. Deidre touched him tentatively, awed by his size and the gentleness of his touch.

His large hands slid down her bare arms and settled on her hips, drawing her against his body. She shuddered, enthralled by the sensations running through her. She didn't even reach his chin. It was like being drunk, but on a person, not alcohol.

"Okay?" he asked again.

She tilted her head back to meet his gaze and smiled. "You're not backing out, are you?"

He chuckled. "Oh, no. You're mine tonight."

There was something primal in his low growl that made her body boil. She felt delicate and feminine in his arms. This was the way it was supposed to be. *He* was the way it was supposed to be.

His next kiss was consuming, hungry yet sweet, teasing her with a hint of promise and driving her body to new heights of awareness. She needed to feel his bare body against hers, ached for his hot hands to brand her as his. She wanted to wake up with his scent ingrained in her skin.

Lost to him already, Deidre sank into his world, not caring if it was the last night of her life, if she spent it with him.

Chapter Four

Mid-morning sun warmed Gabriel's face, drawing him out of the deepest slumber he'd experienced in years. He didn't push himself awake but let his senses register the world slowly. The satiny sheets of the bed smelled of the woman he'd made love to for hours last night. The ocean breeze cooled his back, and his heartbeat was synced to the movement of the tide. The restlessness was gone from his blood, his body relaxed in a way he couldn't remember feeling.

Past-Death took him to her bed most nights for thousands of years, and he'd never woken this sated and centered. He knew why: every night was a test. Every night, he had to be better than the night before: More creative, more sensitive to her body. He'd loved her every way he could, knowing the night she was dissatisfied with him, she'd replace him. She never lost control of herself or failed to remind him that it wasn't her fate at risk each night.

Last night was different in too many ways for him to count. This woman had been wild, uninhibited. She'd held no part of herself back from him and surrendered in a way that made him want to memorize each sigh, the softness of her skin, her silky depths and the way her blue eyes grew dark with desire. She hadn't judged him or restrained him. She touched him everywhere, hungry to consume him. She'd wanted him in a way the other women in his life never had. When her body ceased convulsing from an orgasm, she'd kissed him with tenderness and asked him how she could make him as happy.

He had *fun*. Gabe snorted at the simple thought. She'd teased and flirted with him, adventurous one minute and submissive the next in a way that made him burn hotter for her. He experienced none of the awkwardness he did with Harmony. Though he intended to make the night about the dying woman, he found it was as much about him.

It was one night he wanted to enjoy. His guard hadn't lowered; it crashed as he let himself experience every part of her body, her cries and the passionate spirit that held him captive on the beach. She'd ensnared him with her laughter and touched him with her words about Death.

About him. What he should be. What he used to be, before the events of the past year. He'd once done what she did: faced Death and refused to cower, instead deciding to live on his own terms.

Aroused again, he reached over but didn't feel her body. Gabe twisted his head to see the bed empty. The shower was on, and she was singing. His eyes went to the bathroom door, and he considered joining her. He'd fulfilled his end of the bargain and crossed quite a few things off her bucket list last night.

Gabe roused himself and sat. One night stand. That's all this was. This was a good opportunity to leave. He had a ton of work to do and was no closer to fixing any part of his underworld. He came back to search the body of Logan Myers and figure out what it was that Rhyn wanted him to know. He found a strange woman with pink hair and a blue face, sprawled on the beach, staring at the sky with a childlike fascination. He really thought her some sort of underworldly creature that somehow ended up washed up on the beach.

Last night was an oasis, a slip. It was probably a mistake, but he truly admired her spirit. He'd never been guilty in his role as an assassin or as Death, until sitting with her on the beach. He'd wanted to make it up to her for her life ending too soon. Or maybe, he wanted to get rid of his own regret at the idea of taking such a sweet soul, someone who might've been a kindred spirit in a different time and place. He saw himself with a mate like her, one who was able to remind him what it was like to feel human.

It was one night. He had work to do. He'd see her soul soon in the underworld.

Gabe got dressed, tying one boot as the sound of the shower stopped. He braced himself to tell her thanks for the night and farewell. Hopefully there were no tears, and he was able to walk out instead of tumbling into bed with her like he wanted to.

"Can I ask you something?" she called through the door, an odd note in her voice that made him pause as he pulled on the other boot.

"Yeah," he said.

"Are you one of those serial killers who marks their victims?"

He chuckled. He'd never considered Death a serial killer, but he did kind of fit the bill.

"Like with a tattoo or something? I'm not mad. Curious. Or whatever," she paused, as if waiting for his response, before continuing. "It's pretty. Love the color and the swirlies, like Celtic designs around it. I saw on TV that some serial killers are possessive and do these sorts of things."

Gabe rose and swirled on his trench coat. There was genuine uneasiness in her voice that drew his interest. His movements stilled as he listened.

"Is your name Gabriel by chance?" she ventured.

He froze. His heart stopped in his chest, and for a long moment, he couldn't breathe.

"Show me," he managed at last.

"It's okay. I think I'll stay in here."

He strode to the door. It was locked. Gabe snapped the doorknob with ease. She jumped from her place before the mirror. A towel was wrapped around her and her pink hair clipped on top of her head. Written across the top of her back was his name and the geometric Immortal script marking her as his mate by Immortal law. She faced him, her pink face scrubbed clean.

Immortal Code, Rule 973: An Immortal mate of human origin is marked with its Immortal's name so that other Immortals know to protect and welcome the human into the Immortal society.

"Deidre," he whispered.

She nodded uncertainly.

Deidre. The name past-Death adopted when she took on a human form in her underworld before she quit. Though her hair was pink, there was no mistaking the delicate facial features, porcelain skin and large eyes of the woman who tormented him his entire life then dumped the underworld on him. The eyes that once turned from black to white to every color in between were now blue-green in color, and her face held a human flush enhanced by his lovemaking. Her lips were plump and red from their night.

She was scared, probably because he was a second away from killing her.

Gabe took a step back. His body tensed to the point of snapping. He whirled, called for a portal and left his betrayer, his former lover, the woman who had been his world, until she snatched it from him.

His *mate* by Immortal law!

She'd tricked, cornered and beaten him one last time.

Thousands of years of repressed fury bubbled within him. He was too angry to see where he went as he crossed through the shadow realm. After awakening feeling at peace, he was close to pulling a Rhyn and decimating the world around him in an explosion of raw fury.

Gabe was halfway across the gym where the Immortal foot soldiers were training before he knew where he was. Sensing the pulse of power, Rhyn whirled from the far side. He issued a quick order Gabe couldn't hear through the blood pounding in his head.

"How fucking long did you know?" he roared.

The Immortals scattered while Rhyn remained.

"I'm not going to-" Rhyn started, hands up.

Gabriel smashed into him, picked him up and threw him. Rhyn slammed into the wall above the doors the Immortals were fleeing through. Gabe saw the half-demon's eyes flare silver and pursued, wanting ... *needing* a fight.

"How long, Rhyn?" he demanded again.

This time, Rhyn didn't back down. Gabe drew sword and dagger and unleashed on the half-demon, whose demon magic and quick reflexes responded with power that'd overwhelm anyone but Death himself. Gabe fought, not caring what happened. They smashed the gym around them, two titans dueling.

Finally, after what felt like an eternity lost in his fury, a dagger sliced his forearm. The physical pain penetrated his mental anguish, and he lowered his weapons. Gabe threw his head back, breathing hard and sweating.

"You ... good?" Rhyn panted.

"Define *good.*"

"I figured you'd be by yesterday." Rhyn tossed his weapons. "We've known for a little over a week."

"About the time everything started going to shit with the underworld."

Anger rose, but Gabe reined it in, exhausted. He flung away the weapons and the trench coat. His clothes were strangling him in heat after the match. He pulled off his sweater then dropped back onto the sparring mat, focusing hard on calming himself down. Unfazed by Gabe's attempt to hack him into pieces, Rhyn sat beside him.

"Rhyn?" One of the half-demon's brothers called from the doorway.

"Bring it."

Gabe twisted his head to watch Kiki, Rhyn's right hand and the most dependable of the brothers, walk into the gym. He looked around in disapproval at the disaster that remained of the new gym. Gabe sat up as Kiki approached, and the tall Immortal paused, critical gaze taking in both of them.

"It's Gabe, Kiki. He's not gonna kill you," Rhyn said.

"Yet," Gabe added.

"Neither of you are funny," Kiki replied. He set the iPad he carried on a totaled machine a few feet away without coming closer. "Rhyn, a reminder that Gabriel is a deity or at least, a human-turned-immortal-turned-deity, which means you must use-"

"-discretion," Rhyn finished through clenched teeth.

"Exactly. The first page has the talking points outlining what you can share," Kiki said before addressing Gabriel. "Do you have any idea how much this gym cost to set up?"

Practical and detail-oriented, Kiki was well-dressed and lean. Like all the brothers on the Council That Was Seven, he had the same father and a different mother. His Oriental features were chiseled, his turquoise eyes bright. He'd lived in Tokyo before Rhyn dragged him to the castle as his charge d'affairs.

"Send me the bill," Gabe said drily.

Kiki was unimpressed. "Discretion, Rhyn." He turned and walked out. Rhyn stood and crossed to the iPad, reading quietly.

Gabe heard the voice of Rhyn's mate, Katie, from the direction of the hallway as she greeted Kiki on her way in. Her blue eyes lit up when she saw him. Curly brown hair was pulled into a ponytail, and she wore jeans and a long-sleeved

T-shirt that was tight over her swollen belly. The last of Gabe's anger slid away at her glowing smile.

Rhyn glanced up, gaze lingering on his mate, then shook his head.

"Hasn't hatched yet?" he asked.

She rolled her eyes at him. Gabe watched as she crossed the gym to give her mate a kiss on the cheek. The tension in Rhyn's body doubled. Gabe cleared his throat, amused at seeing the half-demon putting so much effort into restraining himself.

"Good to see you, Gabe," she said, moving to stand near him. Rhyn trailed, never farther than arms reach when she was around.

"You, too, Katie," Gabriel replied. He reached out to rest a hand on her belly, as he did every time they met the past few months. The life within always greeted him.

"So you let Gabe touch you but not me," Rhyn said, bristling.

"Gabe didn't knock me up," Katie replied archly.

"Trade you an iPad for your mate," Gabe replied. He tried to grab the iPad with his other hand. Rhyn yanked it away.

"Take her. Keep her, until she's normal again," Rhyn growled.

Katie ignored him. Gabe lifted his chin towards Rhyn in a silent request. She winked.

"What color are her eyes?" she asked. "Can you tell yet?"

Gabe used his magic to communicate with the small life.

"Silver, like Rhyn's," he said.

"Well, I guess you're right, Rhyn. It is your kid," she said with a sigh. "I wasn't sure there for awhile. Kind of a blur. Nothing memorable."

"Nothing memorable?" Rhyn shifted his attention to glower down at his mate. The edge in his voice and the flash of his eyes made Gabe hide a smile.

Sensing his dangerous mood, Katie leaned into Rhyn and gazed up at him. He wrapped one arm around her instinctively.

"I'm having a mood," she said.

"Gods. What now?" he snapped. "Cheeseburgers? Ice cream? Another fucking week on the couch?"

"More like, you give Gabe the iPad and take me upstairs," she murmured. "Now." As she spoke, she pulled the iPad loose and handed it to Gabe. She tilted her head to the side, exposing the delicate skin on her neck in an unmistakable invitation to the demon side of her mate. Rhyn made no attempt to reclaim the iPad, attention fully on her.

"I'll find you later, Gabe," he said, his fangs growing.

Gabe didn't waste time. He silently thanked Katie and grabbed his gear. With Rhyn nuzzling Katie's neck already, Gabe sensed they weren't going to make it to their bedroom a few floors up.

He returned to his underworld, reading the information on the iPad as he walked. The talking points Kiki had given Rhyn told him nothing aside from the name, date the Immortals found her and the human-Immortal blood percentage. She was ninety eight percent human.

He flipped to the next page as he emerged near the palace, agitated at realizing he'd get no privacy, not with the hundreds of assassins loitering. Instead of taking a portal to his cabin in the Everdark forest, he hiked through the woods. A trail formed in any direction he wanted to walk. The branches of the trees slithered overhead while brush and bramble scampered out of his way.

His cabin was tiny, two rooms, with the walls lined with weapons he'd collected over the years. He stretched out on his back on his bed. The picture of Deidre almost made him throw the iPad, but he forced himself to flip through the various surveillance pictures Rhyn's Immortals had collected. Until he saw the one of her kissing someone.

Then he set down the iPad, reminded of how often past-Deidre teased him by taking other assassins to her bed.

He couldn't think straight. Nothing made sense. The Deidre he'd spent the night fucking was not the same as the goddess who tormented him. And yet they were. The deity had purposely left the underworld in shambles then gone to the mortal world, probably knowing her reincarnated human form was his mate.

His *mate.*

It was too much. By Immortal Code, he was obligated to claim her and protect her as Rhyn had Katie. Seeing her made him want to explode.

Her scent lingered on his skin. Gabe hated her yet couldn't escape the memory of the compassion and spirit that made him take a stranger to bed last night.

Death lets you see the stars and the moon instead of how dark the night is.

He heard the unquenchable life in a dying woman. Her words touched him on a level he didn't expect, one he thought was dead, destroyed by past-Death.

She was alive. She was *his*. She was dying.

He sank into stormy contemplation, clueless how to handle the latest of his challenges. Thousands of years of love-hate memories left him conflicted. How did he follow the Code, when it felt like it was betraying him? He'd never resented the Code before. It was his life, a sense of comfort and structure. This time, it was suffocating him.

The forest outside his windows grew dark, and he forced himself to his feet. Sitting around wasn't going to solve any of his problems. Whenever he was frustrated by her before, he went back to doing what he did best: his job.

He pushed Deidre out of his mind. Composed enough to handle his duties, Gabe left his cabin. Wired energy made him edgy and his step quick. Harmony met him in the woods, coming from the direction of the palace.

"What's broken?" he asked.

"The portals are working."

"Really?"

"Yes. We tested them. Soul radars are still broken, but we can at least travel to the mortal world."

Instead of being cheered by the news, he was annoyed. He didn't know why they broke in the first place or how to fix them if it happened again. She was waiting for him to tell her what to do.

"That's good," he said at last. He rubbed his jaw. "Send half of the assassins to the mortal world. Have them positioned at the Sanctuaries and at Rhyn's. I'm not taking chances this happens again."

"Will do. Are you alright, Gabriel?" she asked.

He hadn't thought twice about running into her in the forest. It was past dark, and she'd come to his cabin most nights for the past two months. Gabe realized she was coming to see him for pleasure, not business this time. And he had a mate, one he refused to touch but who now kept him from finding solace with any other woman.

"I'll survive," he said, waiting for her to get the joke. When she continued to gaze at him, he sighed. "Get it? I'm Death, and I said I'll survive?"

"Interesting," Harmony said.

The Deidre from the beach would have appreciated it. She'd laughed hard when he murmured to her about *famous last words*. He'd found it funny for his own reasons. By the end of their conversation, he understood why she laughed, too.

Anger building again, Gabe strode forward. Harmony followed.

"Is the hole in the sky sealed at least?" he asked, referring to the entry the demons had made into Death's underworld prior to his takeover.

"Sealed this morning. The last of the demons are dead-dead."

"Good. I'm going to see someone about something that might help our radars. You know how to find me." He didn't wait for a response but opened a portal and crossed into the mortal world.

It was daylight here, and he instinctively assessed it was still Sunday on this side of the world. Time passed differently in the underworld than the mortal world. Sometimes, a night in the underworld was equal to seconds in the mortal world, sometimes a night and sometimes, a few nights. A few hours had passed since he left Deidre's bed this morning; it was early afternoon in the mortal realm.

He strode through the crowded Egyptian street market, the Khan al-Khalili, one of the oldest markets in the world. Gabe made his way through the narrow alleys and disjointed walkways that wound like a maze through the market. Tourists and locals alike bartered with vendors, and he entered a tiny silver shop, where he sensed the Immortal he sought.

"Tamer," he said to the small man behind the counter.

He pointed to a set of narrow stairs. Gabe climbed them, forced to go sideways to make it up to the top.

"If Rhyn sent you…" Tamer, Rhyn's half-brother and one of the four surviving members of the Council That Was Seven, growled from across the room.

"He didn't."

"You here for me?"

"No."

The largest of the brothers in size, Tamer's temper most closely resembled Rhyn's. The two were always at each other's throats, and Gabe had witnessed their decision making skills on the Council. Rhyn always won, but Tamer got his punches in. Lounging in a pillowed corner of the room, Tamer resembled a cross between a lion at rest and a desert Bedouin with his muscular form and loose garb. His skin was dark, his eyes turquoise, as their father's had been. He drank hot tea from a glass.

"You're my last resort," Gabe started.

"Great way to start a discussion. I feel motivated to help you."

Ignoring the acid tone, Gabriel sat in the chair a few feet from him. He pulled off the compass and held it out. Tamer studied it. After giving him a moment to examine it, Gabe spoke.

"Two questions. One, can you read the symbols?"

"They're archaic. They predate anything I've ever seen before. I might have a later text with similar symbols I can use to trace the roots of the writing," Tamer answered. "What's the second?"

"Can you duplicate whatever this is?"

Tamer's eyes took it in expertly before he rose. "Come on."

He strode through a curtained doorway in the corner and down a long hallway almost too narrow for either of them to fit.

Each of the brothers on the Council was gifted in some way. They'd never trusted one another enough to share, and their father made things worse by compartmentalizing the Council's business and pitting the sons against one another long before he was killed. Gabriel knew the secrets of all seven from interacting with them over the years. There were things Immortals told Death – or Death's messengers – they dared not tell anyone else. Who better to keep a secret?

Tamer's gift: He was the keeper of the Immortal histories, records not even Rhyn knew about, that only Tamer could read with his magic.

"Shouldn't you know this shit? Since you're Death?" Tamer asked over his shoulder.

"Shouldn't you be in the Alps with Rhyn?" Gabe returned.

"I was *granted* leave. I need goddamn permission to take a piss."

As much as the brothers hated one another, Rhyn and Tamer were too similar for Gabe to feel anything but amused by the open hostility. They emerged through a back door into a massive foyer made of white marble and limestone with ancient carvings on the walls and statues positioned throughout. Tamer continued to a locked door on the other side of the foyer. It led down another hallway lined with wooden doors, each marked with an Immortal symbol.

He pushed open the fourth door, walking into a large room stacked from floor to ceiling with ancient tablets, manuscripts, and books. In the center was a table stacked with more of the records.

Gabe paced as Tamer climbed a ladder to tablets stacked at the top of one limestone shelf. His thoughts kept straying to a certain pink-haired woman whose scent on his skin was driving him crazy.

"You're making me edgy," Tamer snapped.

Gabe stopped and crossed his arms. Tamer descended, one cracked tablet in hand. He tossed it on the table with a thud then set the compass on top.

"Some similar," he said, pointing out the symbols.

Gabe frowned. Whatever Tamer saw, he did not. The writing on the tablet was too faded to make out, and the symbols he did see looked nothing like those on the compass. He sensed magic, though, and understood the Immortal was able to access the tablet in a way Death had no need to.

"The writing on this is from the time-before-time," Tamer said, motioning to the compass. "Before the last great demon raid. Maybe even before the *first* demon raid. It's an interesting piece. Not an original, but probably kept to spec."

"How old is the compass?" Gabe asked.

"Compass? That would've been nice to know."

"Does it matter?"

"It might. Its function could determine the meaning of the symbols, since the most ancient Immortal writing is based on a complex system of symbolic context. A letter in one place might mean something completely different somewhere else," Tamer explained. "This compass is only a few thousand years old. I can spend time researching it or I can try to duplicate."

"Duplicate," Gabriel replied. "I've got an army of bored assassins on the verge of killing off the wrong souls. I'd rather fix that first. If you can duplicate, I'll need as many of those as I can get."

Wariness crossed Tamer's face as he realized what the compass did. He stepped back from the desk, as if fearing the compass would claim his soul right there.

"The magic binding it is Death's," he said. "If I can piece it together, I'll need your help to test it."

"Easy."

"And of course, I'm a businessman." Tamer smiled. "This'll cost you."

"I'm sure you wouldn't dream of charging past-Death."

"She wasn't best friends with Rhyn.'"

"I'll owe you a favor of your choosing, if you can make these work," Gabe said.

"Nice. Deal." Tamer held out his hand. "Come back tomorrow. I'll have something for you."

Gabe shook on it, satisfied he at least had the right person looking into the issue. Tamer pulled out his cell phone and scowled. Gabe saw the screen light up with a text message.

"Rhyn says to send you his way when you're done here. Didn't think deities took orders from half-breeds," Tamer said, shoving the phone back in his pocket.

"Thanks." Gabe left the library. He called a portal when in the hallway and walked into the shadow realm, stopping in place.

The gray door to his underworld was gone. It denied entrance to its own master. Gabriel's temper was close to boiling over, for the umpteenth time since he inherited the responsibilities of Death. If his week was any indication, this was not about to fix itself as easily as the portal shutting out his assassins.

Immortal Code, Rule 22: Only deities can interfere with the duties of another deity.

He suspected Fate was done with smiley faces and polite invitations. Locking him out of his underworld wasn't a summons Gabriel could ignore.

Determined to fix what he'd fucked up, Gabriel drew a deep breath then strode towards one of the sunny portals to the mortal world.

Rhyn stood beside a lake on the property the Immortals owned around the castle in the French Alps. The shade of the forest where Gabe emerged was cool, the spring sunshine warm. The scent of pine and blooming flowers was thick in the air. He sensed the presence of his assassins nearby, relieved a few had made it out of the underworld before the portal disappeared.

"Notice anything out of place?" Rhyn asked, peering into the lake.

Gabriel joined him and cursed. The bottom of the lake glowed with souls. The green gems reflected the sunshine, shimmering through the clear water.

"How many of my dealers made it here?" he asked after a moment.

"Five. I dragged them out here as soon as we found this." Rhyn lifted his chin to the far side of the lake. "Want me to drain the lake?"

"Not yet. I have no way of getting them back to the underworld," Gabe said.

Rhyn met his gaze, surprised.

"C'mere, Harmony," Gabe said, using his magic to project the quiet order across the lake.

"I never thought I'd be the one to say this, but I think you have real issues, Gabe," Rhyn said.

Gabe nodded, forced to admit he no longer had any idea how to fix whatever was broken in Death's domain. Harmony appeared beside him.

"We're shut out of the underworld," he started. "How many made it up?"

"Forty three, five here, thirty eight spread among the Sanctuaries," she answered promptly.

"Can you sense them?" He indicated the souls.

"Within a short distance. We sensed them from the castle but not much farther."

"About five kilometers," Gabe judged. "It's something. Spread everyone out and have them start searching. We need to locate how many lakes are now possessed."

Rhyn chuckled. Harmony didn't get the joke. Gabriel wasn't surprised.

"And then what?" she asked.

"For now, our mission is to protect the lost souls from the demons."

"Very well."

Gabe turned towards Rhyn, in sore need of a pep talk as only his best friend could provide.

"Gabriel," Harmony's voice was hesitant.

He looked at her once more. She considered for a moment then shook her head.

"Later," she said. "I'll catch up with you."

"You're doing good, Harmony," he said, sensing her concern.

She smiled politely then opened a portal.

"Even I know what that was, Gabe," Rhyn said, amused.

Gabriel suspected he did, too. A status check on their relationship, the one he hadn't told her he couldn't have, because he was trapped into mating with a formerly sadistic psychopath-turned-human he was trying hard not to kill. If he slipped and broke that rule, he didn't have to break it off with Harmony. He hadn't made up his mind about either woman yet.

"I have a bet with Katie," Rhyn started. "She thinks you blew up the gym because Deidre is your mate by Immortal law. I said it's because you slept with her."

Gabe grimaced. "You're both right."

"That is not good, Gabe," Rhyn said with a shake of his head. "You realize that means you can't kill the bitch who tortured you for all those years?"

Immortal Code, Rule 10 & 11: An Immortal must regard the protection of its mate above its own safety. It cannot purposely kill its mate.

"I ...no. Son of a bitch." He was quiet for a moment, broiling internally. "None of my dealers can either, if I can't be directly involved in her death."

"Did you read the file?"

Gabe gave him a cold look.

"You couldn't get past the pictures, could you?" Rhyn asked. "I didn't think so. If I saw Katie with another man, there would be nothing left of this world."

"I spent thousands of years and broke the Code twice. The past few months, I've come close to breaking it hundreds of times to keep the underworld from shutting down. Now, I *know* what I should do by Immortal law. I saw the mark with my own eyes. I knew what it meant. And I walked away. I didn't even try. I have an obligation, Rhyn. To the lost souls, to the underworld, to a woman I want to hate," Gabe finished. "I'm failing every one of them."

"I did a shit ton of damage trying not to be Katie's mate. She wouldn't have survived, if not for you, Gabe. From the beginning, you were willing to do what I couldn't," Rhyn said. "You didn't fail me. You won't fail the underworld or *her*."

Gabe listened. He'd watched over Katie every night for months while she and Rhyn struggled to find their paths. He'd helped build the bridge between the two who were sworn together as mates after they barely learned each others' names. He'd talked Rhyn off the ledge a million times then defied past-Death to protect Katie. He'd done it for the people he cared about as much as out of his sense of honor. He did what was right. He always did, no matter what the personal cost.

"What is wrong with me?" he muttered, furious at himself. Somewhere along the past few months, he lost his way. He didn't even know what the right thing to do was anymore. He'd caught himself creeping closer and closer to breaking Immortal Codes.

"She's human now. She can't do to you what she used to," Rhyn said at the silence. "I mean, the deity we knew would never dye her hair the color of a water sprite's."

Or paint her face blue, Gabriel added.

"She's yours by Immortal law, which means you're fucked. I know that much. I can't help you much with any of these things." Rhyn motioned to the souls. "I figured you'd freak out. I've got Immortals keeping an eye on her. The demons want her bad, but they're waiting for something."

"The demons are stealing my souls, too. I can't figure out how they're beating us."

"Their activity is off the charts. It's my responsibility to monitor and deter them in the mortal world," Rhyn said. "I'm as fucked as you. The Council is a mess. My dear half-brother Erik went into hiding and hasn't been seen in weeks, leaving his part of the world completely exposed. We're still trying to recover from the demon raids last fall. We lost so many Immortals, Gabe. I destroy shit. That's what I do. But even I can't keep up with the demons. I'm the only one who can track them, and only when I'm close enough to kill them."

"We've both got issues," Gabriel said.

"Kiki keeps telling me Andre would've figured this out by now," Rhyn continued. "You know how fucking annoying that is?"

"Oh, yeah," Gabe smiled. "I get that a lot, too."

"I know one thing for sure: the Immortal mood beast that is my mate is the only reason I'm making it through this. Pick your battles, Gabe. You won't win this one, so give up now."

Gabe sensed Rhyn's words came from an enormous amount of thought. The Immortal had the temper of a demon, the power of a deity and the self control of a child. His bond to Katie tempered what was otherwise a disaster of epic proportions. That he'd grown a little more thoughtful and a little less reactive in how he handled adversity impressed Gabe.

It didn't mean Gabriel was ready to swallow the reality of being bound to the woman who tortured him. Not yet.

"She's human, Gabe."

"I get that," Gabriel snapped.

"This must be what it's like when Kiki's trying to school me," Rhyn said with a laugh. "No, you don't get it. You're not hearing me. She's *helpless*, like Katie was."

"You're calling me a piece of shit for walking away, aren't you?"

"I'm saying, learn from the shit I went through and go get your mate. Dump her off here, if you don't want to deal with her, then get your ass down to the underworld and fix that shit. You're Death. The only person who can do it."

Everything Rhyn said was right. By Immortal Code, Gabriel was obligated to protect Deidre. He didn't have to love her or live with her or even talk to her. Past-Deidre controlled his life. Now that she was gone, she only ruled his life if he allowed her. He didn't know how to shake off that yoke or his anger.

His thoughts went to the door in the corner of past-Death's bedroom in the underworld. Would walking through it prevent more issues and fix those he had? Would it help him figure out how to deal with Deidre? What about Fate, who'd been hounding him for weeks? Would the deity shed light on what Gabriel was doing wrong?

"Alright," he muttered. "There's something I should've done awhile ago. I need to go do it now."

"Go."

"If the death-dealers give you any issues, talk to Harmony," Gabriel advised. "This might take me a little while."

"I already had a discussion with one of them," Rhyn said. "They understand."

Gabe snorted, knowing his assassins were unaccustomed to being challenged by anyone. If they backed down, it was because Rhyn did much more than talk.

He called a portal and walked into the center. The gateway closed behind him.

"You win, Fate. I'm coming to see you," he grated. Turning in a full circle, Gabe waited for a sign the deity still sought him. It took two full revolutions before he saw it, a mortal gateway that pulsed brighter than the others, beckoning him. Uncertain what to expect, Gabe went through it.

Someone was waiting for him at the Sanctuary, seated on the beach. Gabe's step slowed as he neared the man dressed in a white shirt held closed by two buttons and cream linen pants rolled to his knees, as if he'd been walking in the ocean. He wore no shoes and sat with his arms draped over his knees. His body was wiry and lean, his skin golden from sun. His eyes were white then black then changed from every color in between, his brown hair of medium length and wavy, ruffled by the sea breeze. He was stunning, ageless, as the goddess of the underworld had been, except this deity's smile was genuine.

"I knew you'd come," Fate said.

Gabe studied the deity gazing up at him. He wasn't expecting Fate to crack a joke. Past-Death and Fate had been at each other's throats for as long as Gabe could remember. He'd never met the enigmatic deity, but he'd heard past-Death go off about this man after every interaction.

"You didn't find that funny."

"I did," Gabe said, allowing a trace of a smile to slip free. "I don't know why I'm here."

"Because you're single-handedly destroying the universe. No pressure." Fate patted the sand beside him.

Gabe lowered himself into a crouch a few feet away, recalling the last time he'd been on a beach. He wanted more of the woman he'd sat with yet guessed he'd kill her if he was allowed. Or make love to her again. Or both.

"I'm doing something wrong, aren't I?" Gabe said.

"I'd say so. You've been fighting me since you took over."

"Not on purpose."

"That's what they all say," Fate replied. "Sometimes, you need to acknowledge the path at your feet and just go with it."

"Fucking deities speaking in riddles," Gabe muttered.

"Maybe it's easier than you're making it out to be."

"Or maybe you all should consider making instruction manuals before dumping your duties and walking away."

"You don't need an instruction manual. The Code is flexible for us godlings," Fate said, chuckling. "She was better than me at fucking people over. I warned her about crossing the line. It's one thing to see the Future; it's another entirely to try to change it. You fuck with the Future, you fuck with me."

"I want to do my job. I don't want to fuck with you or any of the others," Gabe said firmly.

Fate studied him for a long moment. "Every chain of events starts with one push, a catalyst, the perfect mix of different elements that craft a path and make an outcome more likely. For example, when you ignored my first summons" - Fate glared at him - "you made the deterioration of the underworld eighty percent likelier. When you ignored my second summons, you forced me to make a choice and start off a new chain of events."

"What choice was that?" Gabe asked, genuinely interested.

"To intervene or not. That eighty percent went to ninety nine. You forced my hand. The alternative was irreparable and too permanent for my taste. I sort of like the mortal world existing."

Coldness trickled through Gabriel. He knew he wasn't performing well in his new role, but to hear Fate tell him he was on a crash course with catastrophe made him sick to his stomach.

"I'm listening," Gabe said. "Tell me whatever it is I'm screwing up, so I can fix it."

"I did tell you. Stop fighting me." Fate grinned. "Stop overlooking the resources you have at your disposal. For example, there's a room in your palace in the underworld where you've refused to go. You know what's there. You know why you haven't wanted to visit."

Gabe looked away. "I don't know exactly what's there."

"You know when you cross that threshold, there's no going back. It's a one way visit, and that is what you fear most, the possibility you turn into what you hate."

"Yeah," Gabe said quietly. "That's it, then. All these issues because I didn't open one door?"

Fate shrugged. "It's one of your issues. You'll have to figure out the rest, first. You had access to that door and didn't walk through it. Now, you get to earn your way back to that choice. Right now, I can't trust you to set up what I'd call *healthy* chain of events."

"Clean up my messes in the mortal world then you'll let me go home," Gabe summarized.

"Correct. Easy, isn't it?"

Fate narrowed down his challenges to those he was able to handle. But only because he fucked it up so bad, there was no other choice. The emeralds in the mortal lakes, the uncollected souls, the broken radars, the demons stealing souls. His challenges on the mortal realm alone were overwhelming.

"Will I know when I'm on track?" Gabe asked.

"It will be so obvious, even you will see it. You now have a thirty five percent chance of succeeding. Isn't that better than one percent? No need to thank me. Just doing my job."

Gabe smiled. He should've known he'd end up liking someone past-Death hated. The deity managing the Future was wise in the way of an ancient immortal that had seen everything since the time-before-time, yet laid back and friendly, two traits Gabe didn't expect.

"Why did my predecessor hate you so much?" he asked.

"Because I had the power to tell her no, and I did it often," Fate replied.

"That sounds about right," Gabe said, recalling how much she liked to be in control. "Why are you helping me?"

Fate winked. "I like having the last laugh."

"Deidre."

"Past-Deidre made a wager with me. I agreed and of course, yanked her Sight so she couldn't cheat. She lost," Fate said. "I've been sitting here all day, waiting for you and debating what I'll say when I see her again."

"What was the bet?" Gabe asked, amused to know the woman who fucked with him had herself been fucked with by the man beside him.

"Ask me again when you decide to follow the path at your feet," Fate said. "Assuming you make it that far."

They were quiet for a long moment, listening to the ocean. Gabe wasn't going to ask what happened if he failed. He wouldn't let himself fail. He'd floundered up until now. Too much relied upon him for him to continue barreling towards disaster. No more excuses. No more personal weakness.

"Thanks," he said and stood. "Is it a safe guess that I now owe you?"

"Only if you succeed," Fate replied. "I already know what I'll ask for."

"Alright. Wish me luck." Whatever favor Fate asked of Death, it'd be huge.

"I'll see you in an hour."

"Not sure I like the sound of that," Gabriel said, eyeing Fate.

"Chain of events, my friend."

Shaking his head, Gabriel left, headed to the place he knew he needed to be. For the first time since taking over the underworld, he had a small semblance of direction. It wasn't enough to salvage his mess, but it was a start.

Chapter Five

Deidre paced on the beach behind her bungalow, unable to do anything but lecture herself over and over about how stupid she was to sleep with some random stranger. Her blood still raced whenever she thought of his hot touch branding her body. She'd done things with him she'd never admit to, things that made her never want to see him again.

Things that made her knees weak and her eyes drift dreamily to the ocean as she remembered. Something about him touched her on a level that left her feeling at peace, as if he, too, understood what it was to face death each day and struggle to see the light instead of the surrounding darkness. She wasn't alone when she was with him.

He was so gentle and tender in bed, savoring every touch. He didn't treat her as an outlet for his own release but as a partner on a sensual journey, one where pleasure was a gift as much as a reward. It was more than sex. It was deeper, beyond the physical joining, the sense of being one. She held nothing back as he drove her to sensations and heights she'd never imagined.

She shook her head and focused on her phone again, willing Logan to return one of her dozens of calls or texts. Dressed in jeans and a tank top, she plopped onto the beach then hopped up. Her body was humming with the stranger's weird energy. She couldn't sit without fidgeting or think straight.

She found herself walking down the beach to where she'd met him the night before. She hadn't considered why he was there, just like she hadn't thought twice about tumbling into bed with him.

"Like some common whore," she muttered.

After seeing his name tattooed across her back and the look of pure murder on his face, she hid in the closet until certain he was gone. The man she'd seen in daylight and the one who'd kissed her so passionately in moonlight became two separate people. One she wanted to spend eternity in bed with; the other she felt the need to flee.

"Stupid, stupid, stupid. This is totally karma," she told herself angrily. "You sleep with a wacko, your boyfriend won't return your calls. You deserve this, Deidre."

It was three o'clock. She wasn't going to be on the beach when dark fell, in case Gabriel came back. Nose wrinkling from the scent of rotting seaweed, she glanced towards the crumbling foundation of the beach house. Her eyes went to the sand in front of the lot. This was where she'd met him, the man who rocked her world. He'd been standing in the brush.

Deidre tried to call Logan again. The phone rang and went to voicemail. From somewhere nearby, she heard someone else's phone ringing and stepped out of the way, off the path running along the beach. Couples and families had been walking up and down the beach all day. Their footprints remained in sand wet enough to become packed but not wet enough to be squishy.

"Hi, Logan. Me, again," she said. "Please call me back."

Hanging up, she shook her head, pissed at him. He really had left her. She deserved it after last night, but still, why didn't he at least answer and tell her he was done with her? He'd taken the car; it was *her* car!

Angry at him, Deidre texted him. She heard a familiar ring tone – the one he assigned her – and looked up hopefully.

She didn't see him. Puzzled, she texted him again.

Again, the ring tone. The sound came from the deserted lot. Deidre tried calling him. She heard the phone ring and followed the sound. It stopped when the call went to voicemail. She did it again and again, moving into the brush, where the scent of rotting seaweed came from.

Dialing one last time, she looked up and froze.

The body a few feet away was bloated and pale, missing its face and dressed in the shirt she bought him for his birthday, the one with his initials – *LJM* – embroidered across the pocket. The phone was ringing from its place in his jeans pocket.

That's what the man, Gabriel, had been doing in this spot last night. He killed her boyfriend. Maybe he meant to kill her, too, but slept with her instead. Or maybe, he planned on coming back for her tonight.

He really was a serial killer. What the fuck was wrong with *her* that she not only drew the attention of such a person but slept with him?

"Oh, god, Logan," she breathed, eyes watering.

Alarm surfaced. She'd gotten Logan killed by dragging him to the ocean. The killer had already marked her with his name.

She was next.

Full-blown panic hit her. Deidre staggered away and ran to the beach house. She snatched her purse and fled out the front door, running as hard as she could down the driveway. By the end of it, she was sobbing. She dropped to her knees, the vision of Logan's faceless body forefront in her thoughts.

She'd cheated on him and gotten him killed. He didn't deserve this! *She* was the one who was supposed to die, not him!

She cried for a few minutes then forced herself up. She had to get out of there and go somewhere safe, her apartment, hours away from where the murderer was. There were too many things she'd wanted to do before dying; now that someone might kill her, she realized how unready she really was. She definitely didn't want to end up like Logan.

Somehow, Deidre made it to town. She pushed her sunglasses on and hailed a cab.

"Atlanta," she told him in a shaking voice.

"Ma'am, that's a three hour drive. The cost –"

"I'll pay it. Please, just drive." The desperation in her voice drew his attention. She willed herself not to cry, but she started soon after he left the beach town.

The cabbie said nothing. She managed to pull herself together after awhile but was unable to forget what she'd seen, what she'd done. It was entirely her fault Logan was dead. She deserved the brain tumor. She deserved to die.

She'd never been so scared.

It was dark by the time the cab dropped her off in front of the high rise where she shared an apartment with Logan. Deidre paid the driver and hurried inside, her mind reeling and her body buzzing with the weird energy of the killer who'd marked her. Whenever she felt overwhelmed from her oncoming death or the doctors' news, she ran to her room until she was strong enough to face the world again. The urge to hide forever made her feel sick.

Deidre left the elevator and went to her apartment. Her hands fumbled with the keys three times before she managed to unlock the door. She flung the door open and slammed it closed, about to run for her room, when she stopped cold.

"Logan?" she whispered, shocked to see the man she'd thought was dead standing in front of her.

He stared back, mirroring her surprise.

"Omigod, Logan!" she all but screamed. Deidre flung herself into his arms, pulling his face down to spread kisses across his features. "You're alive!" She began crying again. "I thought … I saw you .. and the phone I kept calling and calling and you didn't … at the beach and I did something so horrible you'll hate me…" She half-babbled, half-sobbed.

"I didn't understand any of that," Logan said but returned her hug. His body was stiff, as if he wasn't used to hugging her. She found herself comparing him to the stranger, whose body had molded around hers, as if he was made for her and no one else.

Deidre didn't care. "I am so sorry, Logan. So, so sorry. I never meant to hurt you. I don't know what happened. I'm so, so sorry! I thought you were dead!"

"Why would I be?" he returned.

"You wouldn't return my phone calls," she said, calming. "Did you lose your phone on the beach?"

There was a pause. "Yes."

She didn't let herself listen to the instinct that told her the body she'd seen was wearing the clothes she bought him. Too happy knowing he was alive, Deidre hugged him harder.

"Logan, I saw a body on the beach. I thought it was you. I thought I lost you." She looked up at him, eyes watering again.

"I'm right here." He withdrew, and she noticed he was agitated.

"Look, Logan, I don't care why you left me at the beach house. If you don't want to be with me, it's okay. I'm just … I'm so happy you're okay," she said.

"I want to be with you," he said in the same tone he used to describe the deficiencies of the beach house's security.

"You might not after I tell you this." She took a deep breath. "I did something terrible."

He crossed his arms, waiting. Deidre wiped her eyes and saw the mascara smeared on her fingers.

"Let me freshen up a little first," she said with a watery smile. "Give me a minute?"

"Yes."

She couldn't help feeling familiar annoyance at him as she turned away from him. While beyond thrilled he was alive, she realized she still wanted to dump him.

"Wait." His sudden grip on her shoulder was tight.

"What's wrong?" she asked, wincing.

"Gabriel." He read the tattoo visible through the tank top's straps.

"You're hurting me," she murmured.

He released her.

"That's what I have to tell you. I have to go to the bathroom first though."

Deidre crossed to the bathroom and closed the door behind her. She glimpsed the mess that was her face and decided to wash it and redo her makeup. She needed time to compose herself to tell him about her one night stand. He'd probably storm out and leave her. At least he was alive.

Leaning against the sink, she breathed out a deep sigh. She felt horrible thinking it, but she was utterly relieved whoever it was on the beach, it wasn't Logan. Her thoughts clearing, she realized she needed to call the police about the body she found.

With another deep breath, she leaned over to push aside the shower curtain and grab her face wash. Her hand paused as she stared in bewilderment at what sat in the bottom of the bath tub.

Bones. Lots of them. And a human-looking skull. They looked too clean to be real, like props bought from a Halloween store. What was Logan doing with a disassembled skeleton in the bath tub?

Deidre washed her face and redid her makeup before venturing to peek into the bathtub again. The sound of squishing drew her attention to the bath mat next to the tub. What appeared to be red wine was squeezed out of the bath mat at the weight of her step. She lifted it to see the outline of a puddle of the liquid beneath the mat.

Blood, not wine. Wine didn't congeal like this did. Disgusted, she stood. It was more blood than from a razor cut but nowhere near enough to justify a full skeleton in her bathtub.

This entire day was weird. Was she that far gone? The doctor said a sign she was deteriorating would be hallucinations. First the tattoos, now bones.

Deidre leaned down and touched a bone to see if it disappeared. It didn't. It certainly felt solid. There really was a pile of bones in her tub. Was that better or worse than hallucinations?

"You okay?" Logan's knock jarred her.

"Coming." Deidre wiped the blood off her foot onto a towel, unable to piece together what the hell was going on. When did she step into the Twilight Zone?

She left the bathroom, weirded out. Logan was in the living room. The lights were on and glowing, the television on quietly. She thought she heard the door to their bedroom close and glanced back.

"So, Gabriel," Logan's voice was casual enough to tell her he suspected something.

Deidre's shoulders dropped. She sat on the arm of the sofa.

"I did something. If you don't want to forgive me or can't, I understand," she started.

He was gazing at her warily.

"I kind of had … well …" she sighed. "Logan, I slept with someone else."

"Gabriel," he guessed.

"Yes. I don't know who he was and will never, ever, ever see him again." Her eyes watered. "Logan, I think he killed someone. And now, he's going to kill me. He marked me like serial killers do." She turned and pulled her hair aside to show him the tattoo once again. "I found the body and I thought it was you and I lost it. I came straight here. I am so, so sorry! So sorry!"

He gazed at her, emotionless. She expected him to react, but he didn't. She heard a sound from their room again and stood, understanding.

"Oh, Logan," she breathed then rushed on. "You're having an affair, aren't you? That's why you've been acting weird and came back and why you're not upset at me."

"That's … possible," he allowed.

"Oh. You couldn't tell me?" She felt hurt, knowing she didn't deserve to feel upset at him after doing the same thing.

"No."

"I understand, Logan. I'm so sorry about … you know." She motioned to her head. "She can come out. I'm not upset."

It really was over. She should've known. No one wanted a dying girlfriend, especially when she'd flat out refused to marry him. Logan rose quickly as she started down the hallway. Deidre knocked then opened the door to their bedroom, startled.

"Or, I guess you can tell *him* to come out," she said. The man in her bedroom was kind of creepy: tall and lean with blond hair and eyes so dark, she couldn't see his pupils. Logan's choice in men was definitely lacking."It's okay. I know. I'm not mad. My name is Deidre."

"I've heard a lot about you." The blond man's smile was slow, predatory, his teeth sharpened into points and his dark gaze piercing. "I'm Jared."

She took an involuntary step back into the hall. "Nice to meet you."

Jared approached. Unnerved by the strange man, Deidre backed away until she bumped into the wall.

"I like your hair," he said, looking her over. "Reminds me of a water sprite."

The familiar phrase made her chest tighten. The instincts she'd ignored at seeing Logan alive grew louder. Something was wrong here. The bones and blood, the scary man with pointed teeth.

"After you." Jared motioned to the living room.

"Go ahead. I've gotta go to the bathroom," she replied.

He shrugged and padded down the hall.

Deidre turned to the spare bedroom. They kept Logan's baseball gear there, and she felt the sudden need to have a bat in her hands. She opened the door and flipped on the light.

The bedroom was covered in blood. The spare bed was soaked with it, and it pooled around the legs. There were handprints on the windows, as if someone had tried to escape, and blood splattered on the ceiling and the walls.

Unable to process what was before her, Deidre closed the door and swallowed hard. The sense of calm settling inside her was unnatural, like the rest of the day. She stared at the door. At some point, her life had gone from crappy to freakish. It started when she had a one night stand with a serial killer.

Was that it, then? Had she really died last night and entered this strange reality? Was this purgatory? Reparation for bad karma?

Could she leave? Return to her own world?

Far calmer than she'd ever been, she crept down the hallway. Logan and Jared were in front of the television, talking about the basketball game. Like two guys hanging out who thought it was normal to have bones in the bathroom and blood covering the spare bedroom.

She was going crazy. Or she'd died. There was no way this was real. It was a sign, though, that things had gone on long enough. Maybe this was the push she needed to take that final step, the one that'd take her out of this world completely. Hallucinations, fate or some sort of mania brought on by her brain tumor, she wasn't going to wait for the Grand Canyon. Either she was dead and didn't know it, or she was close enough to take matters into her own hands.

Engrossed in discussion, the two men didn't notice her cross the kitchen to the entrance. She yanked it open and gasped at the wall of man before her.

"Gabriel," she whispered, looking up from his chest to his dark eyes. She felt the connection to him again, strong and deep, as if her fate was bound to the serial killer who'd come to claim her. There was no sign of the gentle man who made love to her last night, nothing but the cold, stony features of death. This time, there was no mistaking the weapons lining his trench coat or the sword along one thigh.

Deidre whirled. "Logan!" she cried.

The two men leapt up. Gabriel pushed her aside, into the kitchen, swinging out the sword with ease at odds with his large form. Jared scrambled out of the way, but Logan wasn't so lucky. His head flew off in one direction while his body dropped.

For the second time in one day, she saw the dead body of her boyfriend.

Deidre ran. Her heart and breathing drowning out every other sound, she raced down the hall and around a corner, sliding to a stop as she saw the men headed her way. They carried weapons, too, and their eyes were pure black, their teeth pointed like Jared's. She darted the other direction down the hallway and slammed open the stairwell. Sounds of pursuit came from a few floors down, blocking her escape.

She went up. Eyes blurred with tears and bewildered, she couldn't make sense of anything around her anymore. Whatever this was, she was done with it.

They were chasing her. She heard them and launched herself up the stairs, two at a time. Breathless, she reached the exit onto the roof and pushed it open, flinching at the alarm that sounded. The Atlanta night was muggy and dark; a thin layer of smog trapped the city's light and made the sky glow an eerie yellow-orange. Deidre ran and ducked behind a massive swamp cooler. She shook too hard to pull her phone free from her pocket and call for help.

Several men passed by where she was hidden, and she backed away as quietly as she could. She pressed herself against the warm, humming swamp cooler and turned a corner, only to come face to face with Gabriel again.

Deidre bolted. He snatched her, pulling her into his body before she could struggle. One arm locked around her while his other hand covered her mouth. He pressed her head back against his chest. The reminder of his size and strength scared her. He handled her like she offered no more resistance than a ragdoll.

"Quiet," he whispered into her ear. "As much as I'd like to kill you, I won't."

His breath tickled, and she shivered. Her body roared to life at the scent of his dark spices while she fought the urge to break down into hysterics. Wrapped in his warm body, she couldn't move if she wanted to. A side of her really didn't want to, even knowing he'd killed her boyfriend.

Twice.

His heartbeat was strong and steady, the thick arm wrapped around her as it had been when he held her after they'd made love for the last time before falling asleep. The sense of being protected, safe, floated through her. She fought it. She was his next target. She wanted to go down on her own terms, not lured into a false sense of safety before he chopped off her head.

The sounds of pursuit grew fainter. When they fell silent, Gabriel moved, his grip loosening around her.

"Stay here," he ordered. Deidre stayed in place long enough for him to put some distance between them. He faded in and out of shadows, as if he was part of them, the heavy trench coat making him look like some sort of sinister Batman.

She inched towards the edge of the building. It was fifty meters away, far enough he could catch her, if she wasn't careful. Easing to the edge of the swamp cooler, she eyed the distance and drew a deep breath.

He'd guessed right. She was a jumper. She hadn't planned on jumping off *her* building, but the events of this night made the idea more appealing than having her head severed from her body or ending up a pile of bones in a bathtub. Deidre squared off against the waist high wall between her and her destiny.

She sprinted. She passed the halfway point and forced herself to keep going. If she gave herself a second to think, she'd stop and sob, until someone else came by and killed her. She passed the three quarters point, and tears filled her gaze.

"Deidre!" Gabriel's shout was closer than she expected.

She ran as fast as she could, knowing it was her only chance. Reaching the wall, Deidre ignored the scrape of concrete against her hands and knees as she clambered on top. She paused, gazing down at the street lights thirty stories down. Wind whipped up the building and tossed her hair.

Either I'm already dead, and nothing happens. Or, I'm alive and about to be dead.

With a deep breath, she closed her eyes and jumped.

The sensations of freefalling made her stomach turn. She panicked as she fell. This felt too real for her to be dead. Air roared by her ears. She opened her eyes, forbidding herself from screaming as the pavement below grew closer. She seemed to be moving so slowly, crisply aware of every sensation, every thought.

Someone tackled her. She gave a cry, confused as arms wrapped around her. The flutter of a black trench coat blended with the dark sky as Gabriel twisted them in midair, so he'd hit back first, with her protected in his arms. Deidre couldn't move as they fell in slow motion. She saw the flash of a street lamp. Before they hit the concrete, darkness swallowed them, and they fell through a cold, damp place punctuated by strange yellow doors.

Suddenly, they broke free. Blinded by sunlight and blue sky, she closed her eyes.

They hit the ground hard. The impact jarred her to the core. Gabriel's arms fell away. Her breath knocked from her, Deidre didn't move for a long minute then sat up, gasping. She scrambled off him, senses reeling. Blood soaked into the sand around him. He was unconscious – or dead? – while she stood on a beach near blue-green depths so clear, she could see the white sand at the bottom of the water.

She'd done it. She'd killed herself and Gabriel and landed … here. Did heaven look like an island in the Caribbean? She turned around. Ocean surrounded the small island, upon which a fortress sat, several hundred meters away, up a sloping hill on top of solid rock.

A stunning man with a large smile dressed in white stood a few feet away, his brown hair ruffled by the sea breeze.

"Are you… are you an angel?" she asked, hopeful yet confused.

"That's not as funny as you think it is," he replied. "Dammit. I swore I'd get the first *and* last word in this time. Fifty percent chance of that now."

He moved closer, and she found herself arrested by handsome features and eyes that turned every color in the world. He wasn't human. She had to be dead.

Taking one arm gently, he turned her back to him and pushed her hair away to read the tattoo. He pulled her to face him and released her, satisfaction on his face.

"Is this heaven?" she tried again.

"Oh, no. Nowhere near that," he assured her. "I've waited to tell you this since we met long ago." He paused and drew a deep breath.

Deidre felt the sense of losing it again. She was going to break down any second, but the effort the man before her put into preparing himself held her horrified attention.

"It will mean more to me than you, at this point, but I am at peace with that," he continued. "Ready?"

Speechless, she waited.

"Checkmate," he said and gave her a blinding smile. "*That* was worth the wait."

"What the fuck is going on?" she cried at last, tears bubbling again. "What is this place? Who are you? Am I dead or not?"

"In about five minutes, the big man there is going to wake up. There's an eighty two percent chance he'll kill you, if you're not behind those walls," the man replied. He pointed to the fortress. "I am a fan of free will, so it's your choice. But if I was you, I'd start running." He stepped aside, happy for reasons she couldn't remotely comprehend.

Deidre glanced back at Gabriel. How did a serial killer get into heaven?

The smiling stranger's warning clicked. Whatever reality she fell into, it wasn't over yet. There were no other buildings, nowhere else to hide that might withstand an angry Gabriel. She ran up the gravel road leading to the wooden door in the fortress. The door flew open before she could knock to reveal a stern woman in a monk's brown robes. The gravity of her features fell away as she tilted her head, smiled then flung her arms around Deidre in a tight hug.

"I knew you'd come back," she whispered.

Deidre's insides were cold.

"Come on, come on." The woman said, tugging her into the convent. "We'll have tea."

Shaking, Deidre wiped her face and followed the severe woman through the simple, stone fortress outfitted with electrical wiring and occasional satellites. Did heaven need satellite television?

They entered a dark dining hall, where a pot of tea and two tea cups sat waiting for them next to a carafe of amber alcohol at the table nearest the entrance.

"Sit, dear! I made it the way you like it." The woman before her was truly happy to see her. "I'm Daniela." She held out a saucer and cup.

I dive off a building, and now I'm having a tea party?

Uncertain what else to do aside from have a mental breakdown, Deidre accepted the tea. The china chattered in her trembling hands. Daniela observed her for a moment then replaced the cup with a glass filled with the alcohol. Deidre drank it down, hissing at the burn of the harsh liquid. Daniela refilled the glass without asking, and Deidre drank more. The warmth of the alcohol filled her. It felt real, which meant this place was real.

"Where am I?" Deidre managed at last.

"Sanctuary. A place of refuge. You're safe here."

"Safe from what?"

Daniela shrugged. "Whatever you're running from."

"Gabriel," Deidre said. "He killed my boyfriend."

"Did he?" Instead of the horror Deidre expected to see, Daniela's face warmed even more, softening the skin around her eyes. "He really does care about you."

Deidre couldn't manage a response to such a ridiculous statement. Daniela didn't seem completely insane, but who else said things like that? Deidre drank more of the brandy, until it stopped burning her throat, and the world grew a little less sharp around the edges.

Daniela's head twisted to the side, and she frowned. "I hate it when he visits." She stood and walked to the door, saying nothing more.

Deidre slumped and held her head up with her hands. She heard Daniela outside the dining hall, lecturing someone. Deidre rose, eyes settling on the doorway leading into the neighboring kitchens. Wobbling after the alcohol, she crossed the dining hall, hoping to find a way back to reality. Or heaven. Or … somewhere else.

The kitchens were dark. Loaves of bread were rising along one counter beneath thin cloths. It smelled of chicken and rice and something sweet. The scents were real enough and made her realize she hadn't eaten all day. One whole wall was lined with homemade brandy.

Deidre stretched upwards to grab another carafe. She heard voices in the dining room, one distinctly male. Terrified Gabriel was coming to kill her, she sought a place to hide, finally settling on a small, dark space under a counter.

She sat as far from the opening as she could, brandy clenched in shaking hands. The footsteps of those entering the kitchen were solid against the stone floor. A pair of legs paused in front of her cubby hole.

"You can come out or I can drag you out." While male, this voice wasn't Gabriel's. This one was more of a growl, part human, part something else.

Deidre rested her forehead against her knees, tears on her face. The speaker crouched, a muscular man with liquid silver eyes. He wasn't human, either. He reached in and snatched the brandy. Deidre pushed herself against the wall.

"Why do you insist on giving our women alcohol?" he demanded of Daniela, who stood beside him. "You know it's against the Code."

"If you didn't bring them here either half-eaten by demons or thinking they're dead, they wouldn't need alcohol," Daniela snapped.

Demons. Deidre hadn't landed in heaven; she'd landed in hell. Was it for killing herself or for killing Gabriel? She squeezed her eyes closed, ears buzzing and tunnel vision forming.

The man's arm wrapped around her and pulled her out of the hiding place. She shook too hard to resist. He grunted as he swung her up in to his arms and carried her away. Probably to be thrown into a lake of fire.

"You were banned from here," Daniela sounded angry.

"You're welcome for convincing Gabe not to knock down the rest of your walls to get to this one."

Their voices warbled, until he set her down. A charge of fire tore through her, and Deidre's eyes flew open. She gasped.

"Coffee. Now." The man with silver eyes barked at Daniela.

The woman in brown glared at him but stalked towards the kitchen. He sat down across from Deidre, and she would've tried to run again, if her body worked right. Solid and menacing, the man across from her was staring at her as if trying to determine if she was edible.

"This is hell, isn't it?" she whispered.

"Not even close," he said, amused.

"Am I dead?"

"Yes and no. It's a really good story. Once upon a time - "

"The leader of the Council does not discuss these things!" Daniela said sternly. She emerged from the kitchen with a tray laden with coffee and its accoutrements, a slice of pie and water. "Discretion, Rhyn."

"I'm not dead?" Deidre said. "Or I am?"

"No, you're not dead," Daniela answered with a sharp look at Rhyn. "Gabriel brought you here through the shadow world."

"Which is located near my apartment building," Deidre said, needing the brandy again already.

"What'd you do to piss him off?" Rhyn asked. "He's a raving lunatic out there right now."

"Piss him off?" Deidre repeated. "He killed my boyfriend! Chopped his head off right in front of me!" Her throat was too tight to say more.

"Good man. I would've done the same."

Deidre had the sense of being late to a conversation. She wasn't able to catch up, though, not with the absolute weirdness of it all. Alcohol buffered her from her all-out panic, enough so that she was able to sip coffee without dropping the mug. At the strong flavor, she glanced at Daniela, who winked. The coffee was half-filled with brandy.

"Gabriel is Death," Rhyn said.

Deidre looked up. "You said he was alive."

"*Death,* not dead. Soul collector, grim reaper, death-dealer, assassin, Keeper of Souls. Death," he said. "That's why he wears the trench coat all year round. The underworld doesn't have direct sunlight."

"I'll play along." She held her face in her hands. "He wants to kill me, because he's Death and that's what Death does."

"Oh, no." The man's chuckle was terrifying.

Daniela slapped him on the back of the head.

"Goddammit, woman, I heard you the first time!" he snarled at the nun. With an annoyed shake of his head, he addressed Deidre again. "He'll have to tell you that story.

Anyway, now, by Immortal law, you're his mate, so he legally has to protect you instead of get revenge. That's why his name is on your back, by the way. You have a list of enemies longer than mine, and he's obligated to protect you."

"Of course," Deidre said, fighting tears. She chugged the coffee.

"You're handling this better than I expected."

"Rhyn," Daniela said with a sigh. "You're clearly terrifying the girl."

"She needs to learn her place fast."

Deidre dropped her head into her arms, sobbing. Nothing they said made sense. All she could do was hope she passed out and awoke in her bed or on the beach or not at all. Her body grew heavy, and she slumped.

"You spiked her coffee," Rhyn accused Daniela.

"And drugged her. She'll be out in two minutes, but she should be ...manageable when she wakes up. Now, catch her before she hits her head. She needs to rest."

Rhyn muttered. Deidre felt herself lifted once more. Drunk and crying, she didn't bother opening her eyes. She didn't know where he took her, but he set her down on a narrow bed.

"Come find me if you want to know the story of you and Gabe," he whispered for her ears only.

Out of control, she curled on her side and tumbled into unconsciousness.

Chapter Six

Gabriel stayed on the beach until the sun began to set. Sensitive to the light after years in the underworld, his head felt like it was going to explode. Falling thirty stories onto the hard sand of the Sanctuary did nothing to help. In hindsight, he didn't know why he thought the rocky beach provided a more yielding place to land than concrete. If he ever leapt off another building, he'd choose pavement, which might have some give to it.

His back was shredded from landing on his weapons as well as the stones on the beach. He'd managed to peel off his sweater and rinsed the blood off his body in the surf. Now, he waited to heal and to calm down. He could think of nothing more appealing than kicking his mate's ass, as much for leaping off the building as for making him feel what he did when he saw her jump.

Terror. He'd lost her once. He never wanted to lose her again. He'd ignored the demons swarming her apartment building and followed her over the side of the building. He thought of nothing else but saving her. Of all the reasons he resented her, this was the one that stung him the most. He couldn't forget the energy of the bond that tore through when he held her on the roof. It was unlike what he'd known with his predecessor; this was natural, deep, soothing. Compelling. He understood why Rhyn never let Katie out of arm's reach when they were in the same room.

Deidre was his. Judging by the strength of their bond, she'd be more than a duty to him.

He wanted to hate her and to tell Fate to fuck off. Watching the sun sink into the ocean, he knew it was only a matter of time before he gave in and accepted it, like Rhyn eventually did Katie.

"Rhyn said you'd be here."

Gabe glanced at the Immortal. Tamer dropped onto his knees and held out two compasses: the original and a second without the wear of time around its edges.

"I duplicated it," Tamer said. "The original was put together with magic, and I managed to do the same with the new one. There might be some sort of ..."

Gabe grabbed the new one, and the face flared to life. The hands spun several times while the icons around its edges glowed, danced and finally settled back in place. The brightness faded.

"...or that," Tamber said. He plucked it out of Gabe's hands and held it up.

Gabe sensed some sort of Immortal power.

"You need to test it, but it reads like the original," Tamer said.

Hefting them, Gabe glanced at his forearm. Both compasses lit up as the next name on the list appeared.

"You are the first good news I've had in a fucking week," he said quietly. "How many of these can you make me?"

"That thing cost a fortune," Tamer replied. "I've got enough materials to make you fourteen. If I rope in my assistant, I can produce two a day."

"Fourteen?" Gabe frowned. "I need a few hundred, and I can't wait months. I need everything I can get in a week or two."

"Tell the half-breed to fund it," Tamer suggested. "If you got people, send them my way. I used machinery to cut the pieces. They can assemble it. I'm the only one who can seal it."

"Get started. Rhyn won't say no," Gabe said.

"If you say so. Hope this keeps that dick off my back for awhile."

"He knows I'm going through some shit right now. He should leave you alone," Gabriel agreed. "Do you need the original, or can I keep it?"

"Take them both. I have the specs."

"Thanks." Within the week, the death-dealers stuck in the mortal realm could start collecting souls again. A trickle of relief went through him as he realized he was able to fix one of the many issues he faced. He had a feeling the most difficult was the one hiding in the Sanctuary.

"Alright. I'll check in tomorrow," Tamer said. "Looks like something exploded." His gaze was on the blood-soaked sand where Gabe landed.

"Pretty much."

Tamer shook his head and rose, disappearing into a portal. Gabe climbed to his feet. The sun was down, the afterglow of sunset lingering on the horizon. His trench and shirt were shredded and his favorite sword shattered, along with the majority of his other weapons. He gathered the three daggers that survived.

His gaze went to the Sanctuary. Reluctantly, he walked up the sloping hill and to the door that opened automatically for its master, unlike the portal home. He glared at it and strode into the well-lit courtyard of the Sanctuary.

He sensed Deidre but didn't go to her, instead walking through the open-aired hallways until he reached the quarters reserved for him. Pushing the door open with his foot, he dropped the contents of his arms on the bed and opened the dresser drawers. There were no trench coats outside of the underworld he'd consider wearing, but he pulled on a soft black t-shirt and strapped a few sheaths to his body.

Ready, he left his room and walked through the courtyard.

"You're not going to see her?" Daniela's voice was heavy with disapproval.

"If she's in danger, I'll know."

"Danger isn't the problem."

"She's safe here. That's all that concerns me," he replied in a hard tone.

"She's scared, Gabriel."

Gabe paused then forced himself to continue. He'd deal with her after he issued orders to his assassins.

He crossed through the shadow world to the lake near Rhyn's, emerging near Harmony.

"Take these," he said, tossing the compasses to her.

She caught them.

"These will be replacing our broken radars." He stopped beside her, gaze on the lake that glowed green in the quiet night. "Pick someone as quick as you and start collecting souls. The demons are gathering the ones we're missing. We've gotta curb the damage as much as possible."

"Will do," she said. "Forty seven lakes." She added before he could ask.

"Good. We're bringing all the souls to this one and sending everyone but five guards to the Ancient Tamer. As soon as another compass is ready, send a dealer out with it."

She nodded. "I'll issue the orders."

They stood in silence for a moment, eyes on the eerie lake. Gabe was beginning to feel like he'd be able to clean up the soul mess. He had no way of knowing how many the demons had claimed during the week his dealers had claimed none. Hopefully, they grappled with the same problems locating the souls.

He had little time to redeem himself, and he kicked himself mentally for not walking into the room that would turn him into the Death he was supposed to be. Whatever powers that room contained, he was in desperate need of them. His predecessor had seemed much stronger. Gabriel felt again he was missing something huge, the key to assuming the power he hadn't inherited with his responsibilities.

"Are you okay?" Harmony asked at last.

"Rough few days," he replied. He glanced at her, noticing for the first time that she was worn out. "If you need to rest, take a break before you go hunting."

"I'd rather go home," she admitted. "I'm used to the trees putting me to sleep at night. It's hard to sleep in a forest that's not ...alive." Her gaze went to the pine trees with suspicion.

Death, a word, if you please. Deidre's place.

Gabriel cocked his head to the side at the polite summons. The timing for the demon lord to request an audience couldn't have been worse.

"Soon," he assured her. "I'm getting my shit together, little by little."

"It's not your fault."

"Yeah, it is. But I'm fixing it. We'll get home. Promise."

Some tension faded from her frame. She sighed.

"It looks like the messaging system is back up."

"Oh, thank gods!" Harmony exclaimed. "You know how hard it is to track down everyone one-by-one to relay orders?"

"Take a break, Harmony," he told her. "I've gotta go. We'll catch up later."

She nodded and kneaded her temples with her fingertips.

Gabriel left, returning to Deidre's apartment. The dead demons were gone, but someone was waiting for him. Gabriel rubbed his rough jaw. It was sandpapery, covered by two days of stubble. He needed a razor and a trench coat to begin feeling normal again. He didn't see the demon that summoned him and waited a moment before speaking.

"Odd place for a meeting."

"Neither your domain nor mine. We are equals here." Darkyn, the demon lord charged with heading the Dark One's armies of demons, emerged from a dark hallway. His pointed teeth rested on his lower lip, his dark eyes displaying the intelligence of a being that existed from the time-before-time. Lean and youthful, he was unthreatening in appearance but the single most lethal creature Gabriel knew.

"Everyone comes to me," Gabriel reminded him. "Even you."

"Not today."

"I'm not the talker past-Death was. Spit it out, Darkyn," Gabriel ordered.

"You visited Fate but not my master?" Darkyn asked. "It displeased him."

"Your *master,*" Gabe replied. He fell quiet, studying Darkyn. Assuming the role of Death heightened his senses about dealing with Immortals. Darkyn wasn't giving off the same vibe that other demons – who were roughly equivalent to Immortals in the food chain – gave off.

Darkyn's quiet power was more like Fate's.

"When did this transition happen?" Gabriel asked.

"Not long ago. When my master recalled me from exile, we had a talk. I won and took over," Darkyn said. "I prefer to keep under the radar. The demons and Immortals don't need to fear what they don't know."

"So you can operate freely between worlds."

"Much like you. I'm invoking Immortal Code, rule 7,340: secrets between deities ...."

"... remain between deities." Gabriel gritted his teeth. "Fine. What do you want?"

"Your *mate* owes me a debt."

Gabriel's eyes narrowed. "What debt?"

"You didn't wonder how past-Deidre learned of the loophole that let her become mortal? With her very own soul?"

"I assume she lost a bet with Fate."

"That was part of it, I hear. In either case, she owes my predecessor for the knowledge he gave her."

Immortal Code, Rule 9: All deals made between deities shall be recorded by the Oracle.

"Assuming this is true, what was the price?" Gabriel asked.

"You mean *who* was the price?" Darkyn's smile was cunning. "A certain Immortal. Care to guess?"

"Doesn't matter to me. Even if she promised him a soul, I have discretion on when I claim it," Gabe said.

"You misunderstand," Darkyn replied. "She didn't offer up a *living* Immortal. She agreed to return the soul of one who is dead-dead. That was the condition of the deal."

Gabe's hands clenched. It was a violation of multiple rules within the Immortal Code. No part of him doubted she'd done it. Worse, if she made the commitment, *he* was obligated to fulfill it.

"Whose is it?" he demanded.

"Wynn."

"The father of the Council That Was Seven?" Gabriel asked, not understanding why the Dark One chose the Immortal that was his archenemy for thousands of years.

Darkyn shrugged. "My master's reasons were his own. The debt was incurred before I took over. I am simply collecting on the debt, as is my obligation."

"I have to verify it with the Oracle first."

"As you wish."

"Anything else?" Gabriel asked, sensing there was more to the demon lord's journey from Hell. "Like why your demons are stalking this woman?" He gestured to the apartment.

"She …left something for me."

Surprised by the response, Gabriel followed Darkyn's eyes around the apartment.

"Rather, past-Deidre did," Darkyn added. "I've not been able to locate it."

"Let me know what it is. I'll help you search," Gabriel said wryly.

"Perhaps in time. I will find it, Gabriel." The threat in his growl was apparent.

"Hope I find it first. I'd love to have a bargaining chip," Gabriel said.

"It's a personal vendetta. Mine, not my predecessor's. There's no record of this."

"Gods. I'll add your name to the list of enemies. Never heard of someone in your position making an unofficial deal."

"It's more of a personal debt. One you are not obligated to pay but she was."

At the end of his patience with the cryptic demon, Gabriel left. He returned to the Sanctuary, to the Oracle, who was busy scribbling. He flipped backwards in the book to the portion that no longer changed.

"Show me the deal past-Death made with the Dark One," he ordered the book.

A vision formed before him. Gabe watched it, anger stirring as the Oracle confirmed Darkyn's story about bringing back a dead-dead immortal. The deal was made before Darkyn assumed the helm of Hell.

Immortal Code, Rule 302: Debts incurred by a deity shall not expire and shall be transferred to successors until settled.

"Show me this personal debt between past-Death and Darkyn."

No images formed. If past-Death and Darkyn made any kind of deal, the Oracle would have record of it.

Was it possible to make a *private* deal, outside the visibility of the other deities?

Gabriel leaned against the lectern. Unable to tamper with Fate's court anymore than Death could, the Dark One was taking a risk at wanting Wynn raised from the dead-dead. While he had to fulfill the debt past-Death incurred, Gabriel at least might postpone it until he had time to warn Rhyn. He'd never thought of being locked out of the underworld as an advantage, but the soul Darkyn wanted wasn't likely one of those in the lakes on the mortal world.

Gabriel's eyes drifted in the direction where he sensed Deidre was. Desire and yearning crept into him, knowing she was so close. Doubting she'd welcome him, he was drawn to her in a way he wasn't going to be able to fight for long.

What did Darkyn want from Deidre? What kind of deal had past-Deidre made that the Oracle didn't record?

Gabriel rubbed his jaw and strode out of the Oracle's small room. He followed the instinct that led him to Deidre and trotted up the stairs leading to the top of the fortress. His step slowed as he saw her leaning against the wall, gazing into the darkness. Her features were drawn in the moonlight, and there were circles under her eyes. Her petite, shapely body was clothed in jeans and a tank top. The sight of his name across her shoulders made his body hot with anger and need that left him frustrated. He was so close … and couldn't touch her the way he yearned to.

The ocean breeze brought the familiar scent of brandy. Gabe approached and stopped behind her, claiming the alcohol with one hand. She jumped. Gabe tossed the brandy over the side of the fortress wall and caught her as she tried to escape. The softness of her body combined with the power of their bond jarred him.

"Leave me alone!" she cried.

"I just need a minute," he said in a calm, level voice. He released her, not wanting to make this worse. He braced his arms on either side of her. She didn't face him. She leaned against the wall, trembling visibly.

The sight disturbed him more than he wanted it to. Daniela said she was scared. Gabe saw she was more- Deidre was terrified. Of *him*. He found himself hating the feeling instead of relishing it, like he thought he would if their roles were ever reversed. He didn't want her to fear him. It probably didn't help that she was drunk.

Pensive, he swallowed hard and finally admitted that he didn't want her to be his by obligation, the way he'd been enslaved to past-Deidre. He took a deep breath, making a decision he knew he'd probably regret.

"I need your head clear," he said, irritated about the alcohol. He rested his hand on the base of her neck, the warm energy of their bond moving through him. As tempted as he was to read her mind, he didn't. He cleared it, pushing aside the haze of alcohol and the pain he sensed but didn't understand the source of. It was physical discomfort, not mental, and he was relieved to feel she was in no great mental pain from the loss of her boyfriend.

Her shaking stopped at his touch, the warmth of their connection and his magic soothing her. Her head nodded forward, and her breathing grew steady again. Her shoulders were still hunched, as if she waited for him to hack off her head.

"First, a couple of rules," he started. "One, no alcohol. Two, no more suicide attempts."

She said nothing.

"There are more, but we'll start there. Understood?" He kept his voice firm and cold, unwilling to give on either point.

"Yes," she whispered.

"Second, a compromise." His tone grew yielding. "We are ...bound by magic older than time. It creates an obligation for me that I must honor. However, the same is not true for you. The laws and magic governing the mate of an Immortal are much more forgiving. You have no such duty to me."

He paused, grappling with the truth. He'd never thought he'd hear himself admit it to any woman who became his mate, especially not to her. The urge to claim her was strong, but so was the need to let her have the choice he never had.

"It's your decision whether or not you want to stay with me. We are bound either way, but if you choose to walk away from me, I ...will respect your decision. No matter what, I'll continue to honor my obligations and protect you."

She was listening. Gabe clenched his jaw. He was putting himself at her mercy again, except that, this time, he had the power and chose not to use it. This part of his life was in the hands of Fate, who would probably be pleased.

Gabe was not. Her womanly scent teased him, the heat of her nearness reminding him of how he'd gotten himself into this situation in the first place. He dropped his hand from her body before he turned into a liar about letting her choose.

She said nothing.

Gabe waited a few more minutes then forced himself to leave. Uncertain what he expected, his anger was boiling at the silent rejection. He'd extended an olive branch and come back empty-handed. Like old times. Doing the right thing never felt as dissatisfactory as it did this night.

He left the Sanctuary to help his dealers consolidate the souls. He had to determine if the one he owed Darkyn was present or not and then warn Rhyn that the half-demon's Immortal father would soon no longer be dead-dead.

The Dark One, Darkyn, remained long after Gabriel left. He searched Deidre's apartment from top to bottom several times, seeking the item he needed to fulfill his part of a deal. True, they'd had more of an understanding than an official agreement, but he never failed to deliver, even if he had a reputation for interpreting the terms differently than those who made him the deal. Likewise, *no one* fucked him over when he made a deal. Not even the bitch that was past-Death.

Intrigued by the offer she brought him before she disappeared, he was beginning to think he should've made the deal official. He'd never entered into a private one before and didn't know if his predecessor had either.

The idea she'd hidden it somewhere he couldn't find was driving him mad, along with the scent of the human blood coating the walls of the far bedroom. He ran his tongue over his pointed teeth and stood in the center of her living room, pensive and hungry.

It wasn't here. It wasn't anywhere he'd tracked her during the entirety of her lifetime. The human named Deidre had to have it with her, a trinket or piece of jewelry with sentimental value that she never took off. It was small enough, it could be anywhere. Wynn's soul was an official debt she incurred, and Death would do its duty and repay.

The second soul bartered for in private was flat out missing. It didn't seem possible. Past-Death *wanted* this soul found, and Darkyn's searches the past few years yielded nothing. With the sheer number of demons Darkyn had assigned to watching Deidre over the years and all the leads he'd personally pursued, he should have stumbled upon it by now. The demons he sent to Death's underworld failed. The demons he sent to the mortal world failed.

Furious, he took matters into his own hands. He, too, was failing. Worse, he wasn't able to operate under the radar for much longer, now that Gabriel had claimed his mate. Time was short.

Darkyn had no tolerance for failure, especially not after past-Death interfered in his attempt to capture Rhyn's mate. He was burning through the limited amount of demons qualified to shape-shift. They were a finicky lot, lasting only two to three days in the human world before the serum that change their features wore off.

Deidre's boyfriend, Logan, cost Darkyn two of the valuable shape-shifting demons. Neither of them found any trace of what Darkyn sought.

"Hey, boss."

His least favorite demon crept from the shadows. Jared was a thorn in Darkyn's side, but he was also a friend of the half-demon Rhyn. No other demon was permitted close the Immortal fortress. It was respect for this usefulness that kept Jared from feeling the brunt of Darkyn's anger.

"I went over the beach house with a fine-toothed comb," Jared said. "Nothing."

"I'm missing something," Darkyn growled.

"Are you sure …"

At Darkyn's glare, Jared ducked his gaze and fell silent.

"I need a distraction, Jared, to keep the Immortals out of my hair," Darkyn said.

"Happy to serve."

"Pick a human school to target for breakfast. Take two more demons with you. Make it messy and obvious."

Jared's eyes lit up with hunger. "Kids make the tastiest morsels. Should I be concerned about pesky Immortals tracking me down?"

"With the Ancient Andre dead, they won't be able to find you in time," Darkyn replied. "Keep at it until I send orders otherwise and change locations daily. I want to thin their ranks."

"You intend to attack Rhyn again?"

"What I intend is not your concern," Darkyn snapped. "Go."

Jared bowed his head and fled, well aware of the power of the demon lord's fury.

I intend to claim what will be owed, when I find that fucking soul, Darkyn added to himself.

"Harmony, come." This order he spoke out loud.

The death-dealer on the Dark One's payroll appeared immediately at the summons. Beautiful and slender, she was likewise deadly. Darkyn liked his women willing to fight him before he fucked them and bled them dry. Her fate would be no different, and he anticipated a good, long fight and slow death.

"Report," he ordered.

She held out something that looked like a compass. Darkyn took it, instantly recognizing the magic as Death's. The symbols were from the time-before-time, an era of chaos he barely remembered.

"Soul compass," he said, not expecting the tool. "Death is going old school."

"Our soul radars are broken," she explained. "Gabe is having these made for us while we're trapped up here."

"Trapped?"

"The underworld kicked us out. Even Death."

Darkyn chuckled, a low, dark sound. "Very good, love."

"You are satisfied with my work?" She was nervous.

"Very. And Death? What of his mindset?"

Harmony hesitated, and Darkyn met her gaze, sensing weakness. Not hesitating to hand over the compass, she appeared torn at taking the final step of betrayal. Darkyn gripped her neck, shoving her into the wall. The scent of an Immortal – a female one – made his hunger roar to life.

"When your master asks, you answer," he snarled.

"He's … confused. Angry," she gasped. "Lost. Forgive me."

"Your first lesson." His fangs lengthened.

Harmony gripped his arm, fear crossing her face.

"Twice you resist," he hissed. "There will not be a third time."

She dropped her hand and closed her eyes, bracing herself.

Darkyn had no intention of going easy on her, even if it was her first lesson in the proper behavior expected of a demon's blood slave. Eventually, he'd reveal the fate that awaited traitors and order her to fight him. For now, he was content to make her life miserable while she fed him information about Gabriel.

With a soul compass in one hand and his dinner in the other, Darkyn was satisfied for the first time in months. He'd find the missing soul. It was just a matter of patience.

Chapter Seven

The new world seemed less scary in daylight. Deidre lay awake in bed for quite awhile, sorting through the events of the weekend. Her insides quaked, but she breathed deeply to keep calm and focus her mind. She'd felt the same loss of control and fear when first diagnosed as terminal. She'd broken down for weeks, sobbing and refusing to leave her house.

One day, she stopped. Acceptance came relatively easily when she ceased fighting the idea that she was going to die. She tried to do the same now. Whatever she knew of the world, it no longer pertained to her circumstances. There was an entire subset of reality, and that's where she landed when she jumped off her building.

She was alive. She was still in control of herself and her mind. With a little discipline and a whole lot of open-mindedness, she'd figure this out, like she'd figured out how to live with the reality she was at death's door.

Gabriel's door. The concept of Death being humanlike in form, that she was permanently bound to him...

"Nope. Can't handle that one yet," she said, grinding her teeth. "One thing at a time, Deidre."

The thought of Gabriel made her panic. Tender one day, chopping off heads the next, Death the third and finally, reluctantly telling her they were bound together forever.

She had the shittiest luck. No, she wasn't ready for Gabriel yet, no matter how strongly her body responded to his smallest touch. She did a few more breathing exercises until she felt ready to step outside her room to face the new world. There were clothes in the dresser, not quite her size but not too far off. She took a hot shower in the cramped bathroom off the side of her room then pulled on the clothes.

The Sanctuary was plain to the point of austere, with no luxuries. Her room was tiny, barely fitting a twin-sized bed and a small, wooden dresser. It was comfortable, like a little cave where she could hide. The sounds of the ocean and the sea breeze lulled her to sleep last night and gently drew her awake before sunrise. She opened the heavy wooden door and stepped into an open-air hallway. She'd seen a handful of nuns yesterday, and only Daniela spoke to her.

She took three steps away from her cave. Nothing went wrong. It was a good start.

Deidre walked into one of four courtyards she'd discovered roaming the day before. She couldn't tell them apart yet and looked around to determine if this courtyard was the one near the medieval cafeteria or not.

It wasn't. Deidre went through another courtyard before the scents of breakfast drew her to the correct one. She walked into the dark dining area to see a few others already present: two of the nuns and two normal looking people.

She didn't want to know what kind of creatures they might be. She sat near the door and waited. Daniela had told her the kitchens would serve at any time of day. Deidre was seated for a minute before a red-faced nun brought out a tray with a plate heaped with food and a coffee pot with creamer, sugars and mug.

Cheered by the sight of food, Deidre dug in. She'd barely finished her omelet when the two people from the other table sat across from her. She paused, not at all certain what to do. The man was tall with Oriental features and striking, turquoise eyes. Handsome and lean, he wore slacks and a collared shirt left open at the neck with the long sleeve meticulously rolled in a faux casual style.

"Keep eating," he said, glancing up from the laptop he set on the table before him. "It'll take me a minute to set up."

Deidre's brows furrowed at his no-nonsense tone. The woman beside him was blond, her eyes pale blue. Beautiful and slender, she offered a faint smile. She was more casually dressed in leggings, knee-high boots and a shirt that fell to mid-hip. She wore a glove on one hand that extended to her elbow.

"He means, we're in no rush. Enjoy your breakfast," the woman said. "I'm Ileana. This is Kiki. We're here to do the interview we do for all new members to the Immortal society."

"I'm Deidre," she replied. "You probably know that though, right?"

Ileana nodded.

Deidre nibbled on her food then pushed it aside to drink the coffee. She feared asking what they meant by *Immortal society*. Half-drunk by the time Rhyn explained things to her the day before, she'd come away from that conversation more baffled than she'd been when she fell out of the sky onto the beach. Gabriel's matter-of-fact talk of magic and laws older than time hadn't clarified much, except that he believed she belonged to him.

The way his touch made her feel, she almost believed it herself.

"How long have you existed?" Kiki asked.

"Pardon?"

"How old are you," Ileana translated.

"Twenty six."

"You've been on the mortal world the whole time?" Kiki appeared doubtful.

"As far as I know," Deidre replied.

"You remember being born here and everything?"

"I don't remember being born, but I mean, I grew up in Indiana and moved to Atlanta for college and stayed after I graduated. Pretty sure those are both in the um, mortal ... world," Deidre said. "Does that surprise you?"

"Yes," Kiki said.

"No," Ileana said at the same time.

She looked between them. Neither tried to explain their answers.

"When did the Immortal mating inscription appear?" Kiki asked.

"You mean the Gabriel tattoo?"

He nodded.

"Yesterday morning."

"Awww, you're a baby Immortal mate!" Ileana said, smiling. "Welcome."

Deidre poured more coffee. She understood why Daniela kept feeding her brandy the night before. Kiki's eyes settled on her shaking hands. He met her gaze then closed the laptop.

"We can wait," he said, the edge leaving his voice. "It's not an easy transition. Gods know we almost screwed up the last one beyond repair."

"That was out of our control." A dark look crossed Ileana's face.

"We have a more formal process now for transitioning Immortal mates," Kiki said, as if his explanation was supposed to mean something to her.

Deidre drew a deep breath with some difficulty. "I have to ask. You're saying there's a society of Immortals living in the normal world that no one knows about?"

"Exactly," Kiki said. "We're managed by a council that very poorly oversees Immortal activities in the mortal world and fights demons to keep the underworld dwellers from destroying the human world. We follow the Immortal Code, which dictates our interactions with humans and our obligations within our society."

They seemed to be waiting for her reaction.

"Okay. I appreciate how straight forward you're being," Deidre said. "Why am I … stuck in this new reality?"

"As far as we know, Immortal mates are predetermined. There's an anomaly in your blood that makes you compatible with our kind."

"You have my blood?"

"Of course. When we identified you, we obtained all your medical records, your credit history, basically your entire life," Kiki explained. "We created a file on you, so we could monitor and determine whose mate you became, if you did at all."

"That sounds like stalking," Deidre said.

"It's necessary, so we can protect you. Only two or three people ever see your file," Ileana added.

"You're ninety eight percent human," Kiki said.

"What's the two percent?" Deidre whispered, afraid to know.

"Other genetic material. We don't know. You might have an Immortal bloodline somewhere in your ancestry or a simple mutation."

"That makes me special?"

"Yes."

"Why didn't you find me years ago, if that's the case?" she asked.

They were quiet for a moment. It wasn't a pensive silence, but more of a silent struggle to determine how much they revealed. They, too, had a secret they were keeping from her.

"We didn't know we were looking for you until a couple of months ago," Ileana said at last. "It's been a rough year for the Council. Everything almost blew up a few months ago. Immortal doesn't mean omniscient or anything. We're closely related to humans, and we share many of the same limitations. We have more of an immunity to dying than normal humans."

"Okay." They were making some sense. Deidre didn't want to ask about the part that disturbed her the most. She soaked in the information, and something clicked. "I'm supposed to die in three months. Does this mean I won't now?"

"That depends," Kiki said. He said nothing else.

"What does that depend on?" she prodded.

"We don't really know how that will work out," Ileana said. "By Immortal Code, Death can't kill you, and neither can any of his dealers."

"Because …"

"Because you're his mate," Kiki said. "We don't really know what will happen."

"He can probably take you down to the underworld and you'll be fine." Ileana shrugged.

"Underworld." The sense of being overwhelmed made Deidre grip the coffee mug hard.

"The demons have been stalking you for awhile. We think there's something else going on," Kiki said. "At the end of the day, you're Gabe's, so he can do whatever he wants with you, as long as he follows the Code."

"It's an honor to be an Immortal mate," Ileana said.

Panic stirred at the idea of Gabriel dragging her to some freakish underworld. He claimed he was giving her a choice the night before of whether she wanted to be with a sword-wielding maniac. The Immortals before her seemed more convinced she'd fall into her place as his mate. Because somehow, this was normal wherever they were from.

"Gabriel is Death," Deidre said the words carefully, slowly.

"Yep," Kiki replied.

"His day job is to kill people."

"Exactly and to collect souls of those who have died by other means."

She swallowed hard. "I don't think I can do this."

"It's not as bad as it sounds," Ileana said with a smile.

"How so?"

"It's Immortal law. It doesn't much matter what you want," Kiki replied.

Ileana rolled her eyes. "For what it's worth, Gabe was the most respected and longest serving assassin of Death before he got promoted. He's fair, honorable, a stickler for the Code, and not someone anyone will mess with."

"I could really use some brandy right now," Deidre propped her forehead on her hand.

"Forbidden," Kiki said firmly.

"There's no way out of this?"

"Absolutely none."

Unless I'm dead in three months. If only she hadn't slept with a complete stranger two nights ago. Though, if what they said was true, she was destined for the Immortal society anyway.

Deidre had the sudden urge to go home. Maybe, if she returned to her apartment, she'd find everything was back to normal. She'd break up with Logan and die in three months. The simple plan never seemed more appealing.

"I, ah, think I want to go lay down," she said.

"We can finish later," Ileana said with a kind smile. "It gets easier."

Deidre nodded, unable to think of a response that didn't involve crying or fleeing. She left the dining area and returned to her room. Seating herself on the bed, she stared at a wall for a long time before pulling herself out of the trance.

She really, *really* wanted to go home! Gabriel's strange magic tingled in her body, warming her. She twisted to pull her feet onto her bed and choked back a scream.

In front of the bed, a dark cave had opened in the middle of her room, swallowing the wall where the door had been. It hovered. Beyond its yawning mouth, she saw what looked like yellow doorways glowing. One of them was brighter than the others, as if trying to draw her attention.

Heart flying, Deidre stood and moved to the end of the bed. She reached out to the cave. The temperature beyond its opening was cold, the air heavy and clammy. She'd felt the weird sensations before …

Shadow world.

Daniela said they passed through it on their way to the island.

Suddenly hopeful, Deidre stepped into the in-between place. The cave closed behind her, startling her. She looked around, not liking the feel of the shadow world. She walked towards the brightest of the glowing doorways and hesitated, unable to see through it. For all she knew, the Grand Canyon was on the other side.

"Might not be a bad thing," she murmured. With a deep breath, she stepped through and braced herself to fall.

She didn't. The clingy cold of the shadow world disappeared, and she was left standing in the middle of her apartment.

Relief brought tears to her eyes. She sucked in a steadying breath, praying any sign of the violence from her last visit was gone.

"No bodies, no blood," she observed of the living room.

She walked down the hallway to the guest bedroom, cringing. She opened the door and closed it quickly.

Things hadn't gone back to normal after all. She wasn't about to look in the bathtub. Instead, she went to her bedroom, changed into her clothing and packed a bag. She took the money in her emergency stash, grabbed her purse, and left.

The heavy Southern day reminded her of the Caribbean. Deidre dug through her purse as she walked and pulled out her cell, thrilled to see she had battery power. She could think of one place to go right now.

She called Wynn.

"Deidre?" He answered at once.

Surprised he'd been waiting for her call, she hesitated. After all she'd been through lately, she couldn't help feeling a little wary. She shook her head. This was the doctor who stuck by her for years after her diagnosis. If anything, she owed him at least the benefit of the doubt.

"Hi Doc," she said. "Just calling to uh, say hi, I guess."

"Lovely to hear from you, especially today." He sounded tired. "I quit Friday."

"What? You quit working at the hospital?"

"Emphatically."

"Wow." She smiled, comforted by the familiarity of his unique communication style.

"Yes, wow." There was silent laughter in his voice.

"I'm sorry to hear it, Wynn. You're the best," she said. "You're pretty much all that held me together over the years."

"Your expectations of those around you always were too low, Deidre."

She laughed, waiting for the light to change so she could cross the street. Her gaze passed over the faces in the crowd across the street. Recognizing one, she looked back, tensing. He was gone, but she almost felt the cold stare of the other man who had been in her apartment.

"Listen, I was calling to –"

"Hey, Doc, are you still in Atlanta?" she cut him off.

"Yes. I plan on moving in a month or so." There was a pause. "Is everything okay?"

"No, not really," she said as cheerfully as she could manage. She started across the street and down the road. "Could I possibly come see you?"

"Of course. I've got one more pad of scripts. I can write up some pain meds."

"Oh, no, I'm … well terminal but relatively okay in that area. Just having some other issues."

"Ah, Logan. The world of the living tires of the dying."

"Sort of."

"Come on by. I'll text you my address."

Grateful for somewhere to go, Deidre hung up and waited for his text. The hair on the back of her neck rose, and she glanced around. She didn't see Jared, but she couldn't shake the sense he – or someone else – was following her.

She caught a cab across town and arrived at the swanky suburbs on the south side of the city. Dr. Wynn's massive home was located along a street lined by manicured lawns and gated homes. The cab dropped her off, and she went to the side entrance to buzz in as Wynn directed in his text.

He was waiting for her in the garden, seated at a tea table under an awning. A pitcher of lemonade was on the table. He rose as she approached and kissed her cheek before pulling out the chair for her.

"You look as eager for tomorrow as I am," he said.

Deidre smiled. He'd always had a morbid sense of humor, like hers.

"Talk to me. You only call when it's raining."

"Gee, thanks! I feel like crap now," she said. "You first. Tell me what happened that made you walk out on being a doctor."

"Life," he said with a shake of his head. "Got sick of the politics. I used to be able to help people like you."

"Poor people?"

"Underprivileged," he corrected with a smile. "There are emerging procedures that will help people who need it, but the cost is beyond what any hospital will spend, knowing no one can pay for it. I got fed up and walked."

"You're so good, Doc," she said, troubled. "I mean, you can still help people like me. You extended my life over three years after the others said I had a few months."

"You were an anomaly, like a band-aid. I thought if I had enough band-aids, I'd be able to wait out the politics. There was no one else but you, and I gave up."

"I can't believe that. You always treated me like I was your only patient," she said. "You have no idea how much of a difference that made to me and probably to the rest of your patients. Even if you couldn't extend our lives, you brought us comfort."

"Perhaps."

She hid a smile. He wasn't convinced.

"Your turn," he said. "Oh, and stop calling me Doc. It's Wynn. Now, talk, Deidre. I see it on your face."

She looked away, uncertain what to say. "Logan did break up with me." *Or died. God help me, I have no idea.* "Life got real weird, real fast. I, um, don't even know …"

"I take it you have no place to stay." His eyes went to the bag at her feet.

"That's a different issue entirely," she said. "I didn't come here to throw myself at your feet for a place to stay."

"Or did you?" he asked.

Deidre wasn't certain what made her so comfortable with Wynn. He was always able to read her, probably because he was the first to tell her she was dying. He was one of the only people she didn't shut out of her life when she was diagnosed as terminal. He knew her mind better than she did.

"You never liked him, did you?" she asked.

"Never. He was a band-aid for you. I figured he'd walk out on you sooner."

"Yeah. I guess it was inevitable. There you have it."

"Dying didn't send you scrambling to my door but Logan did?"

Deidre flushed. "Doc … Wynn …" How did she explain her weekend to someone normal? She rubbed her face. "Later?"

He raised an eyebrow. "Very well."

"It's far too weird."

"How weird?" he asked, interest on his face. "Living for three years after a diagnosis of dying in a month weird?"

"Weirder. Like …" she paused, grappling with some way to explain things. "…realizing everything you know about the world is wrong. Or maybe, incomplete is a better word."

"You've intrigued me." He leaned forward, elbows on the table.

She groaned, aware of how many questions he could ask when he was interested in something. She'd seen him take out a hospital administrator with pure logic to get his way to run a procedure on her.

"Please?" she asked, embarrassed to feel tears in her eyes. "Later?"

"Only because I like you."

She rolled her eyes and wiped away the tears.

"Come inside," he said. "We could both use a drink, I think."

She followed Wynn into his home. She suspected he came from money, and a glance around confirmed it. His collection of antiques was unrivaled and perfectly coordinated, as if he'd meandered through history to hand-pick them.

Like someone who was immortal.

She missed a step. Deidre shook her head at the stupid thought. Just because she knew there was a shadow society didn't mean everyone she ran into was part of it! Wealthy people could afford to choose scarce antiques like his.

Her gaze caught on a picture of a beach house on the ocean, and she hesitated. She never did call the police about the body she found. She couldn't shake the feeling she got when she first saw the faceless corpse, that he was Logan. Even though she'd seen Logan in her apartment, before Gabriel chopped him down.

Deidre shivered, unable to move from the picture. She'd left her favorite clothes at the beach house.

"What is it, my dear?" Wynn called. He was leaning over the railing overlooking the massive marble foyer.

"Do you have plans?" she asked.

"It's the first Monday after I walked out on my job. I'm open to suggestions."

She laughed. "I have one."

"Bring your bag up and we'll go."

Comforted by her only remaining normal friend, Deidre followed him to the wing of guest bedrooms, surprised at how huge her room was. She dropped her bag off and joined him in the hallway.

"Where are we going?" he asked, pausing.

"To the ocean."

"I'll bring a jacket." He headed down the opposite hallway.

Deidre waited for him in the lobby. She couldn't help pacing. Being alone meant she started thinking again, something she didn't want to do. Wynn trotted down the grand staircase, keys in one hand and jacket in the other. He wore khakis and a short-sleeved shirt.

The highways were quiet on the Monday mid-morning, and they drove the three hours faster than she was expecting. Wynn was brilliant at small talk, distracting her and making her laugh with his dry, morbid humor. She grew edgy as they passed the town near the bungalow before pulling up the long driveway to the beach house.

Her palms were sweating at the memories the beach house held. Deidre exited the car and paused.

"I've been patient," Wynn reminded her as he closed his door. "Where are we and why?"

"I, uh, rented the place for the weekend then extended it through the week," she said.

"Very good taste," he said, taking in the house. "Why do I have the feeling the place is haunted or something?"

"You're probably not far off," she admitted. "It was a weird weekend. I kinda left in a hurry."

Bracing herself, she opened the front door and crossed through the house. Everything was where she left it, down to the candle on the back porch. Her nervousness grew as she looked down the beach. It was daylight, and there were a ton of people around. Wynn was with her.

Nothing could hurt her.

She didn't wait for him but flipped off her sandals and jogged down the beach, towards the abandoned lot nearby. Relief flooded her as she saw the police tape around the area where she'd found the body. Someone else reported it.

Shaking from more than the chilled ocean breeze, Deidre walked up the beach to the area. No sign of what happened remained. She wasn't sure what she sought; maybe something that convinced her it wasn't Logan she saw. She forced herself to breathe deeply and continued towards the distant road. The police had cordoned off the driveway, too, and posted signs around the entrance.

Reaching the road, she caught sight of something that made her blood run cold again.

Her car. It was parked in the driveway of the neighboring lot, where she'd seen no lights or activity all weekend. Deidre prayed she was wrong as she approached. She pulled her keys out of her purse and clicked the unlock button, mouth dry as the vehicle's lights blinked.

She slowed at the pool of blood on the driver's side. There was more in the car, covering the driver's seat and the mat on the floor.

If Logan's body was the one she found on the beach, who had been in her apartment?

"Weird does not describe this." Wynn's voice made her jump. He stood a few feet away, eyes on the blood. "This is your car."

She nodded. He met her gaze, intent but patient.

"Logan didn't leave me," she said slowly. "He uh, kinda died."

Nothing surprised Wynn. He moved to stand beside her. He observed the car's interior with the clinical distance of a scientist.

"The amount of blood loss and direction and force of the spray looks like his jugular was ..."

She gasped.

"Sorry. I'd say he died violently."

"Yeah," she agreed. Deidre covered her mouth, more confused. Either Gabriel killed him here, or he killed Logan in her apartment.

"When did this happen?" Wynn asked. He opened the door, studying the interior.

"Saturday night," she replied.

"Not possible. It had to be several days ago."

"We got here Thursday afternoon," she said, confused.

"Did you see his body?"

She swallowed hard at the question, panic fluttering through her. At her silence, he straightened to look at her. She nodded.

"Yesterday, around three in the afternoon."

"Was it bloated, or did he look like he was taking a nap?"

"Bloated."

"He'd been dead for at least two days, then, long enough for rigor to set in and the body to start releasing gases," Wynn said. "Which would fit with this mess."

"That's not possible," she said. "Wynn, he was with me Friday and Saturday. I saw him yesterday."

Wynn studied her.

"We had sex Friday night! You can't tell me I didn't see him!" she cried.

"Are you sure it was him?"

No. She wasn't. She hadn't been. He'd been distant and moody, obsessed with security, and much better in bed than normal.

"I take that as a no." Wynn smiled. "Should we have that talk now?"

"No," she said with a groan. "I want to get my stuff and leave."

"Very well. I'll play along. But Deidre, when we get home, you're telling me what happened."

She gazed up at him. He was calm and patient as always, but she wasn't about to piss off her last friend on the planet. If anyone could handle the truth, Wynn could. She nodded at last. With a look at the car, she trailed him to the beach house. She had no idea what this meant. Gabriel knew the body was there; he had to. He'd been standing by it when she first saw him. But if he hadn't killed Logan that night, what was he doing hanging around a dead body? If he killed Logan, why come back to the beach at all?

Worse, who the hell had she slept with Friday night, if not Logan? Who was in her apartment?

They returned to the beach house. Wynn helped her carry her stuff to his vehicle. She didn't know what to do about her car, and he didn't ask. They rode back to Atlanta in silence, hers distraught, his pensive. He carried her things inside without hesitation, lugging everything to her new room. Deidre followed with a second load.

"Freshen up. We'll have dinner on the veranda," he said. "You have any aversion to pasta?"

She shook her head. He closed the door behind him, and she rubbed her face again. A quick shower later, she joined him in the garden once more in a tank top and jeans. The balmy spring air was warm, even after dusk fell. Her thoughts drifted to the island. It seemed so far away, like a dream.

Ever the gentleman, Wynn cleared the table and returned with two drinks: warm, spiced wine. Deidre accepted hers but hesitated to drink it.

"You're a good friend, Wynn," she murmured. She pushed herself down in her seat until her head rested on the back of the chair. "What made someone like you take my case?"

"I enjoy a challenge. The doctor before me said you wouldn't make it a month. Figured I'd try it."

"You really are too good to quit the field," she said again.

"Probably," he agreed. "I prefer to work on my terms. There was a little too much outside interference."

Deidre studied him. Wynn was relaxed, sharp gaze on some point in the distance as he sipped his wine. She frowned. She had the same strange sense she did when she first met Gabriel, that he wasn't fully part of this world.

"Do you believe there are people in our world who aren't like us?" she started.

"You're talking more than the everyone-is-a-snowflake paradigm?"

"Yeah."

"I've seen a lot during my years as a doctor. We are so far from understanding the roadmaps of our DNA. Who's to say there aren't genetic variations that lend people to being different?" he asked, shrugging. "Did you meet someone unlike us?"

"I think so. I, uh, did something really awful Saturday night, and the whole world has gone insane."

"You do something bad? You're too sweet, Deidre."

"I had a one night stand," she admitted. "Logan or …Wynn, if I wasn't with Logan this weekend …Dammit. One thing at a time." She pressed the meat of her hands to her eyes to keep from crying again.

"One night stand? This is awful? I thought you'd admit to killing Logan at least."

"You're going to think I'm crazy by the end of this." She breathed deeply then told him everything. Almost. One aspect of the weekend she wasn't ready to accept.

Wynn was calm. Deidre took some solace from the fact he didn't laugh or throw her out. He listened intently, swirling and sipping his wine. She'd expected horror or disbelief from him during the hour straight that she poured her heart out to him. When she fell silent, he appeared thoughtful rather than surprised.

"Well?" she asked tentatively. "If you want me to get a hotel room, I totally understand."

He smiled. "No, I don't. From the first moment I met you, I knew you were meant for something different. I think that special path is what you encountered this weekend."

"How could you not handle the politics of the job?" she exclaimed. "I told you the most fantastic tale, and you shrug it off like it's natural."

"I didn't say I couldn't handle the politics, just that I didn't *like* them," he replied.

She snorted. "These could be hallucinations, couldn't they?"

"They weren't hallucinations. Of this, I am fairly certain."

"Why?" she eyed him.

He lifted his eyebrows towards the glass in front of her. "I asked you thrice to share what happened over the weekend. After all we've been through together the past few years, you should've been an open book."

She looked at the wine, realizing she hadn't touched it.

"You didn't drink it, because you have an emotional connection to the person who asked you not to. This wouldn't be true with a purely psychological phenomenon like a hallucination." He sipped his wine, eyes on her. "You denied me, despite what I'd call a fairly strong relationship. Which means, what happened between you and this Gabriel was more than a one night stand."

Her face flamed. She cleared her throat, staring into the wine glass.

"Am I right?" he prodded at her silence.

"I don't know," she said finally. "They said ...I'm his preordained mate, a bond that can't be broken. I just met the guy, Wynn. It makes no sense!"

"By our rules, no. By their rules, yes."

"Exactly. I mean, look at this," she twisted so he could see Gabriel's name across her shoulders. "To them, it's permanent like this tattoo."

"And to you?"

She hesitated. "He said the obligation was one way. He had a duty to me but I didn't have to choose him. He said it's my decision if I want to be ... to be with him."

"A noble response," Wynn said. "By their rules, he doesn't have to give you the choice, does he?"

She faced him and slumped. "No."

"You have flirted with Death for three years now. He comes to claim you and becomes enamored instead. What a beautiful story," Wynn summarized.

Deidre laughed. "When you put it that way, it is!"

He was at ease with the bizarre discussion. She wasn't sure if she should be grateful or alarmed that he was playing along with her.

"What will you do?" he asked.

"I don't know. I mean, he killed Logan, Wynn."

"I didn't like Logan anyway."

"He didn't deserve to die," she said, troubled. "It's my fault he was killed. I never wanted that for him."

"I know how you feel," Wynn said. "I lost patients before, people who shouldn't have died. On paper, they had a ninety percent chance of surviving the operation. I performed exactly as I should have, and yet, they died. The unforeseen, Deidre. You could not have predicted Logan would die anymore than I did one of those patients."

"I feel so guilty."

"So do I. For me, it's a professional hazard. For you, a freak event. Life is known for those."

"My god, Wynn," she said, studying him. "I know we talked before, but why didn't we talk like this?"

He chuckled. "Because now, we are friends. Before, we had a professional relationship. I like you, Deidre. I always have."

If she didn't know better, she would've read more into his words. He spoke like Mr. Checkmate, the Immortal that greeted her on the beach and spoke of a history with her when she'd never seen him before. She had a history with Wynn, and he was right. They'd transitioned from doctor-patient to friends this evening.

"You must be exhausted after your weekend," he said. "Go rest."

She straightened but hesitated. "Wynn, I don't want to put you in danger. If anything weird happens, please walk or run away or call the police or something."

"I don't fear Death or these Immortals of yours," he said. "I've faced enough in my time to take care of myself."

He sounds like an Immortal. She shook her head.

"I really am tired," she said, standing. "Thank you so much for taking me in and not throwing me out after what I told you. I'll see you in the morning." She squeezed his shoulder and padded into the house.

"Sleep well, Deidre," he called after her.

As she walked up the stairs, she realized that Wynn read her the same way Gabriel had the night they met. Wynn always spoke differently, she reminded herself. His perspective was unique, unlike that of anyone else she'd ever met. His ready acceptance of her weekend, however, left her concerned. He wasn't curious about the existence of an Immortal society, only about what she intended to do, now that *she* knew it existed.

He wasn't surprised, because he already knew.

Deidre closed the door to her room and leaned against it, struggling to make sense of everything. She tried hard to convince herself that she was misreading Wynn. Reviewing their day together, she couldn't find any instance where he'd directly tipped her off. But he was a politician. He buried his meaning in vagueness and niceties.

He'd called Gabriel noble. The Immortals earlier in the day said the same. Deidre didn't know what to think about Gabriel, not when he seemed conflicted about her to start off with. Making love to her, wanting her dead, saving her life, walking away.

He was more confused than she was.

She changed into pajama boxers. Stretching out on the bed, Deidre was tired but not ready to sleep yet. She stared at the ceiling. Something wasn't right here. She'd ignored the instinct at her apartment, and that ended in disaster. She didn't want that to be true of Wynn, who had helped her for years.

Deidre didn't know what to do. She paced and rolled her shoulders to free them of tension. Wynn had always taken care of her, yet she'd felt safe at the Sanctuary and safest in

Gabriel's arms. She flung herself onto the bed again, restless and scared.

She'd found her way here through the shadow world. Could she find her way back to the Sanctuary? What had she done to get to the apartment? Folding her legs beneath her, she took a deep breath and closed her eyes.

"I really, really want to feel safe. Wherever that is, that's where I want to be," she said. A stir of warm magic, and she opened her eyes, almost screaming again at the cave yawning open in front of her.

As before, one of the yellow doors glowed brighter than the others. Scared, Deidre slid on her sandals and walked into the cold, clammy shadow world. She crossed more boldly this time, terrified of seeing the doorway close behind her before she'd made it through another one.

She entered the balmy Caribbean night. Sand challenged her first couple of steps. She faced the ocean, the moon dangling low and large in the sky before her.

"You learned to use the portals." His quiet voice made her turn.

Gabriel stood a short distance away. He lowered his sword and straightened from a sparring match with Rhyn, whose pewter eyes glowed unnaturally. They regarded her with wary curiosity.

"Is that what they are?" she asked at the awkward silence.

"Yeah. They take you wherever you want to go," Rhyn answered. He pointed, and one appeared where he indicated. "Later, Gabe."

Gabriel lifted his chin in response. She watched the cave swallow Rhyn, unsettled by the idea of moving between places via the shadow world. Her gaze lingered. She didn't want to look at Gabriel, afraid of what she'd see.

He tossed the sword onto the sand and seated himself on a boulder. From the distance, she felt the bond beckoning her to him. When it was clear he wasn't going to be the first to speak, she addressed him.

"Did you kill Logan?"

"No."

"No … what?" She waited.

"I didn't kill him."

"Who did?"

"The demon that took on his form. Shape-shifting demons."

"Oh, god," she said, shuddering. "You mean …I slept with a *demon?*"

"Yeah." There was a note of familiar anger in his voice.

Her insides were shaking again. He'd calmed her with a simple touch last night and quenched her body two nights ago. She crossed her arms and walked towards him, stopping close enough for him to reach her, if he wanted to. He didn't try. Seated, his face was at her level, the dark eyes on her. Moonlight played across his chiseled features. His elbows rested on his knees, his hands clasped in front of him. The t-shirt he wore was tight around large biceps and snug across his muscular shoulders and thick chest. She'd run her hands over his perfect body, marveling at the smooth skin stretched over solid muscle.

"You're Death," she said quietly.

"I am."

His heat and scent were starting to mess with her at such a distance. Her stomach fluttered, her heartbeat fast. She lifted her eyes to meet his gaze at last. She'd imagined staring down Death before, but she never guessed it would be anything like this. Which did she fear more: Death or the man behind the mask? She was compelled towards both, one by emotion and the other by fate.

"The Logan I saw in my apartment was a… a demon," she managed.

"Yes."

"They ate someone," she said, eyes watering. "I saw what was left."

"That's what demons do." He was cool, distant, impossible to read. His tone was matter-of-fact, his answers short. The comfort he'd offered her before was gone.

"It's been a rough few days," she murmured.

"For both of us."

"You were really unhappy about…" she turned and patted the tattoo on her back. "…weren't you?"

"It was unexpected."

"Unexpected," she repeated, face warm. She didn't know why it bothered her. "I thought you were going to kill me."

"I almost did. Twice."

She fought back the urge to run. "We might have a trust issue."

He was shutting her out. It was like their talk on the beach the other night never happened. She was surprised to find it bothered her. She felt very alone, exposed, standing before him. He held her gaze, and she had the sense that he was looking beyond her, to her soul, examining it as only Death could.

"We do," he agreed quietly.

With a trembling hand, Deidre reached out to him, taking one of his. The warm energy crept across her skin and into her blood. She swallowed hard and looked into his dark eyes again.

"Will you…" She wasn't sure how to ask for what she wanted, the comfort only he seemed to be able to give her.

Gabriel responded. His hand slid up to her elbow, and he drew her into him, until his warmth and scent enveloped her. Deidre wrapped her arms around his neck while his went securely around her body. She tucked her head into the crook of his neck, breathing him in. Her body ceased shaking, and her confusion faded, replaced by the hum of the bond between them.

"I asked the portals to bring me somewhere safe," she whispered.

"Maybe they weren't paying attention."

She lifted her head to look at him, unable to tell if he meant it as a joke and ready to bolt if not. His grip around her tightened at the tension in her body. Gabriel winked, the only indication she didn't need to run.

"Is this a decision or a moment?" he asked.

"I don't know."

"I'll make it easier. Do you want me to make love to you or hug you?"

Her face grew hot fast. Her blood was flying with desire. She wanted both, but she wasn't ready for what she suspected one meant. Ducking her head, she buried her face in the nape of his neck again.

"A moment," he said, amused. "You weren't so shy the other night."

"Oh, god," she said in embarrassment. "You weren't exactly forthcoming about who you are."

"What happened to Death letting you see the stars and moon instead of how dark the night is?"

"I must've sounded like a fool to you."

"No." His voice was low. "You made me want to see the world the way you do."

"That's why you stayed with me," she murmured.

"Yeah."

"You must have commitment issues. One night is okay. A lifetime?" she joked. "You flipped out when you realized you were shackled to me and tried not to kill me the next time we met."

"I'm not the one who swan-dived off a fucking building to get away from my *mate*."

She almost smiled. "I was scared."

"You weren't afraid of me when you went to bed with me. I'm the same person now as I was two days ago."

"A lot has changed. It's not normal to wake up and deal with all this," she said. "I feel like I'm missing something. Daniela knew me and there was a man on the beach when we landed. Said he'd waited a long time to tell me something."

"What was it?"

"Checkmate."

Gabriel laughed quietly.

"That means something to you, doesn't it?" she asked, puzzled.

He didn't answer.

"You won't tell me?"

"When you make a decision," he said.

It was her turn to be quiet. She closed her eyes, at ease in the arms of the man who scared her any other time.

"Even Wynn," she murmured. "It's like people know me somehow, even though I never met them."

"Wynn. Unusual name."

"He's a good friend."

"The kind of *good* friend I need to pay a special visit to?"

Deidre gasped. She hadn't noticed Gabriel tense but did now. Looking at him once more, she shook her head. "You shouldn't make those kinds of jokes."

"It's not a joke."

She saw the gravity on his face. Alarmed, she recalled what it was about him that terrified her. Deidre moved away from his touch, upset she'd let the moonlight trick her into forgetting how dangerous he was. Gabriel rose without speaking. Deidre watched him retrieve his sword and replace it in its sheath.

"What're you doing?" she asked.

"Gotta drop someone a visit."

"Gabriel," she said, taking his arm with both her hands. "He's the reason I'm alive. He was my surgeon." She searched his gaze. "You can't hurt him!"

"Deidre." He worked her grip loose gently. "Stop."

"No!" She was panicking. "It's my fault Logan is dead! You can't take Wynn!"

Gabriel gripped her arms. "Deidre –"

"My decision is yes!" she cried. "I'll stay with you, as long as you want, if you just ...please, Gabriel, don't hurt him. *Please.*"

Gabriel released her. His jaw was ticking. Insides shaky again, Deidre waited breathlessly, tears on her face. She couldn't ... *couldn't* bear the thought of another friend dying because of her! Logan didn't deserve to be killed by a demon; Wynn didn't deserve to die because Gabriel didn't want anyone else around her.

"I can't let you do that," he said at last, his gravelly voice tight. He turned and strode away, disappearing into the shadow world.

Deidre watched him go, horrified at what she'd done. She frantically tried to call a portal. The magic didn't come this time. Pacing, she tried to calm herself, as she had been both times the portal did work for her. She forced herself to sit on the ground, to focus, to wish with all her heart to go back to Wynn.

It didn't work.

She'd just killed Wynn.

She slumped and began crying for her friend.

"Deidre, come in for dinner." Daniela's dark form called from the road.

"I'm not hungry," Deidre managed. "I'm just gonna sit here and wait for the ocean drown me."

"Always drama with Immortal mates." Daniela's sigh was exasperated. "For my sake, come in."

Deidre didn't want to move. Daniela hefted her to her feet. Deidre went obediently with her towards the fortress, numb and nauseous. She'd rather fall asleep crying in her bed than on the beach.

I'm so sorry, Wynn.

Chapter Eight

"I was expecting you sooner."

Gabe emerged into the garden next to a southern style mansion. He was getting tired of surprises and men he didn't want to see popping up to meet him. Wynn lounged in his seat at the garden table, an empty wine glass before him.

"You haven't aged, Gabe," Wynn added.

"You look pretty good for being dead-dead," Gabe replied.

Wynn motioned to the chair across from him. A full wine glass sat in front of the seat. Gabe knew Deidre had been there; her scent lingered. He should've taken some satisfaction at the full glass of wine. The knowing look on Wynn's face, however, made him realize the long dead-dead Immortal had figured things out.

"She's charming this time around, isn't she?" Wynn asked.

Gabe sat. She'd truly thought he was going to kill Wynn. Whatever step towards him she seemed to take this day, she'd leapt back about twenty. He'd drooled over her offer, after wrapping himself around her warm body.

"She is," he replied. "She raised you before she crossed over?"

"Yes. Didn't say why. Didn't say anything at all, except welcome back," Wynn said. "I figured it out when I rediscovered her in the human world a few years ago. I assume she knew she'd need something from me, except she had no idea who I was when we met again."

"You can thank Fate for that one. Pretty sure he's the only one among us who was able to out-manipulate her."

"I like this Deidre. Sweet, gentle, trusting."

Gabe bristled, aware of the quiet lethality of the Immortal before him. Wynn hadn't been much better than Darkyn in his pursuit for power. The disaster that remained of the Immortal society and its Council was evidence.

"You always were a good pair."

"Your involvement with her?" Gabe asked.

"Friendship."

"Men like you don't have friends."

Wynn shrugged. "We don't put all our cards on the table at once, either."

Gabe assessed him. The same gleam was in Wynn's eye that he remembered. The Immortal was planning something and intended to use Deidre to get it. Otherwise, he would've killed her after stumbling upon her years ago.

"It's to your benefit to stay away from her," Gabe said.

"I'm not the one you have to worry about. Of the two of us, she trusts me."

"She also thinks I came to kill you."

"We wouldn't be talking, if my name was on your list," Wynn said. "Very honorable of you to give her a choice of being with you after how she treated you all those years."

Gabe was silent, emotionless. He'd been baited by many Immortals in his time and understood Wynn wanted to push his buttons. Deidre trusted Wynn enough to tell him everything. She'd likely never speak to Gabe again after this night. It burned him, but he had to put her safety over whatever he felt. The high road was his curse.

"But, she's not the same person," Wynn said when the attempt to provoke him failed. "Fate is not the only one you can thank for that. She's learned to appreciate life and those around her, following a diagnosis of a terminal illness."

"Is she really sick?"

"She wasn't when I met her." Wynn's smile was cold. "Vengeance upon someone who has no idea what she's done isn't nearly as satisfactory, but it soothes the burn a little. As sweet as she is, I almost wish I'd given her something a little less lethal. How is that for her having the last laugh?"

Furious at the idea, Gabe began to wonder how the reincarnated Deidre made it this far without being slaughtered by one of her many enemies. Even Rhyn had a reason to hate the deity. That the skin around Wynn's eyes relaxed in genuine warmth made Gabe realize she'd survived partially because she really was different. Innocent.

"What did you do to her?" Gabe asked in a level voice.

Wynn studied him for a moment then shrugged. "It's irreparable. A mix of advanced medicine and magic. I intended for it to kill her over the course of a lifetime. I didn't expect her to be ...so different. Instead of a slow, fifty year death, it'll be three years. I connected the tumor – which was completely operable – with magic to her emotions. Happiness causes her pain, the tumor to grow and eventually, death. I thought it fitting, given the amount of misery she caused men like us."

"It's irreparable, even with magic?"

"Completely. Remember that, the next time you make love to her. Pleasure kills, Gabriel."

Despite the bitter words, there was regret on Wynn's face. Wynn never cared for anyone. He killed his wives in cold blood after they gave birth to his sons, until he tangled with the demoness that was Rhyn's mother. She'd slaughtered him. Deidre affected even this cold bastard, which made Gabe a little less resentful of how she made him feel.

"I'd like to see how ... Death handles her," Wynn continued.

"The same way I handle everything," Gabe replied.

"It's not that easy, as I discovered. If you want her tumor to slow its growth, you'll ensure she's unhappy," Wynn advised. "I gave her three months, but it's probably generous, given her sunny nature."

"You're a real piece of work, preying on someone like her," Gabriel said. He wanted to snap the Ancient's neck. "I know how you operate, Wynn. Whatever the rest of your plan is with her, it won't work."

"I know how devoted to the precious Code and your honor you are, Gabriel. I'm counting on it."

Then you don't know me as well as you think you do. The knowledge left him calmer than when he arrived. Wynn had missed the events of the past few thousand years, which meant the changes Gabe went through the past few months were mysteries to the Immortal.

"The Immortals haven't discovered you," Gabriel guessed.

"Not yet. I've been taking a breather from that life. I'll show myself soon," Wynn said, unconcerned. "What news do you have of my sons?"

"Dangerous question."

Wynn leaned forward, interest on his face. "Do they hold the Council together?"

"Barely. Three of your sons are dead-dead," Gabe said. "Andre, Kris and Sasha."

"My Andre?" Wynn frowned, not expecting the news.

"Rhyn leads the Council."

"The half-breed? I intended to have him killed, before his mother acted against me. Did he kill the others to take over the Council?"

"No. Sasha defected to the Dark One then killed Andre and was himself killed by a traitor. Past-Death took Kris," Gabe summarized. "Rhyn is all that holds the Immortals together."

Rare emotion went through the gaze of the Immortal before him. Gabe waited. Wynn was silent, pensive and troubled. For a moment, Gabe almost thought he cared for his sons.

"Yet she brought *me* back," Wynn mused. "You know why, don't you?"

"I'm not obligated to tell you."

"Will you bargain? Your secret for mine? This is a game your predecessor played very well."

"I have no need for your secrets," Gabe replied.

"You will, when you realize what it is you don't know yet."

"I don't play games, Wynn. I never have."

"You know where to find me," Wynn said, holding out his arms. He folded them behind his head. "Probably with your Deidre. Something tells me she'll be back here soon."

Summoning a portal, Gabriel stood and left.

He agreed silently with Wynn's parting words but wasn't certain what to do about it. If he admitted not to killing Wynn, she'd return immediately. If she believed Wynn dead, Gabe had time. Though he could track her easily, he wasn't certain how to prevent her from using the portals. She was untraceable in the shadow world, until she emerged somewhere else. All it took was a few seconds for her to fall under Wynn's influence. The Immortal knew as much as Gabe about the portals and how to evade those who followed.

One thing was certain: he had to talk to Rhyn fast. It wasn't Death's duty to track a rogue Immortal like Wynn, but he had a need to ensure the right person did.

In the meantime, he had to come up with a plan to make Deidre miserable. Gabriel's step through the shadow world slowed. It was getting more difficult to keep his distance from his mate, and he hated knowing he'd have to hurt her emotionally to prevent the tumor from growing too fast. If what Wynn said was true, Gabriel needed as much time as he could find to figure out how to save her.

Because he *wanted* her to live. Gabriel dwelled on the idea with the same irony that made Wynn regret his vengeance. Urgency filled him at the thought of finding a way to save the woman he might've killed a few days ago. Reconciling past-Deidre and human Deidre was enough to give him a headache. How was it possible they looked exactly alike, yet were so different? Would the Deidre that was his mate snap one day and turn into the goddess he remembered?

It didn't matter, if she died in a few weeks. Stymieing her sunny nature now was a small sacrifice compared to seeing it snuffed forever. He had to figure out a way to do it in a way he was able to recover from, if she survived.

Deidre's eyes were puffy from crying herself to sleep. She showered and left her room, mourning the loss of her last good friend. She located the correct courtyard beside the dining hall on the first try and walked in. No Immortals waited for her. In fact, it was empty, except for the nun who brought her breakfast. Deidre didn't want to talk to the Immortals, but she felt alone eating breakfast.

Despondent, she went from the dining hall to the top of the wall and leaned on it. The sight, sound and scent of the ocean helped her relax. She'd never seen such a beautiful body of water. Her gaze flickered between it and the interior of the Sanctuary. She left everything of value she owned at Wynn's. Terrified she'd find him in the tub, nothing more than a pile of bones, she pushed herself away from the wall and focused hard on calling a portal.

It came today. Dread sank into her belly as she entered the shadow world and crossed to the glowing doorway. She stepped through into the guest bedroom she'd left the night before. Her things were where she'd left them. She changed into her own clothes and gathered the most important of her belongings before bracing herself to leave the room.

She went to Wynn's bedroom first. His bed was made, and there was no body on the floor. Heart beating fast, she descended the stairs in the marble foyer, listening. While she heard nothing, she smelled coffee. Deidre followed the scent to the veranda, thrilled to see Wynn seated at the table where they'd had dinner.

And then she remembered the demon that took the shape of Logan. She paused in the doorway to the patio.

"I made coffee. I don't know how you drink it," Wynn said, turning his head to the side.

"Thanks," she murmured. Deidre crossed her arms as she moved to take the seat she'd been in the night before.

Wynn looked like Wynn. Logan had seemed off in hindsight, his gestures unnatural and his talk stilted. Wynn poured her a cup of coffee and sat back, studying her closely.

"Are you well this morning?" he asked.

She nodded. "Are you?"

"Very."

She didn't know what to think about Gabriel after last night. He'd flipped on her again, going from the tender lover to the homicidal maniac. She thought for sure he was coming after Wynn. Yet, Wynn was fine. Was she so wrong about Death?

"I'm happy to see you," she said. "I thought …never mind."

"You were concerned. I'm flattered," he replied with one of his faint smiles. "Did I not tell you that I am not one to worry?"

"Yeah, you did." She released a deep breath. After sobbing herself to sleep, she was almost too tired to appreciate the fact he was alive. "Did anyone come to visit you or anything?"

"No one I couldn't handle, dear," he said. "You're safe here. You know this, I hope. What's on your mind?"

"Just a … bad dream I guess. I'm going crazy, Wynn. Isn't that one of the signs I'm starting to deteriorate?"

"Loss of cognitive function is a sign, yes," he replied. "If you start to deteriorate, I'll tell you. Trust me?"

"Of course. I've always trusted you, Wynn. As soon as I start down that path, I'm ..."

He raised an eyebrow. She flushed and rubbed her face. Deidre drank her coffee in silence, feeling Wynn's gaze and unwilling to look at him after almost admitting to the plan. Gabriel's second rule was at the forefront of her mind. She thought she was going crazy already; if she really started to deteriorate, there was no way she'd be able to handle it.

"We'll cross that bridge when we come to it," Wynn's voice carried a note of sorrow. "In the meantime, I've got to run out this morning to meet with my financial manager to adjust my plan now that I'm happily unemployed."

"I think you'll be okay," she said, glancing at the mansion.

"Only because I take steps to make certain it stays that way," he said. "Will you be okay here?"

She nodded.

"You have my cell number?"

Another nod.

Wynn rose. "I'll leave the coffee for you and check in later to make sure you haven't decided to act prematurely."

"I won't," she said, clearing her throat. "Thank you, Wynn."

"No need to thank me. It's my fault I can't right this."

At the tight words, she looked at him curiously.

"Apparently, I'm not the medical genius people believe me to be," he added.

"You know that's not true," she said firmly. "I'm grateful for all you've done for me."

His smile was polite. "Be back in a bit."

He was unhappy about something. Deidre sipped her coffee. There was no way he was concerned about money. All he had to do was sell one of the original pieces of artwork displayed casually in the marble foyer and he'd be fine for years.

She trusted him without question and yet, there was more to him than she really knew. Their professional then personal relationships had centered around her and her illness. She didn't know more than his official biography. She'd never needed to know, before now.

Deidre waited half an hour then rose. She wandered into the house, uncertain what she sought. Some sign he was an Immortal? Some sign he wasn't?

She didn't really know. She put her cell phone on its charger and explored the house, admiring his taste in everything from furniture to paintings to simple décor. He lived well but not lavishly, surrounded by an understated elegance much like him: aloof and pleasant.

Nothing screamed Immortal or that there was something about him she should be worried about. Frustrated with herself for assuming the worst about her remaining friend, she returned to the veranda. She understood why he liked the spot; the scent of honeysuckle and herbs was thick in the air, the manicured gardens pleasant to look at and the awning providing the right amount of cool shade from the midmorning Georgia sun.

Had Gabriel visited him last night? If so, why was he alive?

No one I couldn't handle, dear.

She hadn't put much weight into Wynn's response, but she considered it now. Another bizarre answer. The coffee was still warm. She poured herself some more, struggling to figure out what she was missing. What the Immortals were hiding from her. The only one who seemed willing to talk to her before being shushed by Daniela was Rhyn.

Rhyn, whose last words to her had been to find him, if she wanted to know the full story. Struck by an idea, Deidre sat up. If the portals took her to Gabriel and Wynn, they might take her to Rhyn, too. He scared her, but it was beyond the time for her to start getting some answers.

Deidre wiped her hands on her jeans and sat up straight. She breathed deeply and closed her eyes, aware the portals wouldn't respond if she was remotely upset.

"Rhyn," she said. "But only if it's safe where he is."

A familiar warmth stirred within her, and she braced herself before opening her eyes. Witnessing the gaping hole to the shadow world form in the middle of the real world was unsettling.

It was there, and one of the doorways on the other side beckoned her. With a deep breath, she crossed through the clinging cold, at a run by the time she reached the other side out of fear the portals might all disappear before she was safe.

She paused, afraid of where this doorway led, and steadied her breathing before stepping through, at once disoriented to appear in a small kindergarten class. There were six students around five-years-old and an older boy on the verge of puberty sitting around a beautiful blond, who was reading a book out loud. The chunky blocks of the stone walls were decorated with art done by children, and colorful mats covered the floor.

Rhyn wasn't there. Did the portals send her somewhere random? Deidre turned around to find the hole between places had closed already. She faced the class. The blonde teacher was staring at her.

"Sorry, I think I'm …lost," Deidre said.

The kids all turned at her voice.

"Are you here for me?" the blonde asked guardedly.

"What? No, I um, was looking for someone else," Deidre answered.

A flush spread across the woman's face, and anger glittered in her eyes. She rose and strode to Deidre.

"You can't have the angels!" she snapped. "And this is for taking Kris from me!" A hard slap accompanied her words.

Stunned, Deidre took a step back. The sense of being in the Twilight Zone returned.

"I didn't … I don't know a Kris," she stammered.

"Who are you here for? Tell me and get it over with!"

"Rhyn."

"Ah. Him you can have," the woman said, whirling away. "About time someone took out that son of a bitch."

Deidre fought the urge to scream again. Couldn't *someone* tell her what the hell was going on?

"Auntie Hannah, this isn't … who you think it is," said the oldest boy in the class. His large brown eyes were studying Deidre. He appeared to be close to eleven or twelve. "She's human."

"Seriously?" Hannah faced Deidre, cool blue eyes assessing. "Are you human?"

Deidre nodded. Hannah relaxed. Deidre guessed she'd stumbled upon somewhere in the Immortal world.

"You should go get the Immortal mood beast," the boy advised Hannah.

"No, *you* go get her, Toby," Hannah replied.

"I just escaped!" the boy whined.

Deidre gasped. No part of her was ready to meet whatever creature they discussed. She was barely holding it together knowing about Death and the Immortals.

"It's okay, I'll … come back later," she said and moved towards the door.

"Fine. I'll go." Toby rolled his eyes. "Stay here. Are you still calling yourself Deidre?"

She gaped at him. He rolled his eyes again and trudged out of the room.

"If you're human, then I'm sorry," Hannah said with some effort. "If you're messing with us, then I'll do worse than slap you."

"I like your hair," one of the kids said, approaching.

"How did you become human?" another asked.

"Did you bring snacks?"

"Can we go to the underworld?"

Deidre stared down at the curious kids gathering around her. Normal kids didn't ask about the underworld or being human. She swallowed hard, not wanting to break down in front of them. One of the girls grabbed her hand to pull her to the blankets where they'd been sitting while another one tugged at a loose lock of her hair. Deidre went and sat when they pulled her towards the ground.

"You look like you're about to pass out," Hannah said.

"Rough week," Deidre whispered.

The kids were talking to her, but she had trouble focusing on anything outside of keeping the buzzing in her ears from pushing her beyond tunnel-vision into the darkness. Everyone knew her somehow or about the Immortals, and she was lost.

Hopefully, I'm dead in three months.

One of the kids handed her a handful of cotton balls while another put a doll in her lap. Uncertain what to do with either, she kept them. The kids seemed entranced by her pink hair. Someone brought her a colorful picture book.

"Read!" the little girl demanded.

Deidre struggled to focus.

"*What Humans Eat,*" she read the title. "Really?"

The girl nodded.

"Okay. Why not." Deidre flipped to the first page. The little girl pushed the pages until satisfied, and Deidre didn't have the mental power to tell her it wasn't normal to start mid-book.

"Do humans eat plants?" she asked, eyes on the illustration.

"Yes!" a couple of voices chorused.

"Yes, humans eat many vegetables, like lettuce, broccoli and carrots," she read and turned the page. "Do humans eat rocks?"

"No!" the kids replied.

"No, humans do not eat rocks. You should never feed a human a rock, even by mistake. Good advice," she muttered and turned the page. "Do humans eat ... uh ... demons?" Unsettled by the image of a cheerful demon on a spit, she flipped to the next illustration.

"No!" more voices joined in.

"No, humans do not eat demons. But demons do eat humans," she read, grimacing at the image of a cheerful man on a platter surrounded by demons. "What kind of children's book is this?"

"Technically, they're not kids," Hanna replied.

Deidre's head was pounding.

The girl in front of her began speaking. "Humans eat plants and macaronis and –"

"Meatballs!"

"Chocolate."

"Oooohhh chocolate!" several kids echoed.

"The little angels have a thing for chocolate," Hannah explained.

"Sure," Deidre murmured, near fainting.

"Someone get Deidre a juice box!" Hannah ordered.

Three were thrust at her. Deidre took one and sipped. The cool liquid felt good on her throat.

She never should've left Wynn's. In fact, if she'd stayed away from the beach this weekend altogether and had dinner with her doctor instead of causing her boyfriend to be eaten by a demon, she wouldn't be facing an Immortal mood beast or teaching Immortal children not to feed humans rocks.

"Deidre?"

She looked up. Toby stood beside a plainly pregnant young woman with blue eyes and a tattoo across her neck that resembled the one on Deidre's back in color and otherworldly script. While *Gabriel* was written at the center of the geometric designs on Deidre's shoulders, the tattoo on the woman before her bore the name *Rhyn*.

Rhyn's mate. Deidre almost understood why the portals brought her wherever this was. She was surprised to see Rhyn's mate looked … normal.

"Yes," she said at last, cringing for another bad reaction.

The woman smiled.

"C'mon kids, let Deidre up," Hannah said to the little Immortals surrounding Deidre.

One of them claimed the doll, and Deidre released it. Hannah accepted the book and juice box. No one came for the cotton balls, and Deidre stood, putting them in her pocket.

"I'm happy to see you!" the dark-haired woman crossed to her and hugged her hard. "What're you doing here? I thought you were dead-dead!"

"Um, not yet," Deidre said, returning the hug awkwardly. "Kinda wish I was, though."

"Mama, she's human," Toby said.

Rhyn's mate withdrew, gazing at Deidre quizzically.

"You don't remember me, do you?" she asked.

Deidre shook her head. "I'm happy to see you instead of an Immortal mood beast."

"Immortal mood beast?" the woman addressed the boy. "Really, Toby?"

The boy's face turned red. Deidre's gaze fell to the woman's protruding belly, and she suddenly understood.

"Sorry, Toby," she said.

"I deserve it," Toby said with a pitiful sigh.

The woman rolled her eyes. "Anyway, I'm Katie. You've met Toby and my sister Hannah. You really don't remember any of us?"

"I'm sorry but no," Deidre replied. "Should I?"

"Well, yeah. We spent time in the underworld together, though if you're human, that might mean ..." Katie drifted off then glanced at the children. "Hey, Toby, can you give her one?"

Deidre followed her gaze, not understanding.

"You can't just assign one because she's human," Toby said.

"Oh no? And how did I end up with you?" Katie challenged.

"That was different."

"Give me what?" Deidre interrupted.

"A basement angel," Katie answered her before continuing with Toby. "They need homes, don't they?"

"You want to give me a … kid?" Deidre asked, baffled.

"Yes, but she has to be screened and compatible," Toby said.

"We know how well that screening worked out, now don't we?" Katie retorted.

Toby rolled his eyes. "Mama, pleeeeeeeeease don't make me pick one for her."

At the end of her rope with the bizarre world and discussion, Deidre fainted.

Chapter Nine

When she awoke, it was to find the face of the boy, Toby, hovering over hers. Deidre blinked. He leaned back, and a recessed, marble ceiling came into view. Its edges were gilded with gold marking a lazy geometric design across the marble. Two brightly lit, massive bronze chandeliers dangled at even distances across the ceiling. She was on a huge, plush sleigh bed with dark wood and pastel coverings. Pushing herself up, Deidre was amazed at the size and furnishings of the room. It was like something out of a television show about castles.

"Where am I?" she asked.

"Didn't you come here through the portals?" Toby asked.

"Yes, but I don't understand how to use them yet."

"French Alps. This is where the Immortals live," Toby replied. "Gabe's not dead-dead, is he?"

Deidre looked at him, surprised he knew Gabriel.

"Not that I know of," she said with a shiver. "I have a headache."

"It's my fault. You hit the ground before I could catch you," he said.

"No, I'd have one anyway," she said, not wanting to admit she didn't think the skinny youth could've caught her anyway.

"Why?"

"Long story."

He reached out to her and placed a hand on her forehead. She was surprised to feel a strange zap of energy, different than Gabriel's warmth but not unpleasant.

"You have a tumor," Toby said, dismayed. "A big one. Does it hurt?"

"Um, I don't know if *it* hurts, but I get headaches," she replied.

"I can't believe you don't remember anything," Katie said from the doorway. She pushed the door closed with her hip, a silver tray of cookies and snacks in her hands. "Hannah said you came here looking for Rhyn?"

"Yes. He's the only one who seems like he'd tell me what's going on. No one else will," Deidre said with some frustration. Her eye went to the snacks. Katie set the tray on the bed then sat at the foot, leaning against the bed frame.

"So you're not Death anymore?"

Deidre stared at her.

"You don't remember that either. Wow."

"We'll tell you!" Toby offered. He climbed over the tray onto the bed with them and sat cross-legged.

"I don't know the whole story, but I can give you the basics," Katie said. "Do you really want to know?"

"I think so," Deidre said uncertainly. "Does the tattoo mean you're Rhyn's mate?"

"Exactly." Katie grunted. "Could've been a little more discreet, but it fits Rhyn's personality."

"Is it something you can undo?" Deidre hedged.

"God no. And I tried."

"Immortal Code," Toby said. "Even the angels can't unmate someone."

"Angels," Deidre murmured.

"Wait, does this mean you have a tattoo, too?" Katie straightened, gaze sharpening.

Deidre nodded.

"Where?"

"On my back."

"Show me!"

Deidre glanced at Toby. He sighed and flopped onto his stomach, facing away from them. Deidre twisted and pulled up her shirt for Katie to see.

Rhyn's mate squealed loud enough for Deidre to jump. She dropped her shirt, startled when Katie flung her arms around her in another tight hug.

"Who! Mama!" Toby demanded.

"I knew it!" Katie all but shouted. She released Deidre and returned to her seat, face glowing. "I called it."

"Mama!"

"Gabe, Toby."

Toby's face lit up. "I bet he was pissed."

"Okay, I need to know what's going on," Deidre said, the buzzing back in her ears.

"Short version. I know this will be rough," Katie started, sympathy on her features. "Once upon a time, you were an Immortal –"

"-deity," Toby corrected.

"What's the difference?" Katie asked.

"Deities are way older and more powerful."

"Whatever. So you were a deity," Katie continued. "Guess which one?"

"Death," Toby supplied.

"Not you, Toby. Deidre, you were Death for let's say, a zillion years. Somewhere along the line, you found Gabe and forced him to work for you as your number one assassin. He fell totally in love with you. You following so far?"

Deidre's mouth was dry and her hands shaking, but she nodded.

"You fell totally in love with him, too, but you were uh … well, I guess deities are sort of…"

"You were a mega-bitch," Toby said. "You took his heart and crushed it, like every day for thousands of years."

Deidre gasped.

"That's a little harsh," Katie murmured.

"Then you dumped him," Toby continued. "So then, one day you told him to kill Katie and her baby, because you were mad at Rhyn and the demons were coming."

Deidre's eyes went to Katie in horror. Rhyn's mate tried to smile, but her gaze was haunted.

"Gabe wouldn't do it. He went rogue and helped Katie evade you in the underworld. I was there, too! And Rhyn and Kris and Kiki," Toby said cheerfully. "You made Kris and Gabe trade their souls for Katie and baby's then you quit."

"That's um, the abbreviated version. You also broke immortal laws to let me go instead of killing me. You didn't quit because you wanted to, but because you had to after breaking those laws to spare me and Hazel," Katie added, patting her stomach. "You helped me escape demons through that awful underworld forest. That's how I found out you really did love Gabe, even though you um …"

"Crushed his will to live," Toby finished.

"Anyway, you must've been reborn as a human," Katie said.

Deidre struggled to absorb the wild story, unable to comprehend most of it. That she was a deity, Death, who lived for thousands of years … None of that made sense. Nothing did, except that she hurt Gabriel. He'd recognized her the morning after their one night stand, flipped out and wanted to kill her since then. In that light, his reaction to her appeared less like that of a moody homicidal maniac and more like one of a jilted lover.

"I did those things to Gabe?" she asked, upset.

"Yeah, you were really psycho to him," Katie replied.

"It's because he was originally human," Toby said. "You hated that part of him, so you tortured him for like –"

"Toby!" Katie snapped. "Overkill."

Deidre sat frozen, aware of their concerned gazes. Suddenly, she wished she hadn't asked.

"That's why everyone reacts funny to me," she managed at last. "They think I'm coming to k…kill them?"

"Yeah. You should be able to see the Immortal markings, too. They're reddish tattoos. I usually see them when I first meet an Immortal," Katie said.

"I have seen those. I thought they were hallucinations," Deidre murmured.

"Did Gabe flip out when he saw the mating tattoo?" Toby asked, giggling.

"Yeah, he did," Deidre said. "But he told me he'd give me a choice about whether or not I wanted to be with him, even though he's obligated by those laws."

"Awwww," Katie's gaze warmed. "Gabe is the reason I'm alive. He's the best man I know, aside from Rhyn. He risked everything to save me."

"Really?"

"He and Rhyn are like brothers. They only had each other for a long time. Then I came along what? Six months ago?" Katie glanced at Toby.

"Seven."

"I guess. I am six months pregnant."

"Immortal mood beast," Toby muttered under his breath.

"Oh, and there's no walking away from an Immortal that's claimed you," Katie added. "I don't give a shit what they tell you. Especially Gabe. He means well, but there's no way he could let you go. He's loved you for like, a million years."

"He doesn't act like it," Deidre said.

"He's hated you that long, too," Toby said.

"Rhyn and I tried everything to get away from each other, and Gabe put the smackdown on it all. He'll come around soon, when he realizes you're not the deity who fucked him over," Katie said. "That explains why Rhyn's been checking up on him so often lately."

"Am I different as a … as a human?" Deidre asked.

"Very. I can tell but it takes men longer to figure out that stuff."

"I can't believe this is happening." Deidre rubbed her face.

"Tell me about it." Katie was glaring at Toby, who grinned.

Their nonverbal exchange made Deidre smile. She liked Katie and Toby. The history they related to her, however, left her wanting to cry. No wonder Gabe hated her one day and tried hard to tolerate her the next. He was stuck with her by their laws, a daily reminder of someone who used to hurt him. If he was half the man they believed him to be – and if she was half as bad as these two related to her – he'd resent her for the rest of their lives. Being Immortal, that meant pretty much forever.

She didn't want to live with someone like Logan, who resented her for something she couldn't control. She wasn't going to be some sort of obligation to someone who stuck around because he had to. It left her depressed, when she wanted to be happy the last few months of her life.

The strange Immortal world was so unwelcoming. Her brain tumor never seemed like a blessing before now.

"Are you okay?" Katie asked.

"Not really," Deidre admitted.

"We can give you an angel," Toby relented.

"What is this angel stuff?" she demanded.

"Toby is a guardian angel. They're assigned to human mothers," Katie explained. "He's the one who dragged me into this whole mess with Immortals."

"You mean those little kids are angels? Real live angels?"

"Yes!" Toby beamed. "They're too young to take care of humans yet, so humans have to take care of them. Death … *you* used to take care of the really old angels, and Gabe visited the little ones all the time. Rhyn is supposed to find the basement angels new homes."

Angels almost made sense. More sense than the idea she was a deity for thousands of years.

"I don't think I can handle a basement angel," she said. "You'd have to find them a new home in a few months anyway, when I die."

"Die?" Katie echoed.

"She has a brain tumor," Toby said. "It's huge."

"You can't die. Gabe won't let you."

"The alternative is that it keeps growing and I turn into a vegetable," Deidre said. "So, yeah, that's not happening."

"Does he know?"

"Yes."

Katie waited for more. Deidre didn't know what else to say. Toby looked thoughtful.

"I guess at least he'll be able to get a new mate in a few months. Then he won't be stuck with someone he hates," Deidre added, comforted by the thought.

"Um, no," Katie said. "Immortals only get one their whole lives, even if they live for a million years."

"Well, he'll be free to date," Deidre said.

"Not an easy thing to do when you're Death."

Deidre sighed. Why did she feel guilty about this whole mess, when she hadn't done anything to get herself into it? Not directly, anyway. Or maybe it was all her fault, created by bad karma she built up when she was some crazy deity in a past life she had no memory of.

Okay, so maybe this wasn't so weird. She was working off bad karma.

"Toby, what do the angel memories say about it?" Katie asked.

"I'm thinking."

Deidre glanced at the angel curiously.

"When they get old enough, they can tap into this encyclopedia of shared memories," Katie explained. "It's kinda cool, except that Toby isn't old enough to research everything yet."

"I can't find anything," Toby said, upset. "But I think that Gabe can fix it. I mean, he has to be able to."

"Unless he can do something my surgeon can't ..." Deidre shrugged. "Oh! Speaking of him, I'm supposed to be at his house."

"You should stay here," Katie said. "It's not safe in the human world for you now. Rhyn said there are demons after you. They're nasty bastards. This is the headquarters for the Immortals. Nothing can get you here, which is why I'm not allowed to leave." She rolled her eyes.

"I think I might've put him in danger, though. I already got one friend killed by a demon," Deidre said, guilt assailing her at the memory of Logan.

"The best thing you can do is just disappear," Katie advised. "That way, no one around you is in danger."

"I guess. I hope it's not too late, though," Deidre said. "I left all my stuff at his house."

"Go grab it and come right back," Katie suggested. "Rhyn knows you're here, which means he'll be checking up on you. You don't want him or Gabe to hunt you down. Trust me."

Deidre suspected the result of provoking either man was death to someone. She shivered. She hadn't intended not to return to Wynn's, but the idea of keeping him safe, too, made her feel a little less guilty about sneaking out on him.

She didn't want to die. She'd always hoped Wynn found some miracle cure, even while checking things off her bucket list. There wasn't anything else Wynn could do, though. Like Gabriel, he was better off without her in his life. It seemed like death was the only way to make up for whatever past-Deidre did.

"Do you need a portal?" Katie asked.

"No, I figured them out somehow."

"You're able to draw off Gabe's magic, like I can Rhyn's. It's how I accidentally learned to use the portals, too."

"Okay. I'm gonna give it a go. Sometimes, it doesn't respond," Deidre said. She swung her legs off the bed and closed her eyes. Focusing hard on Wynn, she willed the portal to appear.

"Yes!" Toby exclaimed.

Opening her eyes, she saw the dreaded shadow world waiting for her.

"Don't be gone long," Katie reminded her.

Deidre wanted to flee and never return, but she nodded at the young woman who almost seemed normal. Deidre hurried into the shadow world. She was halfway to the portal when the low, unfamiliar voice reached her.

"A moment of your time."

She froze in the middle of the in-between place.

"Deidre, I believe?"

She turned to face the figure. Tall and lean, with eyes as black as Gabriel's, the man who stood too close for her comfort wore normal enough clothing, aside from the knives strapped to his thighs. He appeared to be any other Immortal.

"I'm Darkyn, and I work for another of the deities," he said. He neared, assessing her with a level of interest that made her uncomfortable.

"How many deities are there?"

"Several dozen."

"Is this where you live?" she asked.

"No, love," he said with a smile. "I happened to be passing through when I saw you. You came back as beautiful as you left."

"Oh, god!" she groaned. "Not another jilted lover out for revenge!"

He chuckled, a sound that somehow managed to be threatening. He paused between her and the portal beckoning her while keeping his distance from both.

"You're not, are you?" she asked at his silence.

"My relationship with you was …complicated. In any case, I went to visit you at your apartment recently to ask you something."

She waited.

"Did past-Deidre leave you anything?"

"Leave me anything?" she echoed. "I never knew she existed until a day ago, and I'm only now learning how awful of a person she was. I certainly never met her."

"She may have provided it to you in such a way that you thought it yours. A piece of jewelry. A trinket or bauble you inherited from a family member."

Deidre shook her head. "My parents died in a house fire when I was eighteen. It destroyed everything, and I was an only child from a small family. I came to Atlanta with nothing but the clothes on my back."

"No strange gifts?"

"No, nothing." She shivered at his penetrating gaze. Gabriel's made her hot from the inside out; this one left her cold. "What is it?"

"Nothing of interest to anyone but me."

"You can search my apartment, if you don't believe me."

"I believe you. I know when one lies."

"Then you know I can't help you."

"I sense physical weakness. Are you ill?" His head was titled to the side, as if he was trying to determine what was wrong with her.

"I am," she confirmed. "I have a terminal brain tumor."

"Death will not let you die-dead."

"He can't help me. No one can."

"No one?" A smile crossed Darkyn's face. "I can."

"Not that I doubt you, but um, I really don't think so," she said. His predatory smile made her pulse fly. "It would kill me to take this thing out of my head, and Gabriel and all his … uh minions … aren't allowed to kill me. So I'll just die slowly over the next few months." She rubbed her face, overwhelmed by her day. "Wynn couldn't help me. Gabriel can't. You can't either."

"Wynn. I know this name."

"He's my surgeon and the best there is." She looked him over, silently dismissing any notion that this creature spent much time in the mortal world. He appeared normal, unassuming, but there was something otherworldly in his eyes that warned her he wasn't normal. The chances he knew her surgeon were negligible.

Darkyn's gaze turned considering. "My magic is of a different kind. May I touch you?"

She swallowed a refusal at the expression on his face. Deidre retreated, but he took one arm before planting a hand on her head. He tilted his again. Cold energy shot through her.

Shuddering, she backpedaled. Darkyn released her.

"I can fix it," he said. "But you are uncertain as to whether or not this is what you wish. I can kill you, too, if this is what you decide."

She listened. The longer they talked, the deeper the clammy shadows sank into her.

"You're correct. Gabriel will not be able to take you, and he won't be able to cure you. The decision is yours."

"My goal has been to enjoy what I have left then …die."

"A worthy goal. Can you do it before Gabriel falls in love with you? Before you hurt him in this life as you did in your previous life?" Darkyn asked. "Before you start to deteriorate and your body gives out on you?"

"I don't know," she whispered, wondering how he knew exactly what she feared. "I ask myself that a few times a day."

"When you know the answer, come here. You only need to say my name to summon me. Whether you choose to live or to die, you will need my help."

"That's it? You'll just help me?"

"That's it."

"Feels like there should be a catch."

"Find me, love, when you're ready. We'll discuss terms then."

"It won't be today," she said, starting to freak out again at the cold shadows and the scary man.

"By all means, you are free to go." He stepped out of her path.

Deidre moved past him timidly, expecting him to attack her. He didn't, and she paused in front of her destination to glance back. She sensed danger and promise from the freaky guy loitering in the shadow world. His offer was tempting. Of everyone she'd dealt with, he was the first to give her a real choice: Life or death. Slow deterioration or an eternity. The idea she had a choice was strangely empowering. Accustomed to the thought of dying, she viewed the option of living as …weird.

There had to be more to what this creature offered. What kind of stranger – Immortal or otherwise – gave a blank check to someone who probably screwed him over in a past life?

"It can't be that easy," she voiced.

"Life or death? The simplest choice there is," he assured her.

"Was your relationship with past-Deidre good or bad?"

"There were no *good* relationships with past-Deidre. Only quid quo pro. What form that took was almost always of her determination. I respected that," Darkyn replied.

Uncertain how to interpret the response, Deidre shook her head and faced the portal. Life was possible. He'd given her something to think about, but her instincts were screaming at her not to have anything to do with this creature.

She emerged in the gardens. It was later than she thought, mid-afternoon by the heat. She was relieved to see Wynn wasn't on the patio. Anxiety filled her once more at the idea he might've been replaced by a demon by now. She wasn't going to lose her only friend, not after all he'd done for her.

Entering the house, she heard nothing indicating he was home. She felt awful leaving him out of the blue, without saying farewell or thanking him.

He'll be safe this way, she told herself again, hoping that was the case.

Deidre ascended the stairs to her room and gathered her things. She shrugged the backpack on and grabbed the bag at her feet. She couldn't take everything this trip, but she had the most important stuff.

A light knock at the door made her stop in place.

"Deidre? I thought you'd left." His voice came from the hallway.

"No, just ..." *running out on you in the middle of the day after all you've done to help me.* "You can come in, Wynn."

The door opened, and she stared at him.

"What happened?" she exclaimed. His eye was black, one of his cheekbones yellow.

"Nothing to be concerned about," he said with a casual shrug. "Are you leaving?"

"I have to, so I don't put you in danger," she said. She placed her bag on the ground and approached him. She touched his cheek gingerly. "You know you should have ice on this!" she chided. "You're a doctor for god's sake!"

He took her hand. "It looks worse than it is. Really, Deidre, it's nothing."

"Wynn, you have to tell me what happened!" She searched his features.

"It's rather embarrassing," he said.

"Omigod! You've seen me naked and drooling and drugged up. You've cut me open and – "

"I cede your point," he said, smiling. "First, can you tell me if your Gabriel is about seven feet tall, with eyes darker than night and no sense of humor?"

Her jaw dropped.

"I'll take that as a yes. In that case, I understand completely."

"Gabriel hit you?" she demanded.

"It might've been another seven-foot stranger concerned about your welfare."

Deidre didn't see Gabriel doing something like this. He was the kind of man who struck once - and it'd kill his target. But how else did Wynn know what Gabe looked like? There was no mistaking the description.

"I can't believe he did this."

"Full disclosure, I think he was aiming for the … thing beside me. It looked human," Wynn appeared perplexed. "Jared? Sounded human but …"

Deidre shivered. She recalled Jared too well. He was a demon that ate people. Maybe Gabe hurt Wynn while trying to save her friend from the demons. It made more sense than Wynn being hit by Gabe.

"My dear, your eyes." Wynn took her chin and tilted her face up. "It's not a good sign."

"What's wrong?" she asked quickly.

"Your pupils are different sizes. Do you have a headache by chance?"

"Yes."

He frowned.

"Wynn, what's wrong?" she asked again. "Do you think … am I starting to you know, go downhill?"

He hesitated. "Possibly. It might be an early indication."

She swallowed hard. Wynn being cornered by a demon and her body starting to give out on her. It was an awful combination.

"Do you trust me, Wynn?" she asked.

"Of course."

"Will you go somewhere with me?"

His gaze went to her bag. "Weekend trip or longer?"

"Longer, probably."

"Can I pack?"

"Sure. I want to take you somewhere safe."

He studied her for a moment then nodded. Wynn retreated to his bedroom. Deidre grabbed her bag and waited for him in the hallway. He joined her, a gym bag at his side. Handing her the keys, he smiled.

"Um, don't need these," she said. She tucked them into her bag. "Close your eyes and just work with me here."

Wynn raised an eyebrow but obeyed. Deidre calmed, drew herself up and summoned a portal. It came quickly this time. She reached out to take Wynn's hand.

"Trust me," she said again.

"I do, Deidre."

"Okay, come on." Deidre led him into the shadow world at a quick pace. She glanced back at him to make sure his eyes were still closed. She'd been freaked out by the in-between place and wanted him to wait until they reached their destination before he had a chance to panic.

Hurrying through the brightest doorway, she recognized the massive bedchamber where she'd left Katie and Toby. They sat on the bed, playing a card game. Katie looked up as Deidre appeared. Her smile faded as she saw Wynn.

"I know. I should've asked." Deidre cringed. "But he's in danger. This is my friend, Wynn. Wynn, Katie and Toby."

Toby's mouth was agape, Katie's face blanching. Uncertain what to think of their reactions, Deidre turned to Wynn. She released his hand.

"You can open your eyes now," she said. "Don't freak out."

Wynn opened his eyes. No emotion crossed his features as his gaze settled on the two people on the bed.

"You okay?" Deidre asked at his silence.

"Deidre," Katie managed. "What the hell did you do?"

"I was worried about him getting caught up by demons," Deidre replied. "If I'm safe here, isn't he?"

Toby was too shocked to move, while Katie scrambled to her feet. Both were alarmed. A familiar sense returned, the one that made Deidre think Wynn wasn't a normal human.

His attention turned to her. "My sweet Deidre. I expected you to take me to a Sanctuary, not here."

Chapter Ten

Wynn was an Immortal. As she watched, the black eye and bruised cheek healed themselves.

"How do you … oh, god," she whispered.

"Dead-dead," Toby managed.

"I fucked something up, didn't I?"

"This was inevitable. I'm sorry I tricked you into bring me here," Wynn replied. He approached Katie. "The half-demon's mate. My first grandchild, I take it?"

Deidre saw Katie swallow hard before she nodded. Katie didn't move as Wynn placed a hand on her stomach.

"Girl," he said. "Healthy and happy. Very good." He dropped his hand, and Katie eased away.

"Why aren't you dead-dead?" Toby exclaimed.

"Before she crossed over, past-Deidre brought me back."

"Wynn, please tell me you're …" Deidre started, horrified at the latest revelation of what she'd done in her past life. "I don't know. Tell me something. Anything." Her voice trembled.

"I am the same friend you've had the past few years. I happen to be an Immortal rather than a human," he said gently. There was warmth in his gaze. He touched her cheek. "You have to trust me."

"Not any Immortal," Toby said. "The first Ancient."

"Rather than continue to distress you all, why don't you take me to Rhyn, angel?" Wynn asked.

Toby stood slowly and moved towards the door.

"We'll talk later," Wynn promised Deidre, squeezing her arm. "A pleasure, Katie."

"Yeah, sure," Katie replied.

Deidre watched Toby lead Wynn to the door and out.

"What just happened?" Deidre asked.

"I'm not sure. The last time I saw him, he was in a tomb. This can't be good," Katie said.

"Who is he?"

"The father of the Council. Rhyn's father." Katie appeared as confused as Deidre felt. "I've never heard a good story about him, but he seemed ... nice."

Deidre laughed, not caring about the note of hysteria in her voice. She'd just discovered her best friend was some sort of dead Immortal, one she'd raised from the grave after she fucked over Death to the point he hated the only mate he'd get the billions of years he was alive.

"Katie, Deidre." Gabriel's quiet voice came from the doorway. "You okay?"

"I told you so." Katie grinned.

"Not the normal greeting for Death."

"Congrats, Gabe. I'm going to give you a piece of advice you gave me a few months ago." Katie paused for effect. "You're fucked. Deal with it."

"I'm always right, aren't I?"

Deidre faced the door, not at all prepared to see Gabriel. Dressed in black, he was an imposing figure, even in the cavernous room. She felt his pull from the distance. There was a flicker of warmth in his gaze as he teased Katie, and he almost seemed approachable without the bulky trench coat lined with weapons. Not that he wasn't armed; he wore a few sheaths strapped to his body. He was dressed as he had been the night before.

She couldn't remember seeing his chiseled features in full light without being drunk or terrified. With a low brow and piercing gaze, gravelly voice, a perfectly sculpted body and rugged features, Gabriel was the sexiest man she'd ever seen.

"You have no idea how happy I am right now," Katie said.

"Out, woman."

"Fine. I'm two doors down, Deidre. Come find me later."

Gabriel held the door open for Katie, who took the hint and walked out. Deidre's gaze fell to his shapely shoulder, thick bicep and roped forearm as he extended one arm high enough for Katie to walk under. His hands were large, his palms flat. She crossed her arms, too aware of how close to the bed she stood. He regarded her for a long moment, as if assessing if she was going to run or cry, then closed the door.

"You're in one piece," he said after a tense silence.

"That's something, I guess," she replied.

"Rough day?"

"You could say that. Yours?"

"Nothing I couldn't handle." He lifted his chin towards the other side of the bedroom.

Gazing at the muscular man who freely admitted to killing for a living, Deidre couldn't help thinking she never wanted to see something he couldn't handle.

She turned where he indicated, noticing the double French doors for the first time. They led onto a balcony, but it was the eerie green glow beyond that caught her attention. Curious, Deidre crossed to the doors. She didn't notice Gabriel follow and jumped as he leaned around her to open the door. His scent stirred her blood.

Stepping quickly onto the patio, she was able to make out the shapes of tall pine trees. The air was crisp and fresh, the night sky clear.

"What is it?" she asked, eyes on the green glow.

"Lost souls."

Deidre gasped. "Are you serious?"

He nodded once.

"Did I do that, too?" she whispered, dismayed.

"Not directly." Gabriel met her gaze. She felt the shift in him. He was guarded again.

"Never mind," she replied, looking away fast.

"Who told you what exactly?"

"It scares me when you do that, Gabriel."

There was a pause. He wiped his face and sat facing her on the edge of the balcony's railing, arms folded across his chest and legs crossed at the ankle. He made an effort to relax.

"Better?" he asked.

She nodded and moved forward to stand beside him, leaning her hips against the railing. It was too chilly for her to want to keep her distance from the incredibly attractive man. Immortal. Deity. She didn't know what he was.

"Katie and Toby told me what they knew," she replied. "That I was Death for a zillion years and that I fucked you over bad then ran off and became a human."

"Sounds about right."

"And that you hate me pretty bad," she added. She was afraid to ask if it was true what they'd said about him always loving her despite what past-Deidre did.

"Hate is a strong word," he said.

"You have a good reason to use it."

"I don't hate you, Deidre."

"You don't hate me, and I'm dying soon," she said ruefully. "Well then, we're on our way to happiness ever after."

"It's definitely complicated."

Deidre laughed despite herself. His dark, dry humor left her entertained – and baffled. He was studying her.

"Thank you for not killing Wynn. Though in hindsight, I have no idea if that was good or not," she said. "Did you know?"

"When I left you last night, I went to see him. Figured it was no coincidence that a mysterious man named after a dead-dead Immortal just happened to fall into the life of a former deity," Gabriel replied.

"He's helped me through a lot over the past few years."

"He's dangerous, Deidre."

"You aren't?"

"Not to you."

"You kill people for a living and only get one mate for eternity that just happens to be someone who screwed you over for thousands of years who you can say with a straight face that at least you don't hate her," she summarized, aware of the hysteria creeping into her voice. "But you're not a threat."

Gabriel chuckled. "You want to know why I came by tonight?"

"Oh, god. Dare I ask?"

"You remember the two rules I gave you?"

"Yeah."

"And the choice?"

"Yeah."

"You're not walking away from me anymore than I will from you," he said firmly.

"Katie said you'd figure that out," Deidre murmured. "You really want to spend eternity with someone you resent?"

"It doesn't matter how I feel. You're my mate. I'm obligated by divine law to protect you."

No reassurance he'd be able to get past their history, no expression of wanting to be with her. She wasn't sure why she expected either from him, except that she still held half a hope that she might live beyond three months. She wasn't spending an eternity miserable.

"That's not good enough for me," she heard herself saying.

"It will have to be," he replied. "I won't make the mistake I made with you before."

She met his gaze, dreading his words.

"I'll never let myself feel anything for you," he said.

How did a proclamation from a virtual stranger hurt her more than anything anyone else had ever said? If he spoke with anger or frustration or anything other than the quiet, impassioned tone, she would've been able to handle the news better.

"I guess we're both lucky I'll be dead soon," she returned.

"You won't be. I will find a way to stop it, now that Wynn told me what's wrong. In the meantime, I know how to slow the inevitable."

"Because spending *eternity* with someone who hates me is better than leaping off a building how?" she snapped.

"Does it matter?" he returned, irritated. "You'll find it hard to kill yourself when I'm the one who determines who lives and dies."

"You've made your point, Gabriel." She didn't believe for one minute he was going to find a way to prevent her from dying in three months. But if she challenged him on this point, she saw him making it impossible for her to die on her own terms.

"My offer is good whether you expire in three months or an eternity. You can have everything I own, Deidre," he said. "I won't deny you my protection, assistance or my bed. It's a better deal than you gave me the first time around."

"I'll take your word on that, since I don't remember," she said. "What do you expect from me?"

"Everything," he said. "I want all of you. Mind, body, heart and soul."

"And I get what? Your body? A fourth of you? That's not the way a functional relationship works," she said, anger building.

"It's the way ours will."

He was so calm, as if they were negotiating over a car and not eternity together. Deidre sought some flicker of warmth in his dark gaze and saw none. He was wearing his poker face. No part of her thought he was bluffing beneath it. He was accepting his obligation to her while shutting off everything but the physical side of him.

On the surface, what he offered her wasn't bad. But she didn't want to be in a loveless, emotionless relationship with anyone, especially one where she had no partner. With the bond between them all but shoving her into his arms, was it possible to deny their fates together for long?

After a week of knowing him, she already had to concentrate hard to resist leaning into him whenever he was around. She ached to feel his warm embrace, to sink into his dark spices and let him take her where he would. Their one night together made her feel alive, and his dark gaze alone was enough to make her body hot from the inside out.

If he felt the same, he gave no indication. He *wanted* her to surrender, because past-Deidre forced him to do the same. Eternity in such an unequal partnership wasn't even worth considering.

"You and I have different takes on relationships," she said at last. "I'm not interested in an *arrangement* with you."

"Neither of us has a choice about being together. I'm simply choosing the terms."

Deidre bit her tongue to keep from saying what she wanted to, mainly that a relationship consisted of two people, and she was not about to be one of them.

As if sensing her thought, Gabriel reached out to her. He cupped the back of her neck with one large hand, brushing his thumb along her cheek. His gaze dropped to her lips, and his thumb followed, grazing the sensitive skin.

Deidre's body betrayed her, giving a full-form shudder at the rush of heat and energy. Her breath caught. She heard it and knew he did, too. It was so easy to agree and sink into his strength, let the scent of dark chocolate work its way into her skin as his hands moved over her. The idea of waking up to him each morning reminded her of how centered, energized and at peace she'd been after their first night together. She'd woken cradled in his arms. She could have that every night and morning. As long as she was willing to accept that was the only part of him she'd ever have.

No, easy was not something she was willing to accept, even if it meant caving to someone she craved, whose looks drove her crazy and whose touch made her feel more at home than she did in the mortal and Immortal worlds.

"If you're a tenth of the man everyone says you are, you'll stop when I ask you to," she whispered.

There was a pause. "Are you asking me to stop?"

She nodded.

His hand dropped. Deidre withdrew a few feet down the balcony, struggling with the heat streaking through her blood and scattering her rationale. She couldn't think straight when he was close and not at all when he touched her. He knew it, which meant he was counting on her caving at some point. She wasn't going to, anymore than she had to the tumor.

"What are you thinking?" he asked.

She was quiet as she put form to her thoughts beyond the emotional turmoil. Her breathing steadied. Gabriel was waiting with the patience of Death, though he'd started to tense, indicating his guard was going up once more.

"I'm thinking I would've agreed three years ago," she replied. "I spent too long fighting to live on my terms to give in, even to you. Whether I have three months or an eternity, I'm not going to stop fighting to live on my terms. We could really have something, Gabriel. But not like this."

"Let me guess. On *your* terms." The stormy note was back in his voice.

"No. As equals." She guessed what he'd say before he broke the thick silence between them.

"I'm not willing to do that."

Rejection hurt. It was hard to remind herself she'd done absolutely nothing to earn it in this life. Gabriel didn't like past-Deidre and wasn't willing to give her a chance. Or, maybe he tried and couldn't do it. It was a huge pill to try to swallow, knowing someone didn't like her for reasons she couldn't control.

"Then I'm sorry, Gabriel," she said.

He walked away. Deidre sensed his anger, though his movements were as controlled and purposeful as usual. She heard the door to the bedroom close and retreated from the chilly spring air back into her room.

Overwhelmed and upset, she wasn't sure if she wanted to run or cry. Or maybe, just leave. Go back to the real world, where there were no demons or Immortals or the sexy man who wanted to claim her heart while offering her nothing in return beyond his bed. With his looks, he'd have no trouble finding company for the nights he wasn't murdering people and stealing their souls.

She hated the thought. Deidre felt both alone and claustrophobic in the huge room. There was nowhere else for her to go, no more friends for her to run to. She couldn't return to her apartment, and her savings were almost gone. She'd withdrawn everything from her retirement account when she was diagnosed terminal. Determined to do what she wanted with her life, she'd been good with her money but didn't save anything. Dead women didn't need cash.

Unless they didn't die. She had no idea who was right: Wynn, who thought she was deteriorating, or Gabriel, who wasn't going to let her die, so he could exact some sort of passive-aggressive revenge over eternity. Or Darkyn, whose offer seemed so much more objective than either Wynn's or Gabriel's.

Was she a lost soul? Distressed by the idea, she found herself standing before the French doors again, looking at the green haze over the forest. It didn't appear to be far, and it was hours before she'd be asleep on her side of the world.

Anxious to be out of the Immortal stronghold, Deidre dug through her clothes to find the warmest she packed. She didn't need much beyond jeans and jackets for an Atlanta winter. She had a cute hat she'd picked out and stuffed in one pocket of her backpack. Dressed warmly, she left her room and stood in the brightly lit, spacious hallway, not at all certain how to leave the stronghold.

Not wanting anyone to interfere with her plan for air, she drew a deep breath and asked the portal system to take her outside the stone fortress. Crossing through, she emerged outside, in the forest, a short distance outside the low walls around the massive fortress. Deidre was astonished by the size of the stone stronghold. It towered twenty stories tall and sat in a clearing the size of two football fields. It was built on high ground, and the forest sloped downward and away from the fortress.

Orienting herself, she caught sight of the green haze again and walked along the edge of the forest, seeking a path. Multiple dirt deer trails moved away. She needed the time to herself and hoped the connection to nature helped clear her head. She chose a trail that appeared to head in the general direction she wanted to go and began walking.

The forest was cold, the rustle of pine trees against one another faint. A breeze swept over the tops of the trees to make them sway but didn't reach the still air of the forest floor. Night animals stirred. Deidre listened to their rustling and distant cries and focused on placing her feet along the path. The outside world distracted her from her troubled thoughts. She forced herself to notice how dark the sky was, the rich scent of earth in the air, the tickle of the pine needles that brushed her skin.

The path towards the lost souls was anything but direct. The twists and turns led her sometimes towards it, sometimes back the way she came. As she walked, the fear and helplessness uncoiled, loosening their grip on her chest. Her step grew less brisk. She began to marvel at the world around her again, something she hadn't done in days. It calmed her to recall how beautiful and different nature was at night. The forest and darkness created a sense of cozy intimacy, one that held her without crushing her, unlike the rest of the world.

Deidre was breathless and upbeat when the lake came into view over an hour later. It was roughly round with a narrow panhandle that was closest to the fortress. The lake glowed like it was radioactive.

She stopped a dozen meters before the edge of the forest, wondering if there was any sort of hazard in being so close to whatever it was causing the lake to be green in the first place. A form melted from the shadows before her, and she held her breath.

Dressed all in black with weapons strapped in places identical to where Gabriel wore his, the tall man was lean with cold eyes. He scrutinized her for a long moment, eyes narrowing, before he stepped aside to rejoin the shadows. Deidre stared into the forest where he'd disappeared. Nothing moved. He hadn't spoken or drawn weapons on her. If he was a sentry guarding the lake, he'd deemed her not a threat.

She inched closer to the point where he'd appeared then hurried by to the edge of the forest. She couldn't see the far end of the lake from her viewpoint, but she was able to see across the narrow panhandle. The light from the water was bright enough to show who stood on the opposite shore, caught in what looked like a lover's embrace.

Gabriel. And another woman. Deidre stared. They were kissing, their bodies pressed together and arms around each other.

The thought he had someone else – and this was the reason he couldn't commit to her fully – never crossed her mind. Some relief trickled through her to know that his hatred of past-Deidre wasn't the only reason he'd offered her the undesirable arrangement. He wasted no time finding himself a replacement when she refused his touch. At one point, she thought he cared for her a little. Not after this.

"The truth comes out eventually." Wynn's voice was quiet. "I'm an Immortal, and Gabriel has moved on after thousands of years at your feet."

Deidre jumped. She faced the direction she'd come. Wynn's gaze was on the figures across the lake, his impassive features bathed in green light.

"Are you alright, my dear?" he asked.

"Off and on," she joked nervously. "Hard to keep track of what's going on. Who to trust."

His attention shifted to her. "I'll tell you when it's safe to turn around."

"It'll take more than that for me to trust you, Wynn."

"I apologize, Deidre. I didn't think it appropriate to tell you who I was. Things changed when you were dragged back into the Immortal world," he said.

He always was able to soothe her. She found herself nodding, accepting his explanation more easily than even Gabriel's.

"So, who are you?" she ventured. "Or do I want to know?"

"A friend to you. The rest is inconsequential."

"You were dead."

"Yes."

"Why did I or ... I guess, the past-Deidre bring you back?"

"You didn't say." He was amused. "I thought..." He considered her then looked across the lake again.

"What?" she asked. "Were we friends?"

"A little more than that."

"How many people was past-Deidre sleeping with?" she demanded.

"You don't want to know," he said with a shake of his head. "Needless to say, you were efficient and dedicated at ensuring you always won."

Toby's description of her as a mega-bitch was sounding more and more accurate. Deidre didn't know what to do about the trail of broken hearts past-Deidre had left.

"You think I brought you back because of that ...er, relationship."

"At first," he said. "But past-Deidre had motivations deeper than anything I could understand. Whatever her plan was, she probably didn't expect to be reborn as what you are now."

"Someone who isn't a sociopath," she muttered. "I even fucked myself over, didn't I?"

Wynn laughed. She didn't need him to answer. Wynn's gentleness, Gabriel's ultimatum, the radioactive lake. She was edgy again after the hour it took to relax.

"You can look now," he said, lifting his chin.

"I don't want to. I dumped him. He can do what he wants."

"It's never so simple. Do you want to know how many times I walked away from past-Deidre?"

"No. Wynn, I couldn't even dump Logan, and I'd been meaning to for months. I can't hurt anyone and knowing that I used to..." her chin trembled. She shook her head. "Someone told me I had a long line of enemies. How did I make it this far?"

"Sometimes, I think that's why you raised me from the dead-dead," he admitted. "I've eliminated innumerable enemies of yours the past few years. I don't know how you made it before that."

"You killed them?" she asked, startled.

"Only to protect you." His cool smile frightened her. Deidre crossed her arms. How many had she unknowingly killed since being reborn a human?

"My karma is beyond reparable," she said. "Wynn, is it true Gabriel can prevent me from dying now?"

"You cannot die by his hand or the hand of nature," Wynn said carefully. "The tumor is still growing, which means there is still a chance at cognitive deterioration."

"So can I kill myself?"

"From what I know, yes. But, I am not Death," Wynn added. "I cannot be certain what the result might be if you tried to kill yourself or if you died of unnatural causes."

"Unnatural causes," she repeated. "I don't think you mean getting hit by a car, do you?"

"More like demon-induced death."

"Demon-induced!" she laughed. "Oh, god, I think I'm gonna go crazy sometime soon."

"What brings you to the lake?" Rhyn's low growl was unmistakable.

Deidre resisted the urge to shrink back as she turned. He and Gabriel stood nearby, their approach silent. Wynn would've seen them walking over but was unfazed by the two men who terrified her.

"I wanted to go for a walk," Deidre said. She avoided looking at Gabriel, not at all certain what to think after their exchange and seeing him with another woman. He wanted nothing to do with her, and she rejected him. Why did it hurt?

"Not you," Rhyn said.

"Curiosity. Most lakes don't glow green," Wynn said in a casual voice.

All three of them were tense. Their energy made her skin tingle uncomfortably. Deidre moved towards the lake, away from the center of the triangle they formed. She didn't want to be stuck in the middle when one of them snapped. Seeing Gabriel made her insides flutter and the world seem too small to be anywhere but his arms.

But Death on guard was something else entirely, and she wasn't going to be the second woman to revel in the heat of his arms this night.

They were silent so long, she finally risked a look. Rhyn's head was tilted, as if he was listening. She realized they weren't totally in stare down mode; they were talking through their minds.

Could they *read* minds?

Her eyes went to Wynn. Was that how he always knew what to say when she was upset? How he gained her trust? And Gabriel, who she thought she'd bonded with on the beach their first night? He made her feel like she wasn't alone for the first time in years. Was it all fake?

The more she learned of this place, the angrier she became. Everyone was lying to her or manipulating her. Or out to kill her. What frustrated her most: they were all probably justified in how they treated her, based on what she knew about past-Deidre.

But how did *she* deserve it? How obligated was she to make amends for something an entirely different person had done? The only thing they had in common was looks!

Furious, confused, she peered into the lake waters. The bottom of the lake was lined with green gems, the source of the strange light. They were beautiful and tiny, some sort of geological anomaly.

Immortals got their wealth from somewhere. That castle cost a fortune to build. If these were emeralds, it made sense that they sold these to build it.

"Wow," she murmured, gazing out over the lake. The entire thing glowed. How many emeralds did it take to fill a lake this size?

She knelt on the beach area consisting of a stretch of pebbles and dirt. Some of the gems had been carried by gentle waves to the edges of the lake and deposited away from the bulk of the jewels. The glimmering lights were nestled among rocks and dirt.

Deidre pulled up her sleeve to reach the closest one. The lake water was freezing. She grimaced and submerged her arm to the elbow to reach the twinkling gem. Cold energy traveled through her as she gripped the emerald. She thought it a result of the water, until she withdrew her hand and held the gem in her palm.

She'd never seen a glowing emerald. Electricity whipped through her. Images flashed in her mind.

A playground near a mall. Shoddy apartments and an image in the mirror of a dirty toddler in a diaper. Shouting as Mother and Father fought. Gunshots. Pain, white light, peace.

She gasped and dropped it.

"Don't disturb the souls," Gabriel ordered. "They're stressed out enough right now."

She'd touched a *soul.* Not a geological anomaly, but the spirit of a child who died violently. Her eyes went over the lake again. There were millions, maybe even billions of the lost souls! What were they doing in a *lake*? Was this what awaited her? To be dropped into a lake while shady Immortals and an unfriendly Death argued silently nearby?

Was this all there was after one died? If they were stressed out, that meant they were aware. Alive.

The sense that nothing was real filled her again. She couldn't fathom the enormity of a billion souls like the one she'd touched. A billion lives. A billion different stories and experiences. A billion consciences sitting under the serene surface of the water. Had past-Deidre lost them and condemned a billion souls to this existence? Were they scared? Trapped? Lonely?

Deidre stood unsteadily. She was breathing hard; it was all she heard. No longer able to register the world around her, she walked numbly towards the first trail she saw.

"Deidre," Gabriel took her arm, halting her.

"Don't touch me," she said.

He released her. She entered the forest, and the darkness was crushing, suffocating her. A few steps past the tree line, she broke into a run, away from the souls, the Immortals, the nightmare her life had become a few days ago. Deidre bolted, neither aware nor concerned where she went or where she ended up. Trees whipped her body, but she drove herself forward.

As fast as she ran, she couldn't escape her horror, her hatred of past-Deidre, her helplessness. Tears blinded her, and her lungs burned. Her legs grew heavy, but she pushed herself onward into the forest, away from everything that could hurt her and everyone who could stop her from ending this nightmare tonight.

The path neared a ravine then ran along it. Deidre's pace slowed as she took in the area. There was no easy way to the edge of the ravine, and it looked too shallow along most places to make a jump pay off.

She spotted the place down the path, a point overlooking the valley. A form melted from the shadows right before she reached it. She slid to a stop, panting and wild. Eyes blurred by tears, she nonetheless caught the flash of silver eyes.

"Let's just calm down and not jump off any cliffs," Rhyn said, holding up his hands. "Okay? Calm?"

Too panicked to care, Deidre whirled and smacked into something solid. It grabbed her, and a small part of her recognized Gabriel. She struggled. It was like throwing herself against a wall. He gripped her wrists and held them behind her back.

"Deidre, stop."

Desperate and immobilized, she sobbed. Her body gave out. Gabriel wrapped his arms around her, his warmth, strength and scent all that anchored her to this world. He lifted her. Vaguely, she was aware of the cool shadow world followed by the warmth of indoors. She felt the plush comfort of a bed beneath her and curled onto her side, unable to stop crying. Gabriel lay in front of her and nudged her, until her body opened to him. His warmth cocooned her as he gathered her in his thick arms.

A temporary sensation entered her mind, as if a breeze ruffled through her thoughts. It was followed by warm energy that Gabriel pushed into her body to calm her. Deidre clung to the clothing covering his chest. Unable to stop shaking, she at least was able to breathe again and pulled his rich scent into her lungs. Her forehead rested in the nape of his neck, and she focused on the steady, slow rhythm of his heartbeat. Gradually, his warmth sank into her skin, and she lay still, exhausted yet soothed by the heat of his body.

He held her in silence. Fatigued, overwhelmed, Deidre was unable to summon the physical strength to move or the willpower to order him away. Her eyes closed, and she slept deeply, the first peaceful night of slumber since her last night with him.

The next morning, she lay curled in his arms for awhile before moving. One bicep filled the hollow of her neck while his other arm was tight around her midsection. She felt horrible: Mentally drained, hungry, disappointed she wasn't at the bottom of a cliff somewhere.

"I'm not sure I should let you go." Gabriel's gravelly voice reminded her of one of the reasons she'd snapped in the first place. "You have an affinity for jumping off tall things."

"Gabriel," she whispered, eyes watering.

"No," he said. "I'm not letting you off that easy."

"Easy? This week has been hell." She strained to move, regretting she couldn't have one small moment of peace.

He didn't release her, instead drawing up the arm she used as a pillow to force her head against his shoulder. She wasn't able to maneuver in his firm grip. Deidre sighed, her body going lax once more. His body relaxed in response. His arm fell away, and she repositioned her neck over his bicep. She really didn't want to leave the comfort of his arms. Whatever she faced there was a million times better than whatever she faced away from him.

"Can you read my mind?" she asked.

"If I choose to."

"And have you chosen to?"

"Last night was the first time. You were too distraught to speak," he answered. "I needed to know why."

"Doesn't seem like rocket science. I find out I was a sociopathic deity. You issue me an ultimatum I can't live with and then make out with some lady at the lake. Oh, and I picked up someone else's soul last night," she said. "Yesterday was not a good one. We're through, by the way, Gabriel."

"Keep telling yourself that."

"If I'm keeping you from your lover, by all means, you can go."

"You weren't supposed to see that," he said quietly.

"Famous last words."

He chuckled. "Will you try to tell me now you weren't jealous?"

"You read my mind already. You tell me," she replied.

"You were crushed."

Deidre said nothing.

"I didn't mean to hurt you."

"Yes, you did," she said. "You don't tell someone you'll never be able to care for them and think you're doing anything other than hurting them. But your offer won't change."

"It can't."

"Then we're still through."

"I'm upholding my end of our arrangement."

She really didn't want to leave the comfort of his arms, but remaining meant giving up something she wasn't willing to do.

"You're not running," he said cautiously. He smoothed the hair from the side of her face. His kiss on her temple was light.

"That isn't an invitation," she warned him.

"You were a helluva lot easier to bed in your past life." The frustration in his voice was clear.

Deidre moved away from him. He released her. She settled on her belly a couple of feet away, glaring at him. Gabe remained on his side, hand propping up his head. Even relaxed in bed, he seemed ready to take on the world.

"You've got a back-up plan," she told him. "She'll likely take your arrangement."

His jaw clenched, his piercing gaze making her want to crawl back into his arms.

"You know that already," she assessed. "Why are you wasting your time with me? Another part of your duty?"

"After your encounter with the souls, I think you understand why I take it so seriously. There's no room for failure, not when the souls of the dead depend on you."

Deidre gazed at him, her throat tightening at the reminder of the lost souls. She wanted to ask more about them and what happened after Death claimed someone, but it was a lot to deal with. She didn't feel up to it.

"I can see that," she managed. "You have my blessing. Not that you need it." She sat up and hopped off the bed, too aware of how alone she felt. She had no idea what to do with herself or where to go.

"I may have to, if no part of you is interested."

A glance at him revealed he, too, was climbing out of bed. He appeared even more frustrated. She didn't understand it, not when he obviously had another woman. Her jacket was draped over a chair across the room. She went to claim it.

"Do whatever you want," she snapped. "If I'm stuck in the land of the living, I'm going to live a normal life. A *human* life. New apartment, shitty job, boyfriend I can't stand. The whole works."

He was silent. She tossed the coat over her arm and turned. He was frozen in place, bristling. The look on his face was dangerous. Deidre studied him, uncertain what she said that set him on edge. It didn't make sense that there was, especially after he'd admitted to having someone else on the side.

"Don't come after me," she added, striding to the door. "I'm done with this Immortal shit."

"Wait."

She found herself stopping, hoping. Deidre chided herself but didn't move.

Gabriel walked across the room to a dresser. He opened the top drawer and withdrew a key chain with a couple of keys and a tag. He tossed them to her. Deidre frowned.

"What do they go to?" she asked.

"Apartment in Atlanta. Address on the label."

"I can do it myself," she said.

"Unless you have more money than you're carrying in your backpack, I don't see you getting an apartment," he said, amused. "Or going back to the one with the dead body in the tub."

She gasped at the reminder.

"Take it."

"You'll know where I am," she objected. "Not exactly a clean start."

"I'll know where you are anyway," he pointed out. "There's nowhere you can go where I can't find you. The reverse is true as well. If you run into trouble, ask the portals to bring you to me."

She wasn't sure which baffled her more: that he happened to have an apartment in Atlanta or he wasn't trying to talk her out of leaving. Maybe it was his way of fulfilling his end of the bargain she'd refused by making sure she had a place to stay. Every day she spent in this world, she became more confused.

"Whatever. I'll consider this temporary," she said at last. "Until I find my own place." She waited for him to say something else. Shaking her head, she turned to leave again.

"How about a farewell kiss?" he asked.

"You have a lot of nerve."

"I'll consider it a favor. I'll owe you one. You don't know what Immortals would do for a blank check from Death."

She wasn't an Immortal, but a blank check from a deity had to be valuable.

"For a single kiss?" she asked. She turned to face him and leaned against the door, hand on the knob.

"That simple." He was already approaching her and stopped just before his body met hers.

Deidre gazed at the expanse of his chest, all too aware of his strength and heat. Her blood was humming from waking in his bed. Suddenly, a blank check – even from Death – didn't seem like enough for what his one kiss might cost her.

"Deal?" he asked.

She wet her lips and nodded, unable to speak.

Gabriel cupped her face in his large hands and tilted it up. He gazed into her eyes for a long moment, the tenderness she recognized from their night together present. Deidre didn't expect to see it, not after how he'd treated her the past few days. His look melted her anger. She almost believed Katie's words about Gabriel always loving her.

Magic flared through her as their lips met. He was gentle, the man who made love to a woman he thought was dying. It was harder and harder to justify not yielding to his arrangement, if only for the pleasure of his body. She deepened the kiss, and he responded with his own hunger. His hands traveled down her arms and settled on her hips, drawing them against his. With a groan, Deidre leaned into him, tasting and feeling his arousal. She'd wanted a second night with him since the first, and the passion of his kiss reminded her of how incredible it was to be the center of his world.

Any resistance she felt was on fire. He withdrew, kissing her face while his hands slid up her shirt. They burned her sensitive skin.

"Wanna stay a little longer?" he whispered, nipping her neck then trailing kisses towards her collarbone.

"Yes," she sighed. "No. God, I don't know." She had to resist him. What she had left of her dignity depended upon it.

"Make up your mind," he said with a husky chuckle.

"Stop," she said miserably.

"One of us has sense," he said as he obeyed. Gabriel smoothed her cheeks.

Deidre wasn't able to ponder the meaning behind his statement.

"No boyfriends," he growled. "No one else touches you, Deidre."

And you? She wanted to ask. Instead, she was working hard to convince herself she really did want to walk away. She stood in the warm silence, senses intoxicated by their bond, his scent and body.

"If I find a cure, we'll revisit this conversation."

"I won't make it easy on you. You'll have to earn me," she whispered.

"Deal." Gabriel held her gaze a moment longer before his hands dropped, and he walked away. "Fourth room on your left."

She barely caught her balance, stunned she turned him down and even more that he let her. Her gaze swept hungrily over his body as he strode across the room, away from her.

Breathless, she managed to open the door on the second try and made it into the hallway before sagging against the wall. Her hands shook, and she dropped the keys. Deidre gathered her composure with some difficulty and walked down the hallway, pausing four doors down to her room. Suddenly furious and anxious to leave, she pushed open her door and grabbed her stuff. Gazing at the address on the tag, she drew a deep breath and summoned a portal.

She still felt his hands branding her body. The look he'd given her after she told him she was leaving made more sense. He was jealous. But how could he be jealous, agree to send her away and make out with another woman?

He made her head hurt, and her body ache.

Deidre emerged into the living room and turned around once completely, not expecting the views of the city from the bank of windows along one wall. The apartment was a sprawling penthouse. The floor plan was open and relaxed, with wooden floors giving warmth to cream furniture.

Nothing about this place looked like it was something Gabriel chose. Did he kill someone here recently and decide it was a nice place to keep?

She shook her head. The bedrooms were on the second floor, the master larger than her old apartment.

If she had limitless money, this was a place she'd pick out. Struck by the thought, she checked the dresser for clothing.

Her size. Her style.

This place had been hers. How was that possible, when she recalled living a full life in Indiana before moving to Atlanta? There were tags on most of the clothing, and the styles were from fall. A few months ago.

If the place didn't feel so much like she designed every detail, she'd freak out. As it was, it was almost familiar. She checked the master bath, half-expecting to find bones in the tub. The round tub was luxurious, and her thoughts turned a different direction.

Deidre ran a hot bath. The main difference between the penthouse and its contents and her own life: she'd never been able to afford anything remotely as expensive or nice. The rich cinnamon-vanilla scent of the bath bubbles filled the air, reminding her of the candle she'd bought at the farmers market the day her life went to hell. She sank into the hot water. For the first time in days, the tension in her body loosened.

Life or Death? Gabriel or ...Gabriel?

She groaned. Darkyn was becoming her most promising option. What did he have to gain by curing or killing her? Whatever it was, it wasn't going to be free. No matter what he said, she'd heard enough about past-Deidre to understand there was much more to their relationship. It probably wasn't good, which meant Darkyn was going to fuck her over somehow, too.

Just like everyone else. Could he really be much worse?

Chapter Eleven

Several hours after Deidre walked through the portals back to Atlanta, Gabe's soul radar began working again. He felt the subtle shift and stopped on the stairwell down to the gym. With her taste in his mouth and scent on his skin, he was about to go insane, especially after walking away from her.

He tested the portals to see if his door to the underworld was back. It wasn't. He crossed through anyway to the soul on the list to be claimed. It was dark where he emerged, but the body was where it should be.

Along with two demons. Gabe's weapons were out before his second foot was out of the portal. He hacked down one, and the other managed to get in one strike before it, too, fell.

They'd been struggling to beat the demons to the souls, and Gabe stood over the dead demons, furious. How did they beat Death? Granted, Death's soul radar just kicked in. There was no telling how long this soul was waiting.

"Come on out," he told the soul, kneeling over the body of a dead human.

The green fog appeared. Gabe had never been so relieved to see it as he was now. He watched the emerald form then placed it in his pocket before returning his attention to the demons.

He searched their bodies to find another twenty souls they'd already claimed. He knew he wasn't collecting fast enough, but the amount left him horrified to imagine how many he was missing. Disconnected from the underworld, he had no way of knowing.

Gabe shook out the jacket of one demon. Something fell with a clunk to the ground. He tossed the coat and froze.

Soul compass. Gabe swiped it off the ground and studied it. It showed no wear of time. None of his dealers reported one missing, which left two options, neither of them good. He debated which he trusted less: the Ancient Immortal that made the compass or the death-dealers that carried them.

He went to Tamer first.

It was too early for the silver shop to be open. Gabe knocked then took a portal inside, to the foyer he'd walked through last time. He sensed the wards he tripped and waited for the Ancient to appear.

"I wasn't expecting you," Tamer called from the third floor balcony.

"I just need a minute," Gabe replied.

The Immortal sighed and trotted down the stairs. Gabe assessed him. Tamer hadn't bothered to put on a shirt, appearing as if he'd leapt out of bed the moment the wards alerted him. He wore silk pajama bottoms and was barefoot, his muscular upper body on display. He was irritated but not wary, unarmed and relaxed. Gabe knew without touching his mind that Tamer wasn't the one who had betrayed him.

"What is it?" Tamer asked.

"This is one of yours?" Gabe asked, holding up the compass.

Tamer took it then handed it back. He nodded immediately, recognizing his own magic.

"Are you numbering or logging them or anything?"

"Nope. Your people are handling all of that. I oversee their creation then seal them. Why?" Tamer's gaze sharpened. "I know it didn't break. I'm too damn good at what I do."

"It works," Gabe said grimly. "That's all I needed." Dread pooled in the base of his stomach for more than one reason. There was a traitor among the fifty-odd death-dealers he had above ground, and he'd assigned twelve-hour shifts to keep an eye on the apartment where he sent Deidre.

"I heard a rumor," Tamer said. He crossed his arms. "Wynn?"

"He is back," Gabe confirmed.

"You brought our father from the dead-dead?"

"You can thank my predecessor for that one."

Tamer appeared conflicted. Gabe suspected he knew why. While not privy to the Council's business, he assessed the appearance of their father at a time when Rhyn was struggling for control did not bode well for any of them. The Council had been on the verge of splitting for years, severing the effectiveness of their ability to combat Darkyn's demons.

The three eldest sons on the Council were dead. None of the remaining were old enough to remember how Wynn had run things, and no other Immortal in the human world had been around when Wynn was in control. Gabe distrusted the Ancient father of the Council as much as he did Darkyn.

What happened was outside of Gabe's official purview. Personally, he wasn't about to let Wynn hurt any of the people he cared about.

"Thanks," he said and tucked the compass away. "Send all of these to me from now on."

"Will do." Tamer said, distracted. "Hey, you got time to see something?"

"Is it important?"

"No, I wanted to have a fucking tea party." Tamer started towards the locked door on one side of the foyer, behind which were the historical treasures. "I figured out a few of the symbols on your compass. I've been working twenty hour days for you, Gabe."

"You're welcome for keeping Rhyn off your back."

Tamer shot him a look. The Immortal led him down the hallway to a familiar library. A notebook lay on the table next to a few scrolls, an ancient manuscript and another block of stone with carvings too faint for Gabe to read.

"The symbols in the strictest interpretation are largely related to nature," Tamer started. "Snow, rain, one is a tree stump, another a ravine. Of the twenty symbols, I've figured out five."

He flipped the notebook open to show a neatly sketched diagram of the compass with the ones he'd interpreted highlighted. Gabe took it.

"It seems too easy that these are locations," he said.

"I thought so, too," Tamer said. He carefully opened the massive manuscript with a petrified wood cover. "Everything in my library that can be scanned is on a computer. The records I alone can read with my magic are in this hallway, which is a pain in the ass when it comes to searching for things. I have to look by hand." He muttered. He turned a few of the crisp pages carefully.

"I don't have much time, Tamer," Gabe said. "Just summarize what you think it is."

Tamer straightened. "Bear with me. This will sound crazy," he said, taking a deep breath. "Measures of a soul's goodness. I think the compass tells you what kind of soul it is."

"Interesting. Unless they're headed to Hell, I don't need…" He drifted off, mind on the demons. He'd wondered how they were choosing which souls to take and assumed his dealers were beating the demons to some.

What if the demons were choosing which souls they wanted, based on the compass readings? Darkyn was old enough to read the compass.

"Quick notes on what I think I know," Tamer said, scribbling on a piece of paper. "I'll keep working on it."

"Thanks." Gabe tucked the note in his pocket. "I'll check in later."

Tamer gave a salute.

Gabe left him for the lake near Rhyn's. Rather than dread at what lie ahead of him, he felt nothing but anger. Reaching the lake, he tossed the souls he'd recovered from the demons into it and lingered.

Deidre had knelt near here and unknowingly touched a soul. Her reaction – and what he'd read in her mind – left him unable to deny an uneasy truth. This Deidre and the one he used to know were two different people. Same body, different in every other possible way. This Deidre was everything he'd loved about his ex-lover: her spontaneity, sense of humor, beauty combined with the purest human heart he'd ever known.

She really was perfect. She really was dying a death he couldn't stop.

Gabe's fury rose again. He located the nearest death-dealer and approached. The man melted from the shadows, awaiting his orders.

"Mind check," Gabe told him.

The man bowed his head without hesitation. No sense of nervousness, no indication he had anything to hide. Gabe knew it wasn't him before he rested his hand on the man's head. The brief touch filled Gabe's thoughts with a lifetime of visions. He pushed them aside to rifle through the man's mind as he sought specific memories and indications the man was a traitor.

He was loyal, if concerned about being trapped on the mortal plane. Gabe dropped his hand.

"Go here on assignment. You are authorized to kill any threats to the woman you're protecting. Demons are after her. Send the dealer you replace directly to me," Gabe ordered. He held out his fist. The assassin bumped fists with his, and Gabe conveyed the location of Deidre's apartment.

The death-dealer obeyed. He called a portal and strode away.

Gabe waited a few minutes for the assassin being replaced to appear. The small woman was one Gabe had known for years.

"Mind check, Cora," he said.

She, too, bowed her head without hesitation. A quick search yielded nothing, except similar worry to the first man. His death-dealers didn't doubt him, but they weren't exactly convinced they'd see their home again.

"Keep this quiet, okay?" he said. "Any issues with your ward?"

"No, Gabriel. You could've warned me," Cora said, grinning. "I almost ran when I saw her."

"Yeah. That happens to me every time I see her."

"She's been exploring the area today. She hasn't gone far. No demons, a couple of Immortals. I take it Rhyn has an eye on her?"

"He does. Does she seem … well?"

"Distraught mostly."

Gabe nodded, uncertain if he should be relieved she wasn't rejoicing to be away from him or worried that she was unhappy. She needed to be unhappy, he reminded himself. He'd done what little he was willing to do to his own mate to keep her upset. And out of his reach, because he was unable to keep the distance between them without her spearheading the effort.

Gabriel was no closer to figuring what to do about the woman meant for him than when he was when he saw her mating tattoo at the bungalow.

"Soul radar?" he asked.

"Broken."

"Alright. Take up guard here," he said, moving away. Mind on Deidre and the fact he still didn't know how to undo what Wynn had done, Gabe went onto the next death-dealer at the lake then the next.

The fifth death-dealer hesitated to submit. Gabe gave him no chance to run or fight but snatched his neck. The man resisted, but Gabe pried his mind open and found part of what he sought: a deal with Darkyn. The death-dealer before him was newer, with less than a few decades in the service of Death. While not surprised past-Death had taken this man to her bed as well, Gabe was surprised he'd folded so quickly to Darkyn's offer of spying in return for a guaranteed trip to the underworld. He had a handler who passed messages from the demons to him. Unfortunately, the man didn't know who his handler was.

Gabe snapped his neck. It was a much kinder death than he deserved. He dropped the body and retrieved the soul. He gazed at it in the palm of his hand. He saw past-Death handle traitors but never expected he'd have one in his midst, a few months on the job.

With some regret, Gabe crushed the gem in his hand. It turned to green dust. He dumped it on the ground. Darkyn would see this man again soon in Hell.

"There's always one," Wynn said from nearby.

Gabe resisted the urge to behead the Immortal. One day, he'd be able to make love to his mate at will and kill the Ancient that almost killed her. That day wasn't coming fast enough.

"Trust me. You want to check all of them. I led the Council long enough to know there's usually more than one."

"Sound advice," Gabe replied. "If you're here to ask where Deidre is, the answer is no."

"You blocked her, not Rhyn. Guess I shouldn't be surprised."

"We both did, just in case." Gabe glanced at the Immortal. Svelte, charismatic and cool, Wynn was the opposite of Rhyn in every way except for looks. There was no mistaking father and son on that level. "What do you want, Wynn?"

"I came to see if you wanted to negotiate yet."

"I didn't think you had anything wanted, now that I have Deidre safe and secure."

"It's a tiny secret, one that may not alter much of anything." Wynn shrugged. "Or, it might, given it means more to you than it does to me."

"You tell me, and if I find it worthy, I'll tell you who wanted you brought back," Gabe said, crossing his arms.

Wynn studied him. Gabe didn't know which way the Ancient would go. Wynn's alliances and motivations were mysterious, but there was one thing they had in common: Deidre.

"She was born with a tumor. Based on her medical records, the tumor didn't grow until she hit puberty and didn't interfere with her ability to function before a few years ago," Wynn started. "What is of interest to you: the *tumor* in her head is formed around a soul. I discovered it during surgery."

Wynn gave him a knowing look.

"Of interest to the Keeper of Souls?"

"You know it is. Whose soul would that bitch put in Deidre's head?"

"My first guess would be hers. It's what I'd do," Wynn said. "Deities are different but they have souls. Our Deidre is a mix of human and immortal."

"Meaning the soul of the deity we know is likely somewhere else." The information was beyond valuable, and on a level that further altered Gabe's perception on Deidre. Adding another layer of separation between past-Deidre and his mate settled some of his turmoil.

Darkyn. The Dark One's mysterious search for something past-Deidre left behind began to make sense. What would Darkyn want with past-Deidre's soul, unless he intended to add it to the Army of Souls?

Controlling a deity would bring incredible power to the demon lord at a time when Rhyn was struggling to battle demons already. The Immortals were vulnerable, and Darkyn's hunger for power and control of the mortal world was not something Gabriel questioned.

Grimly, he realized he should've taken up Wynn's first offer to barter for the secret. The information was beyond valuable. It might be all that stood between the Dark One and the human world. As nonchalant as Wynn was being about it, he knew what it meant.

"I knew you'd find it worthy. The magic I used to kill her, I also used to seal the tumor. My thought was that it was a like a time bomb, awaiting the right moment for our dear deity to reemerge," Wynn said. "I'm beginning to believe she didn't want me to find her after all, that it was Fate who pushed our paths together."

"Fate has been active lately," Gabe said, pensive.

"Indeed. Summoned me a few days ago. He's scheming."

"Deities always are," Gabe said. "The answer you seek: Darkyn."

Wynn's eyebrows shot up. "She made a deal with him?"

"Apparently." Distracted, Gabe began to think about how *he* might be able to save Deidre using the powers of Death. All souls – even those of deities – came to Death eventually. Would the soul in her head respond to him? "You couldn't get it out?"

"A few years ago, I could have. Now, it's not removable by human medicine or by Immortal power," Wynn added.

"I'm assuming the only reason you told me is because you think I can do something about it," Gabe said.

"If anyone can coax an unwilling soul out of a human brain, you can. I'll still kill her to get what I want, if I must," Wynn said with a cold smile.

"I expect nothing less from you."

"Good. You'll keep her out of my way and make sure Darkyn doesn't stumble upon her or the treasure in her head."

Gabe eyed him. From any other Immortal, it wouldn't have been a threat. Wynn was as likely as past-Deidre to make a deal with the Dark One. Gabriel began to see the Ancient's plan as well. Whoever had the soul of past-Death, had immeasurable bargaining power.

"My part here is done. You've been warned. I don't need to tell you that any further assistance I provide you will not be by my choice."

"Understood." Gabriel tossed his head in dismissal.

Wynn left.

"Harmony, pull in all the death-dealers to the lake in an hour," Gabe whispered the order. His gaze settled on the body at his feet.

Will do. She responded mentally.

Gabe opened a portal and strode into the center of the shadow world.

"Fate. I need a moment."

This time, there was no waiting. One of the portals beckoned him before he'd finished the sentence. Gabe stepped into an apartment. He glanced around the penthouse decorated in dark colors with flashes of burgundy and brown, attention settling on the familiar skyline visible through the window.

"You chose an apartment beside hers," he said with a shake of his head.

"What can I say. She's always had good taste," Fate said from his seat on a couch. Dressed in jeans and a T-shirt, he resembled a college student on break.

"Just when I think things can't get weirder ..." Gabriel crossed to the living area without sitting. "You've done a lot of interfering for someone who believes in free will. Wynn, Deidre, me."

"You are still thinking like a death-dealer and not like a deity," Fate chided and motioned to the couch. "Gabriel, what made you hate your predecessor also made her very good at what she did."

"She regarded the world as a chessboard. I know this."

"What made her good was that she was able to work around the Immortal Code that has you by the neck."

Gabriel listened. He didn't like not understanding what to do. He didn't like not being self-reliant. The Code had always been his foundation in a world that adopted him despite his origins.

"You don't follow the same rules you used to. You work around the rules, between them, on top of them, beneath them." Fate nudged him with the top of his foot. "Are you listening?"

"Yes."

"But you're not hearing." After a moment, the deity continued. "View the Immortal Code like a woman and what I'm telling you to do like ...making love to that woman. She's more than a body, and the things you can do are only limited by your imagination. Did I dumb it down enough for you?"

"Yeah. That I understood," Gabe replied. He wasn't expecting humor at such a time, not when everything was wrong. But he found himself smiling at the enigmatic god's explanation.

"The underworld wouldn't have accepted you if you couldn't do this. I'm pushing you to broaden your perspective."

Gabe sat back, eyes on Fate, who looked little more concerned than any other college kid on spring break. The only real difference: the ancient intelligence in the deity's steady gaze, which seemed out of place in such a youthful face. Grimly, Gabriel realized he was still missing too much, even on the mortal world.

"Ask me what you came to ask me," Fate directed.

"Darkyn wants Deidre."

"And you're running out of time."

"I know." Gabe rubbed the back of his neck. "Wynn told me what he did and about the soul encased in her tumor. If Darkyn wants it, it's gotta be past-Death. I ... can't ...get to it without killing her." Admitting the truth out loud was worse than he expected.

"Then you're both fucked."

He looked up.

"First things first. Darkyn wins now if you don't figure out this simple truth." Fate shrugged. "Like making love to a woman, Gabriel."

He'd finally found a deity who used an analogy he understood. Thousands of years of experience rendered Gabe intimately familiar with both a woman's body and the Immortal Code. He'd never viewed the Code in this light, as more than his master. He'd obeyed the Code and his predecessor without question, until forced to choose between them and his conscience. He broke with both to save Rhyn and Katie.

That the Code was malleable, flexible, *alive* ... like a woman.

Deidre's bucket list came to mind, distracting him from interpreting Fate's cryptic comparison. He'd enjoyed himself that night, more so than ever before, because he let go of the side of himself that viewed sex as either a test by a dictatorial goddess or a necessary release for pent up frustration.

How the fuck did he translate a night of fun, passion – not to mention the most meaningful connection he'd ever made – into his job? The Code? That night, he'd done more than try to please someone else. He *shared* his need and pleasure with someone else for the first time in his life.

Fate leaned forward, studying him intently.

"Are you saying ..." Gabriel paused. "The Code enslaved me as an everyday Immortal. But as a deity ..."

"C'mon, Gabriel. It's gotta click here and now, if you are to create a sustainable chain of events. You understand. I see it."

"The Code is not an absolute for deities but a relationship. One I can determine," he said at last.

"Determine. Influence," Fate said, smiling slowly. "Control, if that's your thing. The handcuffs never hurt, right?"

"Silk ties," Gabriel replied.

"Jealous. She never used silk with me."

"She didn't trust you."

"For good reason," Fate admitted. "Same reason she knew better than to let me tie her. That would not have ended the way anyone thinks."

Gabriel snorted, amused. They both knew past-Death wouldn't let anyone place her in a compromising position. Fate was the single enemy that succeeded in cornering her and only after countless millennia plotting.

"Anyway, for you, those handcuffs will soon be falling away," Fate continued.

Gabe tried to envision the Code as a woman, one that he could negotiate with. What if he approached the Code not as a slave but as an equal concerned about the greater good, a dynamic reality the Code had no way of knowing, due to its own static nature?

"I see it," Gabriel said, frowning. "You're saying a deity must look at the Code as one of many factor instead of the only factor."

"We preserve it and the order of the worlds by any means necessary. If that means we break the Code to save it, then so be it."

"Past-Deidre broke two rules and quit. Are you saying she didn't have to?"

"There was much more to what she did. She broke the rules from the time-before-time, of which there are three: mates, blood, fate. No one can fuck with the bond each of those has to one another. The result of a deity breaking one of the three is basically the destruction of the world. She played the Code the same way she played each of us. We didn't band together to stop her, because she had …dirt on all of us," he explained. "Only the deities can force another deity to resign. No one wanted to cross her."

"Except you."

"You want to know how?" Fate's eyes glittered as he rested his elbows on his thighs. "I revealed her mate to her. You've never seen anyone so angry."

"You told her about me, and she spazzed. Great." Gabe mumbled, infuriated by past-Deidre once more.

"You think I told her the truth?" Fate grinned. "She wanted it to be you. I lied my ass off and told her it was the Dark One. Learn a lesson from your predecessor. Don't fuck with me."

"That was the bet she lost?"

"Yep. Said she knew who her mate was supposed to be. I pulled her Sight, so she couldn't tell I was lying, then asked what she'd wager on it. I lied. I set up the chain of events millennia ago and knew if I could push her enough in one direction, she'd go peacefully over the edge," he said. "She made deals with a few people she shouldn't have to try to outmaneuver a fate that didn't exist, thereby breaking all three – mate-blood-fate – without annihilating the worlds as we know it. She was fucked, though."

"The underworld cracked, and the demons came," Gabriel guessed. "She knew she was done."

"Exactly. I then called in the favor she owed me from the bet I actually lost."

"You made her pay up?" Gabriel asked.

"Damn right I did. At that point, everyone was collecting, or trying to."

"Can I ask what you won?"

"I told her to walk through the portals, and where she ended up, was up to me."

Gabriel studied Fate. "You were kind to her."

"No, I was kind to you and to the human Deidre. I'm a deity, not a monster, Gabriel, and I happen to see the Future. Sometimes I favor an outcome and nudge the chain of events to fulfill it. I restored the path she forsook so long ago, as I was obligated to do," Fate said then added. "I am also the only deity, Immortal or human alive who ever crossed that bitch and won."

"By losing."

"Exactly."

Gabriel found himself laughing.

"What are the lessons here?" Fate asked.

Gabriel's smile faded as he thought. He saw first of all that he'd chosen the right mentor. Or maybe, the right mentor had chosen him. Fate was both vengeful and impassioned in his treatment of past-Deidre, and Gabe sorted through the tangled web that marked the tumultuous relationship between Fate and past-Death.

"Aside from not pissing you off," Gabriel started. "Sometimes you make love to the Code and sometimes you fuck it."

"Well-put. What else?"

"You've been much more ...clear-sighted in how you dealt with her," Gabe said regretfully. "You broke the Code out of duty and pushed her to do so out of emotion, which ultimately screwed her. I'm guessing if I break the rules, to do so out of duty."

"Good. Get the point?"

"I had no idea she cared enough about me to break so many rules. This touchy-feely shit is giving me hives."

"Me, too. You will have to cause me some trouble, so I have a reason to begrudge you," Fate said.

"That can be arranged." Gabriel chuckled. "Doesn't explain why your apartment is next to hers."

"Rarely do I get to see the Future unfold in person. I can see everywhere but cannot *be* everywhere. I chose to be here," Fate replied. "I will not need to interfere, unless you reject all we've discussed when you leave."

"No chance."

"Go forth, and use your resources."

Gabriel rose. He liked Fate, though after the story of how the deity took out past-Deidre, he knew better than to trust the godling completely. He didn't expect his portal to the underworld to be waiting and wasn't disappointed. No, it wasn't going to be that easy. He still had the challenge of the mortal world to knock out.

This time, he knew the secret to succeeding in the human realm.

The Code was no longer his master. Neither, he decided, was his past. What past-Death and the Code had been to him - the one-way relationship they'd forced upon him – would not survive the day. Fate hadn't answered the question he wanted, but he provided the response Gabriel needed to hear. Death didn't live in the shadows as Gabriel had for the majority of his life.

Neither did Death sit back and wait to discover the information he needed to do his job. In all his years, he'd known one Immortal with the unrivaled gifts of not only tracking demons in the mortal realm but manipulating the minds of Immortals and mortals. The same Immortal would balance the damage done by past-Deidre when she raised Wynn and help Rhyn manage the Council and Immortals. Though the power of mind manipulation was far from brain surgery, he might also know how to help Deidre.

It was a long shot, but Gabriel was willing to bet that raising the dead-dead Immortal would pay off.

He was about to fuck the Code hard.

Gabriel returned to the lake. There was no way of knowing whose souls had crossed over to the mortal world, but he was going to trust that Fate was on his side, for the time being. Gabriel stripped off his shirt and weapons then his heavy boots, dropping everything into a pile while two of his assassins watched. He whipped off his belt and added it to the rest of his belongings, leaving a single knife strapped to his thigh.

He dove into the cold water. The souls sensed their Keeper and rose from the floor of the deep lake to hover around him like suspended, tiny green lanterns. Each spoke to him as he swam, filling his head with visions as they told him their stories. Gabriel slowed his movements, quickly overwhelmed by the voices. He stopped trying to sort through everything.

If you're here, come to me, he ordered the soul he sought.

Nothing happened. He swam deeper into the lake. One of the gems touched his face. Images flashed through his mind. He snatched the soul and shoved off from the bottom of the lake, kicking upwards.

Breaking through the surface, Gabriel gasped in a few breaths before swimming towards the shore with powerful strokes. All five of the death dealers on guard had drawn near the lake. He hauled himself out of the cold waters and sat on the shore that turned to mud beneath his dripping body.

He placed the soul on the ground beside him and drew his remaining knife. He heard how to bring an Immortal back from the dead-dead from past-Death but never saw it done. Mainly because it broke a few thousand Immortal Codes. It didn't break the triumvirate of laws *he* was required to follow, though it was likely to put him on the radar of the other deities, who were going to be cautious to trust him after past-Death's antics.

Gabriel sliced his palm and squeezed blood out over the soul. If there were magic words, they were stuck in the manual he never got. He willed the magic out of his body and channeled it into the blood-covered soul, visualizing what it was he tried to do. And hoping it wasn't like Wynn, who was reincarnated without even Darkyn realizing the soul was revived. Green power flowed from the souls in the lake, through him and into the gem. The lake blinked out for a second, the light gone completely, then blinked back on, this time much, much dimmer.

He'd always known the source of Death's magic was the souls, but he'd never seen his predecessor wield the light of the souls. Shut off from the underworld, he could only hope he had enough soul power here on the mortal world to reincarnate one Immortal.

The earth beneath him trembled, which he took as a good sign. The soul sank into the ground. Gabriel grabbed at it, until he saw the shape of a man form beneath a haze of green.

He stood and stepped back, breathing hard from his swim. His death-dealers were fading into the shadows of the forest as the ground shook.

Gabe sat down on a boulder, a thrill working through him. He'd been ignoring the extent of the power available from the souls for fear of violating the Code, which he now understood was not binding in the face of a threat like Darkyn.

If this worked, could he do the same for Deidre? Kill her, remove the soul and revive her? Gabriel's gaze went to the lake. The souls were barely glimmering; there was no way he'd be able to pull the amount of power he needed to save Deidre.

He needed more than access to the underworld to save her; he needed the medical advice of someone like Wynn. From what he knew, if they brought her back, she'd be however she left the earth. He couldn't have the tumor – or half her brain missing – when he revived her.

Gabriel shuddered at the thought of hurting her.

Was this why Darkyn hadn't grabbed her? Had Wynn unknowingly protected Deidre by linking her life to that of the soul in her head?

The haze cleared, and the earth settled. Gabriel rose and approached the still form. The night-skinned Immortal appeared to be either dead-dead or sleeping. Squatting, Gabe shook him. Tanzanite eyes opened, the familiar blue-purple making Gabriel smile in triumph. He was going to win this round against Fate, Darkyn and anyone else who stood between him, the underworld and his mate.

"Welcome back, Andre," he whispered. "A little reminder. I brought you back. I pretty much own you, at least temporarily."

Andre sat, steady gaze on Gabriel. Gabe knew he must look half-wild: drenched, muddied and sizzling with power.

"It looks like a few things changed while I was gone," the Immortal said with the calmness Gabriel remembered always admiring.

Gabe nodded. Soul power rippled through him and with it, the sensation of the invisible shackles he'd worn his entire adult life melting away. He was *alive* after a lifetime banished to the shadows. Things would be different from here on out.

Like Deidre, he was going to live on his terms.

"I need a drink and some clothes," Andre said.

Chuckling, Gabe stood and offered the Immortal a hand.

Rhyn, can you drop by the lake and bring a couple sets of clothes? Gabe asked his friend.

On my way. Rhyn replied.

"What's it like being dead-dead?" Gabriel asked.

"Much more peaceful than being alive," Andre replied, looking around. He sighed. "If I'm here, it's not because the world is operating smoothly." His French accent rolled off his deep voice.

"Not in the least."

"Holy fuck." Rhyn's curse made Gabriel turn. The half-demon paused a few feet away, and Gabe saw the emotion cross his eyes.

The eldest of the seven brothers, Andre was the only who supported Rhyn's petition to be recognized by the Immortals who hated the half-demon. Andre was rendered dead-dead while Rhyn was stuck in Hell, killed by the same brother who held Rhyn prisoner.

Rhyn recovered quickly and tossed them both clothing. Gabriel stripped out of his pants and pulled on the new ones before striding back to the pile of the rest of his things. He figured Rhyn and Andre needed a private moment and snorted as he heard Rhyn start off.

"I'm not going to ask why you two are naked," Rhyn said. "Or why Andre isn't dead-dead. Or why Gabriel looks radioactive."

"Hello, little brother," Andre said with some affection.

Gabriel smiled to himself and pulled on his clothes, replacing weapons. He felt the wary eyes of his death-dealers from the shadows.

"We're all here," Harmony's voice carried a note of uneasiness.

"Line them up. I'll be quick." Gabriel glanced up at her as he tugged his belt tight.

"Will do." She hesitated. "You … changed."

He met her gaze. While he didn't want his death-dealers to fear him, he also recognized the look in her eyes and those of the assassins behind her. They no longer regarded him as one of their own after the demonstration of Death's power. Gabriel mourned the loss of the community he'd belonged to for so long. But things had to be different from here on out. He had to preserve and protect the underworld, even if it meant stepping away from the comfort zone he'd existed in for millennia.

"I'm going to get us home," he said gently and squeezed her arm. "There's only one way I can do that. You'll have to trust me."

"About the other night …" she started. "I didn't … I shouldn't have …I'm sorry, boss."

"Don't be. I've been avoiding talking to you about us for awhile," he said, aware he couldn't push it off any further. "Harmony, I have a mate. I found out a few days ago."

She frowned.

"I owe you an apology for not telling you sooner," he added. "I wasn't prepared for what that meant, just like I wasn't prepared for my new duties. I'm taking steps to remedy those issues. If I hurt you, I'm sorry."

Harmony was quiet for a long moment. Gabriel sensed her emotions, even if she tried to keep her face impassive.

"I understand," she said at last. "You have a duty to your mate. I would never interfere." She turned away, issuing silent orders to the death-dealers.

Gabriel watched her, not at all satisfied with the exchange. She was hurt; he was an ass. He'd fucked over both the women in his life, and neither deserved it.

The assassins lined up obediently. He went one-by-one, checking the minds of each with the occasional glance across to Rhyn and Andre, who were speaking quietly.

An hour later, Gabriel reached the last of the death-dealers in line, relieved yet troubled not to have found another traitor. The assassin he'd killed earlier had a handler, one that acted as a messenger between him and Darkyn. While the dead man hadn't known who the handler was, he'd suspected it was another death-dealer. Gabe checked all of those in the mortal realm, except for …

He turned, realizing Harmony hadn't been in the lineup. In fact, she wasn't anywhere.

Harmony, he called over their internal channel.

No response.

Gabriel felt something heavier than dread in his stomach. He'd just told Harmony he had a mate. It wasn't going to take much for her to put together who, especially with the ultra-secret assignments protecting Deidre.

Landon.

The death-dealer appeared at once. Second to Harmony on Gabriel's list of the most effective, Landon was her back-up when it came to organizing the missions and personnel.

"The protective assignment," Gabriel started. "Double it. Move them closer to their ward. I also need accountability on all of these." Gabe handed him the soul compass he'd found on the demon's body.

"Sure, boss." Landon's response was chipper despite his severe features.

"Send Tymkyn to find Harmony," Gabriel said, referring to the top tracker among his death-dealers. "Tell him to bring her in. Alive, preferably."

Landon absorbed Gabe's word choice, recognizing the gravity of the situation without further explanation.

"Find me when you're done," Gabriel added.

"Alright, boss." Landon disappeared through a portal.

Gabe watched him, rubbing his rough jaw. He'd never thought twice about trusting Harmony or any other death-dealer. Or about the Code. Or about pushing Deidre away when she needed to be by his side to keep her safe. Fate was right; the only thing in his way was *him.*

"I'm liking this new Gabe." Rhyn pulled him from his thoughts. "Snapping necks, breaking Codes, bringing back the dead-dead."

Gabe turned. The brothers were standing beside each other a short distance away. Rhyn was smiling faintly, Andre's controlled expression reminding Gabriel of Wynn.

"I learned a few things recently," Gabe replied. "I need to borrow Andre. We've got some demons to track. And Wynn. I'll bring them both back."

"Do me the favor and don't bring Wynn back," Rhyn said, anger flashing across his features.

"He's our father, Rhyn," Andre said.

"Don't start that mediator shit with me," Rhyn snapped.

"You have much to learn about diplomacy, little brother."

"And discretion," Gabriel added, unable to help but tease his rankled friend.

"Where's your mate, Gabe?" Rhyn retorted.

Gabriel rolled his eyes.

"Children, if you're done, I still need that drink," Andre said smoothly. "Let us get whatever this is over with. As a man of fashion, I'm afraid I won't be able to tolerate this clothing long."

Rhyn eyed him, suspecting it was an insult, while Gabriel recalled how polished Andre was. The peacemaker of the brothers, Andre instinctively used his gift of mind control to counter the tempers of his fiery brothers. It was impossible to stand near him and not relax. Gabriel felt the effect of being near him, and Rhyn shifted away from the subtle magic.

"He's yours for a couple of hours," Gabe said to Rhyn. "I've got a rat in my ranks. I need to find her."

"Harmony?" Rhyn guessed.

"Is it that obvious?" Gabriel complained.

"I have a knack for spotting traitors."

The bitterness in his voice was not lost on Gabe. He slapped Rhyn on the arm. Rhyn lifted his chin in farewell before motioning for Andre to follow him through a portal. Gabriel waited until they were gone. He felt different. Centered. Clear-headed. He had a shit ton of work to do the next couple of days. With Andre's help, he might gain some insight into Deidre's illness and be able to counter the demons tracking and stealing souls.

"Thanks for the pep talk, Fate," he murmured.

You'll pay for it later, Death, came the deity's amused response.

Gabriel smiled. "Bring it."

As he started away, he realized Fate had told him something else this day. The godling promised to tell Gabriel about he bet that took out past-Death, only when Gabriel was on the right path.

For the first time in months, he had confirmation that he was headed the right way.

Chapter Twelve

No Immortals showed up on her doorstep the first two days after she left the French Alps. Deidre began to relax. She settled into the luxe penthouse and learned her way around the neighborhood. As the third day came to a close, she suspected they – more specifically, *Gabriel* – had really let her go. After the first glass of wine, she was convinced. A second glass led her to think it was all her fault. After the fifth, she was certain she'd dreamt it all up. Or died and gone to hell.

A bottle of wine later, Deidre found herself sobbing on the couch. She didn't try to test the portals, fearing they wouldn't work. It was clear he wasn't coming for her. He'd spent the past three nights in bed with another woman after completely destroying her whole world!

Her wine headache stuck with her throughout the morning on the fourth day. Not even Wynn – who claimed to be her friend – came to find her. She didn't expect to be so suddenly written off by everyone. Like she was dead.

But she wasn't yet.

Deidre forced her attention from her own issues and outward as she walked through the street fair in downtown Atlanta. Her sunglasses and hat blocked the sun but not the heat, which fed her pulsing head. She wore one of the dresses past-Deidre bought. It wasn't something she'd consider any other time, a form-fitting jersey knit with spaghetti straps probably more suited for sleeping than wearing out.

She caught sight of herself in a store window. At least she *looked* good and was comfortable, even though she felt awful. Would someone like Gabriel notice her, if they crossed paths as random strangers at the festival? Her gaze fell to the tall woman in a slip of a dress that walked by her.

No way in hell. She was too short. No wonder she settled for Logan. Not that it mattered, but she'd need five inch heels to catch the gaze of someone as sexy as Gabriel. And maybe, a different body. A bigger smile. Larger breasts. Definitely some advice from someone who understood make-up better and a real hair stylist who could figure out how to un-pink hair.

"Dammit!"

She had to get him out of her mind. He'd made her an offer. She'd refused. He was moving on while depositing her back at the same crossroads where he'd found her last week. How long until he kicked her out of the apartment, the final act of abandonment after disrupting everything in her life?

The tattoo hadn't faded either, just like her memory of the sweet man who made love to her.

It wasn't fair.

She wasn't going to let a serial killer who chose not to kill her derail her day. No, she'd do what she'd always done: grieve then look for the silver lining. She had a beautiful apartment, a wardrobe, a pantry that magically restocked itself every time she left the place.

Calmed by the reminder, she left her spot in front of the window. The only thing she didn't have was nature. She found herself missing the ocean and the forest near the Immortals.

Chili pepper lights distracted her. Her step slowed as she neared a booth with an assortment of kitchen décor. The sight of something attainable from her bucket list lifted her spirits.

Deidre bought the lights she'd wanted for years. Logan thought them hideous, and Gabriel had laughed. Screw both men; she was getting her chili pepper lights.

They proved to be the turning point in her day. The painkillers she'd taken kicked in soon after, and she bought ice cream. Her mood improved, Deidre returned to her penthouse with newfound resolve to enjoy the last few months of her life.

She spent a grueling hour putting up the string of red lights in the kitchen and stepped back to admire her work. Proud of herself, she sipped from a glass of wine.

"You little bastards aren't going anywhere," she told them triumphantly, admiring the shoddy combination of tacks, tape and nails holding the strands in place along the wall. The sight of the lights thrilled her, reminded her she needed to stop moping around and live her life like a glowing chili pepper.

Leaning back against the counter, she laughed out loud at her absurd thought. It felt good to laugh after the events of the past week.

"So you *meant* to do that."

"You're not going to ruin this for me!" Deidre refused to face him and admired her handiwork. "You destroyed my life. Let me enjoy the shattered pieces you left."

As if sensing Death was in the room, the string of lights fell away from the wall on one side.

"You mean the shattered *peppers,*" Gabriel said drily.

She willed herself not to laugh at his joke, but it was hard. He had her kind of humor. There was something else in his voice she couldn't quite place. He was normally tense around her, his frustration clear. Though he always sounded quietly confident, the new note in his voice was one of calm self-assurance.

"They're plastic," she said in a flat tone. "Like your heart."

"Not to interrupt this lover's spat, but I could use a glass of wine."

At the unfamiliar voice, she faced the two men standing outside her kitchen. She didn't even notice the stranger; her gaze was arrested by Gabriel. The muscular frame, black gaze, dark clothes all looked the same. But *he* was changed. It was in his relaxed stance, the steadiness of his gaze. She'd always known he was strong. This time, she sensed restrained power of a different kind. Worse, whatever tormented him since they met was no longer an issue. He was comfortable with himself.

The other Gabriel didn't know what to do about her. This one might. After rejecting then pining for him for a few days, she wasn't ready for him to be less confused than she was.

"What's wrong with you?" she asked.

Death smiled so faintly, she barely saw it. He tipped his head towards the man he'd brought with him.

"I made an attempt to teach him to dress," the night-skinned man in front of her said as she met his gaze. His eyes were the most beautiful blue-purple she'd ever seen.

She liked him immediately. The air felt a little heavier around her as he spoke, compelling her attention to him. Deidre cocked her head to the side.

"You don't remember me," he said.

"I don't know you from Adam," she retorted.

Gabriel chuckled. "It really isn't funny."

"Be of use, Gabriel, and fix my chili peppers," she ordered then addressed the stranger. "I'll get you some wine."

She turned to the wine chiller and pulled out the bottle she opened when she returned home from the street fair. She grabbed a glass, returning to the counter. Gabriel had dumped her wine before starting to replace the lights.

It was hard to ignore him when he was only a few feet away. Overly aware of his presence, Deidre stepped outside the kitchen to the breakfast counter and poured two glasses of wine.

"I'm Andre," the newcomer said. "Deidre, I presume?"

"Yep. I'm sure I screwed you over in my past life, too."

"Only to kill me."

She met his gaze. "Another dead guy. Like Wynn."

"My father."

"How is he?" she asked with more eagerness than she intended.

Andre motioned for her to sit on one of the stools at the counter. She did, waiting for his response as he sat.

"He is well enough."

"Ah. Of course." She rolled her eyes at the vague response. "What brings you all to my neighborhood?" She found herself watching Gabriel as he stretched upwards to fix the lights. His shirt stretched tightly over his shoulders and across his back while his biceps flexed and the roped muscles of his forearms rippled with his tinkering. His lean torso, narrow hips and the outline of muscular thighs reminded her too well why she wasn't able to get him out of her mind.

She was overheating just looking at him. Andre ceased talking, and she realized he'd been speaking while she ogled Gabriel.

"Come again?" she asked, sipping her wine.

Andre raised his eyebrow in polite disapproval, the same way his father did.

"Wynn's not dead, is he?"

"No, dear. You were friends?" Andre had Wynn's patience and manner, though she sensed more genuine warmth in the man before her than she had during the tenure of her friendship with Wynn.

"*Are* friends, you mean," she replied. "As far as I know."

"That's expensive wine, my friend," Andre said suddenly.

Deidre twisted to see Gabriel at the wine chiller. He had a bottle in his hand and twisted the cork free with little effort. He gave her the look, the one she knew was meant to remind her of his rules, before he dumped the bottle into the sink. A thrill went through her at the silent dare.

"Perhaps, if you promise him not to drink it except with me, he'll spare the rest of those precious bottles," Andre said, gaze on the wine going down the drain. "I'm French. I cannot bear this level of abuse. Would that appease you, Gabriel?"

"She knows not to drink," was the firm response.

"Judging by the stack of wine bottles near the door, there needs to be a middle ground you can agree on," Andre advised.

"Middle ground, sweetie," she repeated with exaggerated innocence. "Some sort of *arrangement* we can both live with."

Gabriel's jaw ticked as held her gaze for a long moment. "Very well."

"Who are you and what have you done with Gabriel?" she asked, surprised.

"I can always say no," he reminded her.

"So can I." She turned her back to him.

"I think we have an agreement," Andre said, smiling. "Yes?"

"Yes," Gabriel replied.

"I guess," she said grudgingly. "Now, about this unexpected visit."

"Without Gabe to distract you this time, perhaps you will listen," Andre said.

She flushed, grateful Gabriel wasn't able to see her face.

"My talent lies with the mind. I read, control, manipulate and anything else I need to do to the mind, I can," Andre started. "I am here simply to assess what is in your brain."

"You mean the tumor or my thoughts?" she asked.

"The tumor."

"Tell me why."

"To see if there's something I can do in order to prevent the inevitable, of course."

Gabriel moved into her peripheral, thumbs looped through his belt as he leaned against the counter on the other side of the breakfast bar's island. Deidre looked at him hard for a moment then shook her head and gripped her wine, padding into the living area. She sat in the oversized armchair, curling her legs beneath her as she drank her wine.

"No," she said at last.

"No, what?" Gabriel asked in a growl. The edge reappeared.

"You heard me."

"Deidre, I'm offering my expertise to assist you," Andre said. His tone was calm. The Immortal sat at the nearest end of the neighboring couch while Gabriel remained standing opposite her on the other side of the ottoman.

"I'm not interested in your help," she said. "Your father did everything he could. There's nothing else I'm willing to try."

Andre's eyebrows both shot up this time. His brilliant gaze turned to Gabriel, who shook his head. She was missing something again. Another secret. Every time she learned a new one, her life went to shit.

"Then perhaps you'll agree to let me try for my own edification?" Andre's words were accompanied by a smile.

The air around her grew heavy again. She felt confused, suddenly unable to recall why this request was objectionable.

"I guess," she murmured.

"Sit forward."

She unfolded her legs and sat on the edge of the chair. Andre perched likewise on the sofa and reached out, placing the cool tips of his fingers on her temples.

"Close your eyes," he instructed.

Deidre did. The coolness of his touch turned to gentle electric currents that worked their paths through her skull. She shivered at the tingling massage traveling across her scalp and into her brain. His examination didn't last long, and the sensations faded. She opened her eyes when the light pressure of his fingers left her face.

Andre gazed at her, quiet and thoughtful. His head tilted to the side, and she assessed that he and Gabriel were speaking mentally.

"Happy?" she asked and eased away. She folded her legs beneath her once more on the chair.

Gabriel rubbed the back of his head and paced towards the windows.

"Now you'll go away, and leave me in peace," she said.

His eyes flickered to her, his response clear on his face. She sighed and rose.

"Let yourselves out." Deidre returned to the kitchen and placed her wineglass in the sink.

"I'm working on curing you," Gabriel said.

"Good luck. If the *Ancient* Immortal surgeon I had for years couldn't do it with modern science and magic, and Death doesn't know the answer, then I'm assuming it's not gonna happen. I want to enjoy the rest of what I have, Gabriel."

"If there was a way, and I knew it, would you listen to me?" he asked as he approached the kitchen.

"Depends. Are we talking a five percent chance of success or a ninety nine?" she returned. "Because I've been through everything in between. It takes a lot to prepare yourself to die, Gabriel, which you of all people should appreciate."

"You'd rather give up." His voice was hard.

Deidre looked up at him as he entered her personal space, at once flustered and irritated. She leaned back against the sink. Gabriel stopped in front of her, his heat and nearness like a subtle siren song that tried to lure her closer.

"I want to hear you say it," he said. "I want to hear the woman who lives by the motto of no apologies, no regrets, who told me once that her own soul searching taught her to live, doesn't want my help turning that three months into eternity."

She heard his anger. He wasn't bristling, as she expected. His tone was controlled, his features calm, his eyes the only indication of the fire in his blood. Whatever happened to him over the past few days, he was no longer willing to walk away or back down.

"I can't handle the *chance* that I might or might not have hope," she replied. "You tear me away from the only stability I have in my life, expect me to change my view on the entire world overnight, reject me and now, you're asking me to take a chance on something you can't guarantee. What part of my … my pure confusion doesn't make sense to you?"

"You don't trust me at all," he said.

"No shit. What reason have you given me to trust you?"

Gabriel studied her. She'd expected to piss him off. If anything, his anger melted into the contemplation of a man who had a new problem he intended to solve.

"She's gotta hear it from you, Andre," he said at last, stepping out from front of her. He leaned against the counter beside her, his arm touching hers. The deep connection and warmth moved through her.

Deidre shifted away then eyed him when he reestablished the touch. His attention was on Andre. She let herself stay where she was, intrigued by the electricity and calmed by the heat of his body.

"I think she should hear it from Wynn," Andre said in clear disapproval.

"Wynn won't tell her."

"Are you certain?"

"We've had the discussion. Twice."

Andre frowned. Deidre suspected they were baiting her. The mention of Wynn was almost enough for her to pounce, but she resisted.

"It's not my place," Andre said. "You're her mate by divine law. It falls on your shoulders."

"If there is any part of you that believes she'll accept the truth if it comes from me, then you're the worst judge of character I know," Gabriel replied drily. "Wynn owes it to her."

"I know you're messing with me," she said through clenched teeth. "If Wynn had something to tell me, he would have."

"Right. Let me guess. Your *friend* didn't come to see you this week, did he?" Gabriel asked without looking at her.

"No one did. If anything, you probably didn't tell him where I was. I know you don't like him."

"You trust Wynn more than Gabriel," Andre observed.

"Yes," she said.

"If Wynn were to tell you something about your illness, good or bad, you'd listen?"

"Of course."

Gabriel shifted in either frustration or anger. He didn't break their touch, so she focused on Andre.

"Gabriel," Andre said. "Bring Wynn here."

"I don't like that, Andre."

"She will not be open to you until this is cleared up."

Deidre clenched her jaw to keep from speaking. She wasn't going to fall for whatever trick they played.

"Son, bring him here," Andre said with the gruffness of an older brother. "I'll make sure he talks."

"Yeah, Gabe, bring him here," Deidre echoed. "That way I know you haven't killed him."

"When you hear what he has to tell you, you'll wish I had, Deidre."

His quite regret made her uneasy. Through their connection, she actually *felt* the emotion. He was reluctant, because he didn't want to hurt her. She broke the contact. Gabriel cared about her. Sometimes. She didn't understand him.

Without another word, he summoned a portal and left.

"I should've taken the bait, huh?" she asked Andre.

"It wasn't bait, dear. You are between Death and well, Death, right now."

She laughed, not expecting the joke.

"Would it have been easier on you if you heard it from either a complete stranger or someone you can't quite figure out? Yes," he continued. "But easier is not the choice we made. You're right. You've been backed into a corner, and you've shut out everything. We have to open you back up."

"Sounds painful."

He didn't deny it as he moved around the kitchen. He retrieved her glass from the basin of the sink and poured her more wine. Her hands were sweating as she accepted it. She deliberated over how strange it was to experience Gabriel's emotions, even if briefly.

Gabriel reappeared at the other end of the penthouse, trailed by Wynn. Her longtime friend was impossible to read, as usual, and she saw the similarity in features between him and Andre.

"We'll leave you to talk," Andre said, raising his glass in greeting to his father.

She watched, curious about how father and son might interact. One warm, the other cold, both self-assured, polished. Aside from the greeting, there was no warmth between them at all. Andre waved a wary Gabriel away from the kitchen. He took up a protective stance within direct sight of them, so still, he seemed like a statue.

Deidre felt the heaviness in the air again, only she felt no confusion.

"Hello, darling," Wynn said as he entered the kitchen.

Deidre felt herself relaxing around him. She kissed him on both cheeks then waited as he poured himself wine. He'd lied to her to get her to take him to the Immortals, but she still felt safer with him than anyone else. He'd had a million chances to harm her while she lay unconscious and vulnerable on the operating table and never did.

Whatever it was they wanted him to tell her, it couldn't be that bad.

"I figured they'd killed you," she said.

"Not yet. It's likely not too far down the road." He swirled his wine as he leaned against the counter opposite her. "You look well. Very cute clothing."

"Thanks. Today was a good day," she said firmly. "Until about an hour ago. Every time Immortals show up, things go right down the shitter."

He smiled. "Yes, well, I won't be breaking that mold."

"It can't be that bad," she replied. "We've been friends for years, and you've been enamored by me for what? Two lifetimes at least?"

"I think you know by now that even those who loved past-Deidre also hated her," he said. "Her affect on those around her was the opposite of yours. She brought nothing but terror. You bring a smile to people's faces."

"That's sweet of you, Wynn."

"Yes and no. I didn't know that when I met you this time around. I thought you were the same person as past-Deidre," he started.

She listened, dread fluttering through her, and sipped her wine.

"It influenced how I handled your illness."

"So, what? You didn't try as hard to cure me?" she asked, perplexed.

"I went several steps farther. The experimental surgeries I performed the first six months were not geared towards curing you at all."

Her heart felt like it was slowing. Rationalizing that he was upset at past-Deidre like everyone else was, she wanted to stop Wynn before he said something worse. Something she wasn't able to live with.

"I am the brilliant surgeon you believe me to be," he said. "Partially due to my magic. The power of an Ancient is beyond anything humans can understand. With a penchant for medicine and science and my magic, I can cure what others could not."

"Except for me," she said.

"Including you," he said slowly. His gaze was steady as he spoke. "On my first surgery, I discovered what exactly was in your head. There's a soul encased in a tumor."

"My soul?" she gasped.

"No. I don't know whose it is. I didn't need to know," he said too casually. "I was trying to figure out what was there, not to remove it, but to ensure no one else could either. Deidre," he paused. "Your tumor was operable when I met you and for the entirety of first year. I told you the opposite from the onset and convinced you to let me conduct experimental surgeries."

She heard the words, but they made no sense. At her silence, he continued.

"The surgeries that first year integrated the tumor into your brain using science and magic in a combination that even I was unable to reverse, when I finally realized you weren't the same woman I recalled. All the surgeries the third year" he shook his head "desperate attempts by me to undo what I'd done."

He was quiet.

"What made you change your mind?" she managed.

"Seeing you for the beautiful person you are. You are now everything I wished you were in a past life."

She looked away. Her hands were shaking too hard for the wine. Wynn stretched across the distance to grasp it as it started to slide from her hands.

"At least you tried to undo it, right?" she half-joked. "That counts for something."

"Deidre, love, you're not hearing me," Wynn's voice was gentle. He set down his wine and settled his hands on her shoulders.

Deidre swallowed hard. She was trying hard to push away the gathering emotions that told her Wynn was not the man she wanted, *needed* him to be. He was the remaining pillar of the foundation of the reality that existed before her trip to the beach. If he crumbled, so did she.

"I didn't just want you dead." He spoke the words in the cool, detached tone that she recognized from their interactions at the hospital. "I wanted you to suffer a long, painful death and was willing to do whatever it took to make that a reality. My vengeance was so well-planned,. Death himself cannot figure out how to save you. Deidre, I'm the one who will kill you."

Speechless for a long moment, she did nothing but stare at him. Her mental wheels began to move again as she grappled with not only what he'd done, but why Andre and Gabriel – who knew the truth long before she did – chose now to have it revealed to her.

"I, um, think I need some air," she said hoarsely. "A swan dive off the roof sounds good right about now."

"No, love," Wynn replied. "Trust me one last time and go to the Sanctuary. It welcomes people like us."

People like us. "You mean sociopathic, indiscriminate killers who can't sleep a night in their own beds without someone trying to kill them."

"Exactly."

"I'm not *her*!"

"I know that now. Not many others do." Wynn released her shoulders and returned to his side of the kitchen.

Deidre's insides were cold. A familiar sense of calm filled her. It was the same sensation as when she opened the door to the guest bedroom in her apartment for the first time to see the mess the demons made of some poor human. It was the moment she realized her nightmare was beginning.

"Tell them I'm going to the Sanctuary," she said. The portal formed before she'd finished the sentence. Without looking back, Deidre walked through it and emerged on a familiar beach, the same one she'd ended up on when she leapt from her apartment building.

At once, the rhythm and scent of the ocean soothed her. She'd missed nature while staying at the penthouse. Deidre sat down on the beach, mesmerized by the movement of the clear teal depths rushing ashore. Nothing made sense to her numbed mind, aside from the fragrant ocean, the fine sand that slid through her fingers like silk, and the warm-cool sensations caused by a combination of afternoon sun and sea breeze. The world outside her was calm, but the storm within her brewed. She hugged her knees to her chest and rested her cheek on one knee, closing her eyes.

"Am I right in assuming I'm the last person you want to see right now?" Gabriel asked quietly.

"I want to be alone."

"I don't think that's a good idea."

"So, what, you plan on riding in like a knight in shining armor to rescue the vulnerable damsel in distress?" she snapped.

"Gods, woman." Gabriel settled behind her, his long legs stretching out on either side of her. His arms circled hers, and he drew her against him. "You've never done what I wanted in either life. I don't expect you to start now."

She wanted to tell him to leave, but whatever bond existed between them, it filled her with warmth and energy that quelled the meltdown she was about to have. His heartbeat was as steady as the tide, his strength needed when hers was fading. It felt too natural for him to hold her. She loved being in his arms, as much as she hated him right now!

She relaxed and pressed her bare legs into the sand in front of her. Gabriel's arms tightened around her body, his chin resting on her head. Deidre let her full weight settle against him. She'd never been able to sit like this with Logan. She'd never felt as secure or protected as she did this moment in the arms of the person who would claim her soul soon.

They sat in silence throughout the afternoon, until the sun sank far enough out of the sky to perch on the ocean. Gabriel adjusted whenever she shifted but never let go, his strong arms wrapped around her possessively. With the sunset came a chilled breeze. Deidre pulled her knees up and pressed her back into Gabriel. She buried her feet in the sand to keep them warm.

He said nothing, even as the last finger of light faded from the horizon and starlight replaced the sun. She didn't expect him to sit with her for hours; she definitely didn't expect him to stay solely for her comfort without trying to force anymore Immortal bullshit down her throat. He made it clear he didn't have to curry her favor, not with the Immortal Code on his side and the *arrangement* he proposed.

What did it mean that he didn't have to be there but chose to?

"Can you be away from your ... underworld this long?" she asked at last.

"The dead aren't going anywhere."

Deidre snorted but forbade herself from laughing.

"You wanna know something?"

"No more secrets that make me cry," she warned.

"Trust me, it won't. I'm doing such a shitty job as Death, I got locked out of the underworld," he said, amused. "That's the other issue I've been dealing with, when not hunting you down to make you cry."

"Seriously?"

"Yeah."

"So you're a lost soul, too, like the rest of the lake and me."

"Pretty much," he replied.

She shivered at the memory of her interaction with a single soul. What was it like to have the duty to protect billions of them?

"Why did you choose today for me to learn about Wynn?" she whispered.

He was quiet for a moment before responding. "I didn't realize things were bad enough between you and me that you'd trust the man who hurt you over someone trying to help you."

"Now I don't trust either of you."

"I can recover. He can't."

She wasn't going to admit out loud he was right. There was nothing Wynn could ever do to make things right. She'd always known there were deep, dangerous levels of potential with Gabriel, if he ever figured out whether he wanted her or not.

"I feel lost," she murmured.

"You're not." He squeezed her. "Think of me as your anchor. Something you want badly to shove overboard."

"You're so not funny!" she said, unable to stop the laugh that slipped free.

"We have a similar sense of humor, I think."

"You're locked out of the underworld, herding lost souls into a lake and yet you're here trying to win over the woman destined to be your mate by divine laws but who doesn't trust you," she summarized.

"Is it working?"

"You've taken the first step on a very long path. At this rate, I'll be dead long before you succeed."

"I'm one step ahead of where I was this morning."

"You took that as encouragement, didn't you?" She twisted to meet his gaze, frowning.

Gabriel smiled.

"Aren't you worried?" she asked. "About the souls and your issues? I mean, why spend the day with me?"

"I'm where I need to be," he replied simply.

She studied him. He was no longer the conflicted man she'd met on a beach a few days before. Was he still the reluctant mate that didn't know what to do with her? She didn't ask for fear of discovering he was going to stop playing his keep-away game and offer her an arrangement she couldn't refuse. Deidre sighed and sank back into his arms.

"Did Andre figure anything out?" she asked in a level voice.

"We're working on it."

"You were bluffing? There was no option you were considering?" Anger fluttered through her.

"There is. But you were right to say what you did at the apartment. I need to respect you enough not to provide false hope. I can't be half-assed about this. I have to look at a few more angles before I can determine if the option we found is feasible." He spoke with thoughtfulness.

"I appreciate that," she murmured. "You realize if you save me, you'll have a much larger issue."

"I'm listening."

"You'll have to court me like a normal person."

"We'll cross that bridge when we come to it," he said in a husky tone.

Her heart quickened. Was he capable of being genuinely interested in her as more than a duty? She wasn't willing to consider it, not when there was the issue of her pending demise between here and there.

"Gabriel, are the issues you're having with the underworld and souls and whatever, are those issues my fault?" she asked.

"Not directly."

"You said that before. What does it mean?"

"The deity you were in a past life started the chain of events that put us here by breaking laws from the time-before-time. The underworld cracked, and the demons came to claim the souls. Past-Deidre walked out and left me to clean up the mess, which I did poorly. I managed to get the demons out and repair the fissure. By that point, other things fell apart that I couldn't fix. I was exiled here," he explained. "I have to address the issues in my domain on the mortal world before I'll be allowed to return and finish repairing the underworld."

"That's a yes," she said, troubled. "I'm directly responsible for all of this."

"*You* aren't. Past-Deidre is."

"Is there really a difference? I mean, I thought there was ... is there?"

"Absolutely. You are two separate people. You look alike, but you couldn't be more different."

"Then why is a crap ton of her bad karma killing me?"

"Don't look at it that way, sweetheart," he said so gently she felt tears prick her eyes. "Some events seem connected but really aren't. You were the victim of someone who couldn't see what was right before him. Pretty much all of us made the same mistake when we first met you."

"I guess it really doesn't matter. The past is the past and I'm fucked either way," she said. "Gabriel, if you can't find an option to save me, will you swear to let me live out what I have left in peace?"

"You mean alone."

"I mean *happy,* whether that's alone or not."

"Yes, Deidre. I promise you that."

"Thank you," she replied. "Did you really come here tonight to start trying to win me over?"

"I don't know." His response came after a lengthy pause.

"You sat with me for hours and don't know why?" she asked, amused.

"I have no fucking clue what to do with you."

"Good," she said, satisfied beyond her expectations. "You confuse the hell out of me, too. Though of the two of us, I'm the one who can't read minds, so it makes sense I'm clueless."

"I've only read your mind once."

"I know that how?"

The sea breeze seemed to pierce her skull and ruffle through her brain. She shuddered.

"That's what it feels like when I read your mind," he said.

"Weird. What did you see?"

"Most people don't want to know," he replied with a chuckle. "There are conscious thoughts that you're aware of and subconscious ones that you're not. Emotions, random sensations, memories, disjointed images. It's like walking from reality into a dream and back again."

"Can you make sense of it while you're in there?"

"Only because of what I am."

"Tell me what's in my head," she ordered. "I can't sort through it."

"It's like someone dropped a stone in the lake. The impact was noticeable, but it's the ripples that are tearing you apart."

"Yeah," she agreed.

"You're in denial about Wynn. You're in denial about dying. You've accepted the Immortals and even taken on the burden of wanting to right the wrongs of past-Deidre. You don't want to die, but the idea of living terrifies you as well."

She listened, dismayed but also interested in someone interpreting the insanity of her mind in a way she could grasp. She held her breath, suspecting what might come next.

"You feel the same way towards me that I do towards you." There was laughter in Gabriel's voice.

"Which is ..."

"You'll figure it out."

"I'm guessing I confound you the same way you do me. One minute, telling me you don't want anything to do with me beyond your duty and the next, sitting on the beach with me for hours because you're worried I'll find a tall building to dive off of," she grumbled. "Am I right?"

"Close."

"Then why ..." she stopped.

"You're not ready," he said wisely. "I saw how much you don't trust me, too. We have a long way to go."

"And no time to get there," she murmured. Something Darkyn told her returned to the forefront of her thoughts. He'd asked her if she'd take herself out of the equation before she hurt Gabriel. Katie was convinced Gabriel had managed to love past-Deidre; was he therefore in danger of falling for her? Before this talk, she didn't think so. He was too cagey for her to understand what he felt.

Some small part of him cared enough to sit with her tonight. There was much more to Gabriel than what she saw. Darkyn saw it somehow, and Deidre suspected Gabriel's here-gone approach to her was his way of hiding how much he did care.

Chapter Thirteen

"Will you tell me what the chances are for the option you're looking at?" Deidre asked him, troubled.

Gabriel hugged her more tightly out of instinct. Her small body cradled in his arms, he wasn't able to remember the last time he felt so relaxed. Or aware that what he did was mostly wrong. He didn't have a solution to her tumor. He was endangering her life by giving her hope and risking his emotions by remaining with her. Fate's lesson was a good one. Past-Death was beaten only by acting out of something other than duty.

He wanted to throw duty out the window when it came to his mate.

"Under ten percent," he replied.

"Wow. How far under?"

He hesitated. "Closer to one percent."

"That bad? And you're a deity?"

"A baby one," he said with a snort.

"Didn't I leave you an instruction manual?"

"Fuck," he muttered. "You would've burnt the place down on your way out the door if you could."

She laughed. "I am so sorry for what I was, Gabriel."

"No. You aren't apologizing for her."

"If I knew three years ago, I might not have trusted Wynn."

"Deidre," he said. "I can't fix that. But I might be able to help you."

She didn't ask how. She either didn't believe him or didn't want to know. From what he'd read in her mind, it was both. His plan took Wynn, Andre, the oldest of the Healers he knew and his own magic, and the best he was able to come up with was given a one percent chance by Wynn, whose mind Gabriel stripped to the core to ensure the Immortal didn't deceive him.

"Will you let me try?" he asked, heart pounding hard.

"I don't know, Gabriel. I'm kinda tired of having my brain cut open. If you fail, I get a shitty quality of life my last few months. If I succeed, I get to …" she stopped herself.

"Deal with this Immortal bullshit?" he finished for her.

"Pretty much."

"What if I made you a new deal?"

"Oh, god. Another attempt at an *arrangement?*"

"Relationship," he corrected with a smile.

"What do I get this time? Your left arm, two teeth and the trench coat?"

"No way in hell on the trench coat."

She gasped. His arms tightened around her as she tried to squirm away. Gabriel hugged her tight, entertained and enjoying the feel of her in his arms.

"Easy," he murmured. "I'm joking."

She growled but settled, her head dropping back against his shoulder. His eyes went to her shapely legs. The knit dress she wore fell to mid-thigh when she was standing. With her knees pulled closer to her chest to guard against the sea breeze, the dress crumbled to the creases of her thighs and hip. A little higher, and he'd be able to tell what color underwear she wore.

Obliviously unaware that half his thoughts this afternoon and evening were on her naked, Deidre melted into his arms the moment he touched her. Her vulnerability shimmered around her in a way that left him unable to leave her alone, until he was certain the worst was over. The last part of her world shattered with Wynn's confession. She was mentally tough but fatigued by the events that occurred since they inadvertently met on a night similar to this one. He was enjoying the sensation of her in his arms as much as he was there to comfort her.

"The deal," he said, redirecting his thoughts. "Give this option we figured out a go. If it works, you define our relationship."

"Not bad," she allowed. "I notice that there's only a one percent chance I get to make the decisions."

"It was zero this morning," he reminded her. "Positive steps."

"Gabriel …" There was too much pain in her voice. "Maybe you should just take this thing out of my head and be done with me. Start over with someone who doesn't look like your ex. The woman you were kissing was gorgeous."

He grunted.

"I'm gonna have to train you, aren't I?" she said and elbowed him. "When a woman says something like that, she's waiting for you to fill in the details."

"So it's like a question, but the complete opposite," he replied.

"Yep."

"Her name is Harmony. Yes, I was sleeping with her before we met. No, I'm not anymore," he said, thoughts growing dark. "She betrayed me to the demons. Another of my issues."

"Oh. How do people mess with you? I mean, me, I'm tiny and blonde. But you're ... kinda scary, Gabriel, even if you weren't Death."

"One of life's growing pains. Trusting people you shouldn't."

"Can I trust you?" Her question was hushed.

"I haven't killed you, have I?"

"Your standards are low."

"You can trust me. I'm flawed, but I will do my best."

Deidre was quiet. It was not a good silence. He resisted the instinct that told him he needed to peek into her thoughts. She was thinking, which was good. She hadn't rejected him, and he already glimpsed what issues he was going to have to overcome.

Assuming he was able to do what he and Andre planned. The alternative was that they killed her when they retrieved the soul in her head. The idea infuriated him. He wasn't about to murder this Deidre to fetch the soul of past-Deidre. No, his predecessor wasn't going to win this round.

Andre had another idea, one that might increase the chances of success, based on ancient myths from the time-before-time. When they left Deidre's apartment, Andre was headed to ask his half-brother, Tamer, for help researching histories for more information. Gabriel wasn't getting his hopes up, let alone encouraging hers.

"Deidre, will you do it?" he asked again.

"One percent is a death sentence," she replied.

"I won't let you go through it, if I don't think it'll work. What would it take for you to trust me enough to take a chance?"

She was pensive again. Gabriel suspected there was nothing on the planet that might make her interested in an option that currently stood at failure rate of ninety nine percent. But he waited for her response.

"If I did, and if it worked ..." she started, paused, then continued. "Gabriel, what would eternity be like? I mean for us."

He was silent, uncertain how to answer.

"I don't know how you offer me nothing one minute then let me decide the next," she added, frustrated. "Meanwhile, I'm dying and my world keeps crashing. Tell me something. Please. Give me some reason why one percent and an eternity with you beats out the alternative. Convince me you aren't telling me we can have a real relationship just so I go through with this procedure you want to try."

He heard the edge of desperation in her voice. As with the underworld, he'd tried to act in a way he thought was best since meeting her. Wynn's information – *pleasure kills* – was still an issue. Meanwhile, Wynn's level of Ancient magic made him almost untraceable. He was able to bypass Gabriel's death-dealers too easily during his frequent trips to the lake. If he chose to disappear, the plan wasn't going to work. If Tamer didn't find the tidbit of history from the time-before-time about forced soul extraction, the plan was never going to have more than a five percent chance of working, even with Wynn.

Gabriel didn't have time, and Wynn's assessment that Deidre was starting to deteriorate made Gabriel afraid to give her more than he already had this night. He'd come close to saying too much since arriving at the beach. At the sound of her despair, he wanted nothing more than to reassure her that she was everything he needed – everything he wanted – in the mate he planned to spend eternity with. Beautiful, brave, funny, sweet. The gods couldn't have molded a more perfect woman.

They had a journey to make together before they were in a functional relationship, but they'd never have that chance, if he didn't find a way to buy them all time.

He couldn't risk it. He couldn't risk her. He'd been trying to walk that fine line all night. He was left feeling dirty, like he was leading her on with enough encouragement to keep her from taking matters into her own hands but not so much that her tumor grew.

"Okay then," she whispered. "Never mind. Just ... hold me."

Doing the right thing was painful. Gabriel held his tongue. Their connection was strong, its calming affect on her the only comfort he was able to offer.

"Who's soul is in my head?" she asked.

"We don't know," he lied. "Probably an anomaly."

"Does that happen often?"

"Not that I know of."

"It's kinda weird, isn't it? To have someone else's soul in your head?"

"Yeah."

"Do you want me to take the one percent chance?"

"I do," he replied as evenly as he was able to. "One percent now is better than zero percent in three months."

"Ugh."

He waited. She was deliberating silently. At last, she sighed.

"I want to live," she said, sounding unconvinced. "I think. The idea of this being my new reality terrifies me. Even if ... even if *you* don't want me, I want that chance. I guess if the operation fails, I'll die anyway, right?"

You have no idea how much I want you. Aloud, he replied, "Instantly. No pain, no comatose state."

"Never thought I'd consider that good news."

Secretly relieved, Gabriel drew a deep breath. He needed her agreement to try, even if they weren't ready yet. He'd figure something out. He just needed to find the right combination of factors that would allow him to withdraw the soul from her head without killing her. If that meant he took Wynn with him everywhere from here on out to ensure the Immortal didn't disappear, he'd do it.

If it meant he went to Darkyn and made a deal as a final alternative, he'd do that, too.

"Maybe we can adopt an angel," she added. "Toby said they need homes. So bizarre."

"Gods. Let's get through this before we talk kids," he said gruffly.

She laughed.

"Trust me?"

"I don't have much of a choice, if I want to give living a go," she said.

"Good enough. You ready to go home?"

"Yeah."

Gabriel stood carefully and pulled her to her feet. She took his hand but didn't look at him, the odd melancholy stirring his instincts once more. A death-dealer outside her door – or better yet, on her couch – was all that would make him easier about leaving her alone.

He took her home through the shadow world. She released his hand as they walked into the living room. Gabriel watched her walk away, loving how much the clingy dress revealed of her body.

"I'm assigning someone to sleep in the apartment," he told her firmly.

"Because of demons?"

"More or less."

Deidre curled up on the couch, eyes thoughtful as she studied him. She was contemplative and calm, sad but not suicidal. Gabriel returned her intent gaze.

"You okay?" he asked, bothered by something he wasn't able to pinpoint.

"I think so. I've lived with the idea of dying for so long, I'm kinda freaked out by the alternative," she admitted. "It's a lot to think about."

"I'll come by to talk later," he heard himself saying. "Tomorrow sometime." During daylight, when he wasn't fighting the desire to make love to her that grew with the disappearance of the sun.

"I'd like that," she said with a small smile.

"I'll send someone over in about half an hour."

She nodded.

He'd gotten what he wanted from her, but he didn't feel like he'd won. If anything, Gabriel sensed something was off again. He pushed the thought away and took a portal to the lake near the Immortals' fortress. It was dark and cool, the forest quiet while the waters before him no longer glowed brightly enough to be seen from the stronghold.

Landon appeared at once, and Gabriel waited for his new second-in-command to join him.

"It's working!" Landon exclaimed. "The Ancient Andre's mind magic. He implanted it in the mind of two Immortals. We tested them today. They were able to track the demons attacking schools. The spell lasts twenty four hours, but it works."

"Excellent," Gabe replied.

"We're testing it out on death-dealers tomorrow," Landon added.

"If we're able to find the souls before demons, we'll be back on track."

"I still can't find Harmony," Landon said.

Gabe said nothing, suspecting he knew where the death-dealer was hiding out. He almost felt sorry for her. Darkyn was not a kind master. Why she'd chosen to serve a demon over him... was there any part of her that cared for him? Or had he been a simple source of information for her and Darkyn? He grieved her choice but also believe she got what she deserved for betraying the souls they were all charged with protecting.

"We'll keep looking," Landon said.

"Thanks. Let me know how tomorrow goes with Andre's mind tricks. I'm going to pick up more compasses from Tamer," Gabe said. "Send Cora to guard my mate. Tell her to sleep on the couch."

"Got it, boss."

Souls, demons, Deidre. For the first time since taking on the mantle of Death, Gabriel was hopeful. He had the right people helping him, a mate who reluctantly agreed to his plan to help her, a better understanding of when to break the Code and a plan to repair all that was broken within his domain on the mortal realm.

He'd turned a corner. It was time to pursue his duties relentlessly to continue to build momentum. By this time next week, he'd be back in the underworld. With Deidre in his arms and the souls in the otherworldly lake where they belonged.

For once, things were going in Death's favor.

Chapter Fourteen

Deidre waited for the portal to close before she rose. She paced and caught sight of her reflection in the windows. For a long moment, she stared. Her insides were shaking, no longer settled by his gentle magic.

She'd told Gabriel she wanted to live. There was no uncertainty about dying. Living promised much more that she'd be unable to control: the Immortal society into which she'd been sucked, a potential boyfriend who still seemed to waffle about whether or not he wanted to be with her, absolutely no sense of normalcy or stability. Did Immortals have jobs? Houses? Pets?

Did it matter, if she was able to live a full life? To turn her bucket list into a to-do list? Her gaze went to the kitchen, and she smiled as she recalled Gabriel putting up her latest find. She wanted a life filled with chili pepper lights.

And a chance with Gabriel.

Her smile faded. He didn't answer her plea to reassure her some part of him cared for her. She thought him sitting with her so long on the beach was an indication. Why then wasn't he willing to admit it?

Deidre wiped her face and forced herself to face another possibility. Was she willing to give life a second shot, even if Gabriel wasn't in the picture and she had no more normal friends after Wynn's betrayal?

Yes. Maybe.

Still cold from the chilly beach, she went up to her room and changed into jeans and a sweater. Tying comfortable shoes, she drew a deep breath.

"One percent chance my ass," she muttered. "Not when I have a guarantee from some freakish stranger I met in a dark alley."

Her confidence faltered. She reminded herself that the man named Darkyn promised to help for free, whichever way she decided to go. She could always double-check and walk away, if he decided not to honor his deal.

Deidre called a portal and stood before it. She breathed deeply several times, nerves and instincts unsettled. She was going to do it. She was going to live - and maybe even share a life with someone like Gabriel. It was terrifying, but she felt invigorated, hopeful.

She strode into the shadow world and stopped.

"Darkyn," she called, uncertain where he hid out.

"I thought you'd come back."

Deidre whirled, startled at how quickly he appeared. His slow smile scared her while the penetrating gaze chipped away at more of her resolve.

"I, uh, thought about what you said," she said.

He clasped his arms behind his back, waiting politely.

"I want to live. But" – she rushed on – "I want to clarify that I'm not going to owe you anything and there's no weird contract with fine print that says you get to claim my firstborn child or anything."

"There is one catch."

"Oh." Her heart tumbled. "In that case, I'll just go home."

"Aren't you curious?" he asked. "There's no obligation in knowing what it is. I never offer deals without revealing the terms."

She hesitated, growing uncomfortable in the clammy in-between place with the scary stranger. Maybe Gabriel's option was best. If it didn't work, she'd die while under.

Death wasn't what she wanted.

Deidre considered how long it took for her to accept her impending death. Did she ever? She'd faced the reality but held out some hope it wasn't inevitable. In a matter of a couple of days, she not only accepted there was a chance to live, but she'd decided to pursue whatever she had to in order to guarantee it.

Gabriel was right. She wasn't ready to give up. The logical side of her understood that Darkyn's offer of fixing her was a better option than dying on the operating table. Her instincts, however, were telling her to run.

Feeling trapped before hearing his terms, her eyes grew misty. Suddenly, she was afraid she'd be tempted to pay whatever price he demanded, no matter how high. He didn't have the pointed teeth of a demon, which she hoped was indication enough she wasn't about to make a deal with the devil.

"Yes, I want to know the terms," she whispered and braced herself for disappointment.

"To save you, I need to remove the tumor Wynn caused to expand in your head."

She flinched at the painful reminder. Darkyn appeared amused.

"The deal is simple. Your life in exchange for keeping the tumor I remove."

"That's it?" she asked, surprised. "I won't be turned into a vegetable or an animal or anything else weird?"

"You will be as you are now. The only difference is that you will not have a tumor killing you. You will have an eternity with your mate."

Her chest tightened at the thought. There was no guarantee Gabriel wanted her, but she'd have a chance. After all, he promised that he'd try and let her rewrite the awful terms of their relationship, if she survived.

There was a soul in her tumor. Thus far, no one seemed interested in it, aside from Darkyn. Unable to shake the memory of her interaction with the soul from the lake, she felt protective of the one in her head. She wished she had a moment to talk to Gabriel, the deity charged with protecting the dead, to make sure she wasn't doing something wrong.

"What will you do to the soul inside?" she ventured. "You won't hurt it?"

"Absolutely not. I plan on restoring its life as well."

"Really? Why?"

"That is not a concern of this deal."

This ... deal sounded too good to be true. He wanted the soul in her head badly. Why not kill her and take it? Would it be hurt if she died before they removed it? Was that what no one was willing to risk doing? Was that why Gabriel promised her the world if she survived the operation? Because they wanted to keep her alive long enough to extract it then walk away?

No, not Gabriel. Sometimes, she heard longing in his voice, the same yearning she experience for him. Perhaps he feared getting close to her if she was going to die in a few months, seeing as how past-Deidre crushed his heart, too.

Deidre needed that chance with him. Darkyn alone was able to give it to her.

"Okay," she said slowly. "One more thing. I'm sick of pain. I don't want *any* of this to hurt."

"Not even a little?"

"Everything completely painless from here on out."

"You drive a hard bargain, but I agree." He reached out to her. "Take my hand, and the deal is official."

Deidre approached but hesitated again to take his hand. It was too easy. Nothing yet in the Immortal world had been as easy as this bargain. Reluctantly, she took his hand. Cold fire shot through her. She shivered.

"The deal is done." Darkyn dropped her hand.

"How can you do what Gabriel and the Immortals can't?" she asked.

"My magic is that of the forbidden," he said. "Every deity has a different nature and source for their magic."

"What does that mean?"

"I will show you." He strode towards a dark wall of the in-between place. Deidre followed, barely able to make out the shape of a doorway that pulsed darker than night. "We must remove it in my domain in order for my magic to work properly. It will take a great deal of power to preserve you, remove the tumor and heal the damage."

Dread filled her. He paused at the doorway. As if sensing her fear, Darkyn held out his hand once more.

"Come," he said.

The deal was done. Deidre accepted his hand and let him take her into a new part of the Immortal world. The moment the shadow world cleared from her sight, she wanted to run. She stood on a covered landing of a fortress made of black stones overlooking a parched desert beneath dual suns too faded to provide anything other than indirect light.

"Welcome to Hell," Darkyn said, releasing her.

"Oh, god," she breathed.

"There are a couple of things we must establish up front."

She whirled. The portal was gone, and Darkyn was in front of her again. Deidre watched in growing horror as his teeth turned from normal to sharpened, and two long canines half the size of her index finger lengthened from his gum. Like a demon's.

"It will require a great deal of effort on my part to keep this painless. Pain brings me pleasure. It goes against my nature to avoid it," he was saying.

Forbidden magic. Hell. She made a deal with a demon. Starting to panic, Deidre sought some escape route.

"Pay attention." He snapped his fingers in front of her face. "If you ever want to leave here, you will follow my instructions."

"We have a deal," she whispered.

"A deal is as much about the spoken terms as the unspoken ones," he replied with a predatory smile. "You didn't bargain to leave here once you arrived. The portal system does not work in Hell for mortals. You bargained for your life and pain. Do you want to leave?"

She nodded, forcing herself to listen.

"You will find your chances improve if you do exactly as I say," he said. He circled her as he had upon their first meeting. "You also didn't bargain against not becoming a blood monkey while you were here either."

"Blood monkey?"

An image not of her own creation pushed itself into her mind. It was of Darkyn's fangs sinking into the delicate skin of her neck. Her body began to shake, and her hands were clammy.

"I have your attention now," he noted. "To keep things … painless for my new blood monkey, it will require discipline on both our parts. I won't hurt you. You don't run, and you don't fight me. I love a chase and a fight, but the chances of me forgetting not to dull the pain increase if you resist."

Another image flashed, and Deidre gasped, covering her face with her hands in an effort to block it. It was of her running and Darkyn tearing out her throat, after doing much more horrible things to her.

"Understood?" he asked.

Gabriel's one percent was a cakewalk compared to this.

"Why is this happening?" she asked. "What did I do wrong?"

"You will get what you came for," he assured her. "In the meantime, I can't have you running from the Dark One. He is not merciful."

"Dark One. My god."

"Only a deity can turn a human immortal, which is what it'll take to keep you alive while we remove the tumor. Be brave, love. You've made it this far." The words were mocking rather than encouraging.

Deidre did her best to stabilize her breathing. She wiped away tears. She deserved whatever happened. If she didn't, past-Deidre did. She wasn't about to get her throat torn out before she found some way to get out of here. Gabriel would come for her, if she didn't return.

She hoped.

Her gaze traveled from the gloomy fortress to the sickly sky to the creature before her, whose fangs seemed to have grown even longer.

If Gabriel didn't come, it was because she fucked up bad making a deal with some shady creature she found wandering in the shadow world. Her life was about to enter its next phase of the nightmare.

"What are your rules?" Darkyn asked, pulling her from her mind.

"N…no running. No fighting you," she said in a hushed voice. "No pain."

"We'll see how badly you want to leave. Come here."

It took every ounce of her willpower not to flee hysterically or give in to the desire to collapse and sob. Shaking and terrified, Deidre nonetheless held his gaze as she closed the distance between them, until she stood less than a foot away.

Darkyn gripped her neck with one hand and tilted her head to the side.

She closed her eyes and prayed.

"Humans are a delicacy. Female humans in Hell with a soul unblemished by evil? I can't remember the last time I tasted one," he whispered. He nuzzled her neck.

Deidre braced her hands against his chest, tunnel-vision forming. She felt his fangs sink into her skin and heard him sucking out her lifeblood. Disgusted, she was also relieved there was no pain. From the visions he showed her, he was capable of things she'd never dreamed of. He didn't drink long, and she was too afraid of moving to wipe away the tears rolling down her face.

"Sweet," he said in a thick voice as he withdrew. "Like honey. You won't like trying to earn your way out of here, but I will."

"Is it even possible for me to leave?"

"Possible? Yes. Probability is an entirely different issue."

She opened her eyes at his response. He released her and turned away.

"Come. Wynn's magic is killing you faster than anticipated. You need to prepare."

Deidre trailed him numbly from the landing into the fortress. It was dim inside the stronghold, and the first torch they crossed that burned with black flames mesmerized her long enough for her to lose sight of Darkyn around a corner. She hurried to catch up. He led her past closed doors and through hallways carved out of black stone.

Deeper into Hell.

Breathe. Focus. Live.

She wasn't going to make it long here if she lost control.

The demons they passed bowed to Darkyn, their eyes riveted to her once the scary creature strode by. They all looked hungry.

She quickened her pace, not wanting to end up the dinner of some demon before she had a chance to try to plan an escape. Assuming she hadn't missed more fine print in her deal with Darkyn, she wanted to survive the removal of the tumor.

Darkyn paused in front of a door guarded by two demons. One opened it for him, and she trailed him into a large bedchamber complete with a hearth burning black flames.

"The mate of a deity will be provided what hospitality we offer," Darkyn said.

"I take it that doesn't extend to blood monkey status."

She backed away as he approached, feeling the threat without needing to see it on his face.

"It extends as far it pleases me to extend it." His sharp tone made her jump. He reached for her neck again.

Deidre sucked in a breath and held it, squeezing her eyes closed. Instead of grabbing her, he slid something cool around her neck.

"To mark you as my blood monkey," he said. "You have five minutes to change."

She didn't open her eyes or release her breath until she heard the door close behind him. Deidre choked back a sob.

"I am so sorry, Gabriel," she whispered.

She had to stay focused. Swiping at tears, she registered Darkyn's words as her eyes identified the dark clothing laid out on the bed. Deidre lifted the dress with trembling hands. It was muted black, made out of material smoother than silk that draped over her arm like a second skin.

"I can do this," she told herself. "I kinda don't have a choice, since I fucked up."

She changed out of her familiar clothing into the dress that matched the black world around her. The simple cut reminded her of something she'd seen in movies about ancient Rome: loose-fitted and airy, it was secured by a thin cord around her neck. The material hugged the natural curves of her body, pooling at the top of her feet. It was light enough that she felt naked, especially with the cut that left her back, arms and shoulders completely exposed.

Her fingertips touched the metal choker he slid around her neck. It was solid and slender with no release mechanism or clasp. There was scarring on her neck from where he'd bitten her. Deidre dropped her hand quickly from the knotted skin, alarm pulsing through her.

He was going to turn her Immortal. What did that mean?

Fuck the tumor. If she saw an escape route, she was gone.

"Do as Darkyn says, Deidre."

She spun at the voice, startled to see Mr. Checkmate, the man she'd met on the beach when she arrived at the Sanctuary the first time. He was out of place, a bright light in the corner of the dimly lit room, dressed casually in jeans, T-shirt and hiking boots.

"This will not provide much comfort, but Darkyn was your only real chance of living," he added. "Assuming you survive what he does to you."

"I'm kinda hoping I don't right now," she said. "Who are you? How did you get in here?"

"Deities tend to do what they want," Mr. Checkmate replied.

"You're … you can't be the Dark One."

"I am not," he said with a wide grin. "I'm worse. I'm Fate."

"You got that right," she muttered. "You've been kicking my ass for awhile now. I don't suppose you're here to cut me a break?"

"I just did."

"Obey the psycho demon that wants to suck my blood."

"Exactly."

"If I do, will everything be okay?" she asked, searching his face for any indication she survived the ordeal and left Hell.

"That's not how the Future works. There is no single event that determines the outcome of one's destiny," he said with a shake of his head. "But, if you do this one thing, you increase your chances of being relatively okay by about thirty seven percent for a total of just under fifty-fifty."

"Do what the demon says and almost have a fifty percent chance of surviving. Disobey him and I have like, a ten percent chance."

"You've got it."

"I'm under the impression your kind doesn't do things for free. Why are you helping me? Do you have an even worse vengeance planned?" she demanded.

"Better. I have a preferred outcome, one that involves you surviving and the soul embedded in your head not."

She touched her head self-consciously. Darkyn wanted the soul alive while Fate wanted the opposite. Who was she more likely to side with? As if sensing her doubt and growing panic, Fate drew near her, face grave.

"Deidre, you must do exactly as I say," Fate said. "You must obey him, no matter how much you do not wish to. Your life is not the only one dependent upon this."

"Gabriel," she breathed. "Oh, god, have I put him in danger?"

Fate's eyes changed colors rapidly. His subtle magic brushed by her, through her. It was warm, like Gabriel's, not cold like Darkyn's. Comforted by the familiar sensation, she sensed she was better off trusting Fate than the Dark One.

"No," he replied. "If you do as I tell you, you will increase his chances of surviving the destiny Darkyn intends to inflict upon him."

"I'd never do anything to put Gabriel in danger," she whispered, distressed by the idea. Surviving her own plight meant nothing if there was no Gabriel for her to return to. "I'll listen to you. I'll do whatever Darkyn wants me to. I swear it."

"Good. I like Gabriel," Fate said, the intensity leaving his features. "He makes me laugh."

Her brow furrowed at the odd sentiment.

"It's not easy to do, when you've been alive since the time-before-time," he added with a wink. His eyes went to the door suddenly. "Darkyn comes. Don't tell him I was here. We're not on good terms right now."

She heard the door open and turned. Without looking, she felt the loss of Fate's warm energy.

"Come," Darkyn ordered without entering.

Deidre obeyed. Afraid of what the demon was going to ask her to do, she was resolved not to hurt Gabriel by ignoring Fate's warning.

"Rules," Darkyn stated as she joined him in the hallway.

"No running. No fighting," she recited anxiously.

He reached for her neck. She flinched but didn't otherwise move.

"Good." He dropped his hand and started down the hallway. "Come meet the Dark One."

Swallowing hard, Deidre followed. He strode through more corridors than she was able to count, down several flights of stairs and finally to a short, dead end hallway with a ceiling that towered ten stories above. One set of massive metal doors was all the hall contained. Darkyn strode to them and placed his hand on one. It cracked open silently with enough room for them to enter.

Her courage almost gave out at the idea of walking into the devil's personal hangout. Deidre felt woozy and paused to steady her breathing. After a moment, she entered the room.

It wasn't what she expected. There was no way for her to measure the size of the chamber, for the darkness inside was more impenetrable than night, with the exception of a circle of light ten meters from the door. Darkyn waited for her in the circle that stretched about five meters across. She went to him, unable to see through the darkness even while walking through it.

The door closed with an ominous boom that echoed throughout what sounded like a massive but empty chamber.

Her tomb.

Skin clammy with nervous sweat, Deidre concentrated on taking deep breaths.

"You may want to close your eyes." Darkyn's laugh was sinister.

She snapped them closed, but not before she saw him slide into the darkness. There was a long moment of silence from the chamber around her, filled by the sound of her breathing as it grew more erratic, louder. She thought she heard something stir once, twice, before she was certain. The scraping of leather against leather, the hollow clatter of stone and shale, the rustle of whatever creature settled behind her.

Near full-blown panic again, Deidre was midway through her second step towards the door when the creature snatched her. At first, the thick leather around her neck felt like a whip.

A second settled across the lower half of her face and two more around her torso. They adjusted around her like fingers, leathery and long enough to wrap around her body.

I can do this for Gabriel. She repeated the sentence over and over to try to block out what her senses told her about the size of the monster.

The fingers around her mouth and neck maneuvered her head to the side until her ear was near her shoulder to expose the delicate area before both fell away. She stayed in place. At the touch of the first fang, her eyes flew open. There was no pain, as promised, but the canine was the size of butcher knife.

It slid into her neck, the sound making her nauseous. The second canine slid into her body, just below her collarbone. The creature took a sip of her like from a straw. It left her lightheaded. The second sucked the strength out of her body and brought tunnel vision. Instead of a third drink, a flash of cold fire was forced through the fangs into her body. She felt the cold circulating but no pain.

The creature's third sip drove her into the darkness between consciousness and sleep. Her body no longer under her control, Deidre sank into the state, clinging to the words of Fate about helping Gabriel. She registered nothing but darkness and cold for awhile before the cold began to fade, and the night behind her eyelids lightened. Her head felt heavy and like it was stuffed with cotton, the way she felt when she came to after surgery.

"Deidre?" Dr. Wynn's voice penetrated the haze.

What had he tried this time? Deidre didn't remember what this operation was supposed to do.

"If you can hear me, give me a sign."

She gave him the same sign she always did: a small smile.

"Good. Relax. Come back when you're ready."

She knew if she woke up too fast, she'd feel like she had a hangover. So, she hovered in the quiet darkness for awhile, until the sounds of the outside world were too loud for her to ignore.

Deidre opened her eyes and blinked rapidly, realizing the black she tried to clear from her sight was the black ceiling of the operating room. Confused, she tried again to remember what procedure Dr. Wynn was performing today. She'd been through so many …

"Good news or bad news?" he asked, appearing in her vision.

"Bad," she replied. Her mouth was dry.

"You're going to have more scars."

"Good."

"It's gone."

"Okay." She closed her eyes. Her head didn't hurt, but it felt weird. Heavy.

"Darling, did you hear me?"

"Maybe," she replied. She reached up to her head, surprised it wasn't bandaged and she still had all her hair. "Wait, what happened?"

"I'll show you. Can you sit up?"

Deidre felt groggy but not like she normally did post-op. She sat up. If anything, she was exhausted and in a recovery room unlike any she'd ever seen before. The advanced medical equipment and sterile scent in the air were the same. The walls, however, were as black as the ceiling.

Stone fortress. Hell. She wore the black dress still.

She gasped. Wynn looked up from his position nearby.

"Oh, god, what did you do to me this time?" she asked, grappling with fuzzy memories.

"Believe it or not, I helped. Look."

She focused on the chart he held up to the light. It looked like a cat scan of a brain, but it wasn't hers. This one didn't have a tumor. It was normal.

Dark chamber. Leathery fingers wrapped around her body. Fangs.

Shuddering, she touched the places where the beast's canines sank into her body. Wynn was right. These scars were huge and knotted.

"You mean ... it's gone?" she asked, the world registering at last. "Just like that?"

"Gone," he replied. "You will live a very long life."

"What are you doing here?" she demanded. "This is Hell, isn't it?"

"I got dragged down here involuntarily to make sure you survived, unlike someone who made a deal with the Dark One." He frowned at her and lowered the chart. "You have no idea what you've done, Deidre."

She shivered. She pushed herself off the bed and tested her body. Aside from fatigue, her body moved and felt the way it should.

"I've been instructed to show you to your chamber, after which I'll be released. Allegedly," Wynn said. "Then I'm off to tell Gabriel his mate is stuck in Hell."

Adrenaline started through her system again, clearing some of the fog in her mind. Deidre met the gaze of her betrayer.

"One might argue this is my fault," Wynn added. "If I hadn't tried to kill you in the first place, you wouldn't be a blood slave to the Dark One."

"Silver lining," she whispered. "Please."

"There is no silver lining when you make a deal with him."

Except that Fate said there was. She couldn't voice the words. Her chest was too tight. Deidre said nothing.

"Come. I'm anxious to leave this place," Wynn said and strode to the door.

She trailed, glancing over her shoulder when the two demons outside the recovery room followed. She rubbed her arms and touched the slender choker at her neck.

Their deal was done. The tumor was gone. How long did Fate expect her to stay here?

They didn't go far, for which she was grateful. Wynn led her to a door guarded by another demon and stepped aside.

"Thank you, Wynn," she murmured. She wasn't sure why she expected him to speak but found herself wishing he'd say something.

He didn't.

The final nail in the coffin of their friendship left her feeling depressed. Deidre opened the door into the familiar chamber and closed it behind her, leaning against it. She was in a lot of trouble, but at least, if Wynn left, he'd tell Gabriel where to find her. From there, she didn't want to think of what might or might not happen.

She pushed herself away from the door and glanced at her reflection in the mirror. She was halfway across the room when what she'd seen registered. Her reflection was seated, and her hair was blond. It wasn't a reflection.

Deidre froze.

"What have you done to my hair?" the female voice asked.

Oh, god. Not this bitch. Deidre took a deep breath and faced the deity previously known as Death. Gabriel's ex-lover was identical to her in every way, even garbed in the same dress. The only difference was her hair and the eyes that turned from white to black to every color in between. She sat in a chair by the black hearth.

"I like pink," Deidre replied. "What are you doing here?"

"Recovering, like you."

"From.... Were you ...?" she pointed to her head.

Past-Death's cold smile did not reach her eyes. Deidre studied her, picking up other signs of how different they were. There was no human color in the woman's pale cheeks, and her expression was emotionless, as if carved from marble. She stood, her bearing regal and her walk smooth, without the cheerful bounce Deidre had in hers. Everything about the deity screamed careful control.

"I experienced your life with you. I admit, I expected a human existence to be a little less boring," past-Death mused.

Deidre was still as the creature walked around her, scrutinizing her.

"So you just rode around in my head for twenty six years?" she asked, confused.

"Pretty much. Darkyn was supposed to find me much earlier, according to our agreement." Past-Death shrugged. "It's for your benefit he did not. Wynn's work on us kept you safe and me trapped."

"I don't think that was his intention," Deidre muttered under her breath.

"I want to thank you for the use of your existence," past-Death continued. "You let me see my Gabriel in a whole new light. Tender, compassionate, weak, like a human, and failing miserably to take my place. Also, no surprise, given his origins."

Deidre suddenly liked her even less. No Immortal alive had a good opinion of the deity, and the mocking way she spoke about Gabriel infuriated Deidre.

"I made you in my image. Incredible handiwork, don't you agree?" Past-Death stepped away from her, admiring her like she was a clay pot kilned in the backyard by a bored goddess.

"Fortunately, I'm nothing like you, or I would've died long ago as a human," Deidre replied. "Gabriel wouldn't have fallen for me, either."

This drew the deity's attention. "Interesting. You don't realize you're disposable to me. I needed you for awhile, and I no longer do."

"Thank god. I can go on living a normal life."

"No. You are the preordained mate of a deity, just as I am. Your fate still lies within the Immortal society."

Past-Death turned and drew her hair to the side in one elegant motion. Deidre's breath caught at the name scrolled across the narrow shoulders.

Gabriel.

Deidre recalled what Katie told her about how Immortals only got one mate in the entirety of their lifetimes. How were they both Gabriel's mates?

"With your deal with Darkyn complete, you'll live a very long life." Past-Death appeared amused by the idea. "As will I with my Gabriel."

"You made one with Darkyn, too?" Deidre asked. She purposely didn't take the bait that Gabriel might choose his ex over her. She wanted to deck her mirror image. "Or you wouldn't be hanging out here."

"I did, and it's complete. We have one other small matter between us, but" past-Death smiled again "I don't lose. The others thought they trapped me, and here I am, against all odds."

"You left Gabriel a mess. You really think he'll welcome you back?"

"He will if he thinks I'm you."

Deidre laughed. "My god. You might have a better chance if you tell him you're *you.*"

"Are you that blind, human? Gabriel wouldn't let himself near you in order to protect you. He fell in love with you .. with *us* ... the first night on the beach. Unwillingly." Past-Death's chuckle was as warm as her eyes. "But you did what I knew you would. You made him love us in a way he never loved me."

The coldness of fear settled into Deidre. How did she warn Gabriel from here?

"You think Darkyn will let you leave here?" she asked. "Or do you have an escape plan you'd like to share?"

"Darkyn won't stand in my way," past-Death said with confidence. "There are strings attached to anyone raised from the dead-dead, but these are of no concern to a deity like they might be to a little human like you."

Toby was right. This woman was a mega-bitch. Deidre wanted to wring Gabriel's neck for wasting thousands of years with someone like this. Was it true what past-Death said about Gabriel? Did he love Deidre?

She'd never understood his waffling. Whenever she started to think he cared for her, he flipped. Was it to protect her? Or to protect his own heart? Did it matter, if he loved her either way?

Past-Death was going to replace Deidre in Gabriel's life. Deidre rubbed her face, her head still fuzzy from whatever the Dark One did to her. Gabriel would know. There was no way he couldn't. It took him almost two weeks, but he'd figured out that Deidre was nothing like his ex-lover.

She needed to get out of here, to warn him before the deity did something horrible to Gabriel. Deidre paced to the fire. It gave off heat despite the black flames. She thought hard about all she'd learned since arriving to Hell.

"Can I ask you something?" Deidre asked.

"Ask away." The mocking note in past-Death's voice irked Deidre.

"Am I … am I an Immortal now?"

"Darkyn turned you. Like Gabriel, you'll always be of human origin."

"Okay. You probably won't consider taking me with you when you leave here?"

"You are expendable," past-Death replied. "The purposes for which I created you are complete. I do not need you any longer."

Ouch. Past-Death was going to be brutal to deal with, if Deidre ever got out of Hell. The powers of a deity with the sociopathic tendencies of a mass murderer? The jealous bitch wouldn't hesitate to kill off the competition, along with probably everyone else within miles.

What did Gabriel see in her?

"Final question. I thought the Immortals said they only get one mate," Deidre started, puzzled. "How can Gabriel have two?"

"He doesn't. He has one. The deity originally preordained to be his mate."

This response was more guarded, less amused, enough to tip off Deidre that there was more to the story. She had no clue what.

"We both bear his name. I mean, I guess there could be two Gabriels in the Immortal world," she said.

"Only one of us bears his name." Past-Death's smugness was back.

Deidre clenched her jaw in irritation. If Gabriel didn't see the difference between the two women when past-Death showed up on his doorstep, he deserved a lifetime with this arrogant bitch.

"Pretty sure we both do," Deidre replied.

"Are you certain?"

Deidre clenched her fists, uncertain what game the deity played with her.

"Have a look," past-Death urged her.

Deidre turned to see the blonde woman standing in front of an open wardrobe. A mirror lined the inside of one door. Foreboding filled her at the expression on the deity's face, like she'd just won the lottery.

Deidre crossed the room, terrified she'd find Gabriel's name gone.

"We are destined to become the mates of deities. Deities, Ancients and Immortals all have a match," past-Death explained. "I'm Gabriel's preordained mate. I created you long before I ceased to exist by morphing a part of my soul with yours. You are mostly human, but you are also part of me. You were enough me to convince the laws governing Immortal mating that you were Gabriel's mate, until I reappeared a few hours ago and set things straight, including telling Fate to fuck off."

"You're the two percent of me that's not human?"

"Correct."

"I don't think I get it." Deidre shivered and paused a few feet from the deity. She had a mild headache, and the tension between her shoulders was aching from the stress of the discussion. Wired, emotional energy made it hard to concentrate as she listened.

"I don't expect a human to understand. What should matter to you is that you're going to be the mate of a deity. It's no small honor," past-Death said.

I want Gabriel, Deidre screamed silently. "I need to get out of here."

"You'll never leave Hell," past-Death continued, oblivious to Deidre's growing distress. "Darkyn was recently promoted to the Dark One. He won't let you go."

Somehow, Deidre wasn't surprised the creepy demon everyone bowed to was the Dark One. If Fate looked like a frat boy and past-Death like a sorority girl, the Dark One's youthful human form didn't seem out of place among the deities she met.

"He said I could earn my way out," Deidre said.

"Maybe in time. Or Gabriel or another deity can make a deal to get you out. There are possibilities. Only one issue you have to overcome."

Past-Death took Deidre's arm and spun her back to the mirror. Deidre was relieved to see the Immortal script, until she saw it wasn't Gabriel's name on her back.

Darkyn.

"One of us was intended for Gabriel. The other for Darkyn," past-Death said. "Luck of the draw, I guess. Darkyn will never let you go."

Deidre stared, horrified. "Gabriel won't let this happen."

"He will if he thinks I'm you."

"He won't. There's nothing you can do to fool him. He will know before you have a chance to kiss him," she said, her fury building. "We're too different!"

"Gabriel will love me as he did you," past-Death returned. "I will make sure of it."

Something within Deidre snapped. She faced the goddess, rage streaking through her along with the terror of being mated to the Dark One.

"What are you?" she demanded. "Getting me assigned to Darkyn and taking Gabriel, who won't want anything to do with you when he cares about me? You can't just swap us out in his life!"

"We are the same person." Past-Death's eyes narrowed. "You don't want to piss me off, human."

"I don't give a shit! Whatever happened, whatever this is" Deidre gestured wildly at the tattoo on her back "Gabriel will find a way to fix it. Even if he doesn't, and I'm trapped here forever, you are too fucking selfish to understand that you can't *make* someone love you. He'll send you packing by day two."

"Do you have any idea who you're talking to?" past-Death shoved her.

"Do you have any idea who *you're* talking to?" Deidre shoved her back. "The woman who captured his heart in a week, something you barely did after millennia! And he *still* hates you!"

Past-Death appeared surprised. A flush of anger crept up her neck and into her face.

"If any part of you cared about him, you'd want him to be happy, not force him to love you!" Deidre cried. "Even if that meant sacrificing what you want or that he ended up with me instead of you."

"I *created* you and broke laws older than time to do it! You are nothing," past-Death shouted. "I sacrificed everything for the chance you would bring us together!"

"You didn't do it for him. You are throwing me away like garbage when I'm the one he cares about!" Deidre pushed her again. "There is nothing on this planet that will make him fall in love with someone like you. I'd bet my fucking life on it!"

"Would you really? Do you know what happens if you lose a wager to a deity?" past-Death challenged.

"It can't be fucking worse than being trapped with the fucking devil!"

"Fine. Name your bet!"

"Gabriel," Deidre said promptly. "If you can't do what I did in a week, he's mine."

"You cannot wager something you do not own," past-Death said scornfully.

"Then good luck and fuck you." Deidre whirled, tears on her face again. Her deal with Darkyn sealed her fate. The catch she'd discounted as simple was going to damn them all.

Mr. Checkmate was probably not smiling anymore.

"Cowardly humans," past-Death snarled and strode to the door.

Suddenly, past-Death's words about how Deidre became Gabriel's mate clicked. Would the reverse also work? If past-Death was dead again, was Deidre next in line to be Gabriel's mate?

She faced the door, mind working quickly.

"Wait!" she called. "Your soul. If you can't do what I did in a week, I get your soul."

"Fuck off, human."

"Who's the coward now?" Deidre demanded. "You're incapable of loving him the way he deserves, and you know it."

Past-Death froze at the door. Her face was red, her eyes glittering. "You will wager your soul as well?"

"Yep," Deidre said. "Deal?" She held out her hand and drew near. "One week. Your soul and mine on the table."

Past-Death shook her hand. Cold energy shot through Deidre, and she flinched. The door opened, and they both looked towards it.

"Which one of you is mine?" Darkyn's growl made her blood run cold.

"As I promised. My payment for your services." Past-Death snatched Deidre's arm and yanked her to the side for him to see the tattoo.

The demon lord smiled. Past-Death pushed Deidre towards him.

Deidre dug in her heels before she reached him. The heat of her anger vanished, replaced by fear.

"Deal settled," Darkyn said, stepping aside. "With regards to our arrangement about reviving you..."

"We'll talk later," past-Death said and brushed by him.

Darkyn watched her go. Deidre saw the look on his face, the same one past-Death gave her when admiring the product she created. His attention returned to Deidre. His fangs were lengthening. She backed away, unable to fathom the idea of being trapped with him in Hell for eternity.

"Rules," he reminded her and entered the chamber. He closed the door behind him.

"No running. No fighting."

You must obey him, no matter how much you do not wish to. Your life is not the only one dependent upon this.

She stopped in place as Fate's words returned her. Unable to quell the panic flying through her, she wasn't willing to test the waters to discover if demons were restricted from harming their mates like Immortals. In a week, when past-Death lost her end of the bet, Deidre would be free.

She just had to survive.

Deidre closed her eyes as Darkyn's arm snaked out to grab her neck. He dragged her against him. Breathing ragged, she tilted her head in submission.

One week.

"Welcome to your new home, love," the Dark One said a moment before his teeth sank into her neck.

For Gabriel.

Chapter Fifteen

At the Caribbean Sanctuary, Fate watched the Oracle record the latest batch of deals made between deities. They were routine. Boring. Nothing he really wanted to see.

And then it came. The one he was waiting for. He leaned forward, intrigued as the Oracle scribbled down the agreement.

Immortal Mate (Death – current) and Immortal Mate (Dark One - current)

This much he predicted. Sometimes, he kept himself entertained by forecasting what happened without letting himself peek at the details. This was one such instance where he refused to look, instead reveling in the thrill of anticipation. Now it was time to see if he'd guessed correctly.

IM-D given one week to make Death fall in love. Deal: IM-D, IM-DO souls. Winner takes all.

Fate contemplated the deal between Gabriel's new mate and the Dark One's new mate. A week was generous to one woman and dangerous to the other. His guess had been three days. Little Deidre was going to have a rough go in Hell, especially when she discovered what it meant to have the Dark One as a mate, while past-Death was going to find herself unprepared for the mortal world.

Prior to the details of the deal, Fate was considering going on vacation. Seeing the bet, he decided he wanted to stick around long enough to observe a few more events in the women's futures. Both were on the courses he laid out for them, though that was not always an indication his preferred outcome was inevitable.

Straightening, Fate smiled.

He had a good feeling about this one. He was definitely sticking around.

Checkmate.

Rhyn Eternal series

"Gabriel's Hope" (Dec 2012)
"Deidre's Death" (Fall 2013)

ABOUT THE AUTHOR

Lizzy Ford is the hyper-prolific author of the Rhyn Trilogy, Witchling Trilogy, Foretold Trilogy, and War of Gods series as well as multiple other single-title paranormal romance and YA fantasy novels. She loves to hear from readers.

Contact her:
Website: http://www.guerrillawordfare.com/
Amazon author's page: http://www.amazon.com/Lizzy-Ford/e/B004XTTYOC/
Facebook: http://www.facebook.com/LizzyFordBooks/
Twitter: http://www.twitter.com/#!/LizzyFord2010
Google+:
https://plus.google.com/b/106728579413949863215/#

Email: LizzyFord2010@gmail.com

Also by Lizzy Ford

The Rhyn Trilogy
Katie's Hellion, Book I (May 2011)
Katie's Hope, Book II (September 2011)
Rhyn's Redemption, Book III (March 2012)

Rhyn Eternal Series
Gabriel's Hope (December 2012)

The War of Gods series
Damian's Oracle (October 2011)
Damian's Assassin (November 2011)
Damian's Immortal (December 2011)
The Grey God (May 2012)

The Foretold Trilogy
Elle's Journey (December 2011)
Shadow Rising (2013)

Anshan Saga
Kiera's Moon (June 2011)
Kiera's Sun (2013)

Single-titles
A Demon's Desire
The Warlord's Secret
Maddy's Oasis
Rebel Heart

Damian Eternal (War of Gods spinoff)
Xander's Chance – 2013

The Witchling Trilogy
Dark Summer (late summer 2012)
Autumn Storm (autumn 2012)
Winter Kiss (2013)

35310458R00150

Made in the USA
Charleston, SC
04 November 2014